1

The Girls School

Donna Emerich

&

Bella Reign Flanagan

Acknowledgments

Thank you, Les Paul Deal for sharing your knowledge of

European history and courtesan training

Table of Contents

Prologue

In the 1940's, there was The Gulag. It was a prison run by the military. Half a million people were incarcerated here. There were murderers, serial killers and rapists sentenced here. It was also a place where anyone who opposed the moral, societal or political norms was sent. There was no hot water and inmates were fed on about sixty cents per day. The Gulag was its own small city, complete with a fire brigade and saw mill. Anyone sentenced here was forced into sixteen hours a day of manual labor. Those who refused to comply were shot or sent to "The Pit." That was basically a concrete block of cells that no one came out of. Ninety percent of the inmates were men who were deported to the NKVD prison in Moscow or to the Gulag. If women were pregnant or gave birth here, the children were sent to government sanctioned orphanages.

Stalin liked young girls. He was always looking for perfect girls for breeding and bearing his children. He would send comrade Max, a trusted member of his cabinet to bring girls to him for sex. Families gave their daughters up with no questions asked. Girls in the orphanages were inferior in breeding but above average in intelligence and appearance. Instead of being executed, they were sent to a finishing school that provided the NKVD (secret police) with a new breed of undercover sleeper squad. Stalin personally reviewed their medical history, intelligence scores, athletic ability and purity/lineage. Parents willingly sent their daughters to school. They were promised a monthly stipend and a dowry to ensure their daughters would marry well. They sold their daughters under the illusion of giving them a prestigious education. Parents were blissfully unaware that the daughters they sold to the government would be trained in combat, weapons and defense as well as social graces. They would become the perfect sleeper agents whose sole objective was to protect the mother land.

Chapter 1: The Indoctrination

Many of the students who attended the school came from small towns in the Ukraine or farming communities. Females were unwelcome additions to families. Sons could work the farms or be hired out to help support their families. They were married off for the highest dowries in hopes of keeping familial lineages going. Daughters were considered useless burdens. Their only skills were eating and reproducing. Sometimes a pregnancy meant a girl would get married, but more often than not, she became an unwed mother with a mouth to feed. For this reason, families were eager to accept when a government agency offered a monthly stipend in exchange for allowing their daughters to attend a private school. Parents were assured this would prepare their daughters to be worthy of wealthy husbands because this was a prestigious finishing school.

Parents knew if their daughters married well, they would receive large dowries.

As the local girls hugged their families, they were taken away to begin their education and new life. Isabella got cold chills not knowing what to expect as the girls were boarded onto the bus. After Isabella, Anastasia, Ingrid, Ursula and Rena were seated, the handler started the long drive to the school.

As Max pulled up to the school, he announced, "This is your new home. Today begins your indoctrination into a new life. *The one your families sold you into"* he thought to himself.

As the girls walked single-file up the path to the large oak door, an older stout woman greeted them announcing "Welcome. I am Headmistress Agnes." As the girls entered the school, the dampness of the concrete chilled them to their very souls. Headmistress Agnes issued them a bunk, a uniform and a list of rules and punishments that they would incur if rules were broken in any form.

"Meals will be served at 7:00 a.m., noon, and five p.m. The school day begins at 8:00 a.m. sharp. Classes go until three p.m. Chores will be done by five p.m. Then it's dinner and homework. You will be in bed by 9:00pm. Weekends will be spent doing chores, studying and attending worship. There will be no visits from your families. You need to concentrate on your studies. Physical education and training will be important in your new lives."

Isabella and her four comrades were about to embark on an adventure they were not prepared for.

At 5:45 a.m. the sound of a tolling bell woke the girls. This was followed by the Chancellor screaming "Get up!" and the cracking of a whip. While standing in front of their bunks, they were given instructions on dressing, making their beds and inspection before breakfast. "You have fifteen minutes to eat breakfast and prepare for your first class!"

On the first day, it was discovered these were not normal classes. The girls were started in advanced Mathematics, Science, World History and English. The second half of their day was spent in shop class to learn to forge weapons and bombs. Physical education was set up like military basic training along with marksmanship and hand- to-hand combat.   The girls endured this pace for seven years. When their work was not up to the Chancellor's expectations, they were brutally beaten until they could perform satisfactorily. The girls that failed to meet the expectations were reassigned in the kitchen, then to work as domestic servants.

When the girls reached thirteen, new training was added to their regimen. They were taught to be visually attractive and soft spoken. Learning the art of seduction came at a hard price. Their education on sexuality and how to please men came from a brothel owned by the school. This is where girls were sent if they were deemed sub-par. After a day of school and hand- to- hand combat training, the girls were sent to the brothel to earn their dinner.

It was Madam Chanel's job to teach them the art of seduction and pleasing men. The Madam started her speech. "There is more to being a consort than being great in bed. A good consort listens to her companion. She does not question anything. Pillow talk always reveals the best kept secrets." Isabella raised her hand. "Yes?" "Will we have to sleep with strange men?" "Yes. Your job will require you to engage in sex!" "Do we have to like it?" asked Ursula. "No, but it helps if you can enjoy it. Seduction is not sex. Seduction is teasing, a slight caress or touch, the promise that there could be sex. You girls need to know there are many forms of sex. You will be taught all of them before you leave the school."

"We will now have our first lesson in dressing and applying makeup to entice a man. First order of business, undress completely. I will need to see what I have to work with. "You mean naked?" Rena whined. "Yes, naked! Are you going to seduce a man wearing a burlap sack?" Chanel asked. Stripping down, the girls tried to cover themselves.

"There is no need to be shy" cooed Madam Chanel. "You're all beautiful young women. Have you noticed the changes in your figures?" "Yes" was replied in unison. "Your breasts are becoming full and round. Your hips are widening, giving you an hour glass shape. Let's discuss breasts. You need to wear a brassiere. It helps to keep your breasts firm. When you go without a brassiere, your breast tissue breaks down and your breasts will sag like cow udders." Giggling, Anastasia said "We are not cows!" "I see. Tell me, Anastasia what happens when the elastic breaks in your underwear?" Chanel pressed. "They stretch out and do not stay up" Anastasia stuttered. "Exactly! That is what will happen if you do not wear a brassiere. Breast tissue is like elastic. It stretches out and your breasts will not stand upright. They will sag." "Yes, ma'am."

Inspecting each girl from head to toe, Chanel yelled for her seamstress to take measurements of each girl and find them the proper undergarments. Chanel then split the girls up into pairs for makeup lessons. The remaining three girls were sent to a private room to learn what Chanel called "touch. "I want you to form a circle. Now, lightly touch each other's arms. Do the same to each other's legs. How do you feel when someone touches you? Are you scared? Does it feel tingly? Are they pleasant feelings? Alright, now I want you to touch each other's breasts." "Do we have to?" "Yes! Light caresses. Now I want you to touch lightly between your legs." "Do we have to?" "Yes, you have to. Tell me how you feel." "It's a tingly, funny feeling." "I want you to

9

practice touching yourselves in the bath for our next class. You three go over there and learn makeup. Send the other two girls to me."   Madam Chanel gave the same instructions to the next two girls. "Everyone line up for your dress and undergarment fittings. Isabella, may I ask how you got those bruises?" "They were punishment from the Chancellor" Isabella said dryly. "I see. My makeup skills can cover many sins, but these bruises just won't do! Go over and get fitted. Ladies, I will see you at our next meeting. Do not forget to practice touch."

As the students walked to the side entrance, Rena noticed some of the girls that had washed out of physical training were now working in the brothel. "What happened?" "Ursula whispered. "This is where you get sent if you're not good enough." "Where's Lizzy and Iris?" "They were sickly. I think they were shot. There are fresh graves by the woods!" "Oh God! No!" "Work hard or they'll put you here with us!" Tears streamed down Ursula's face. "Do Not Cry! It is weak!"

Headmistress Agnes emerged to walk them back to school. "You need to eat and ready yourselves for bed!" she said sharply. "Ma'am, are these classes really necessary?" "Oh yes, these classes are just as important if not more." "But?" "Your rich husband will expect you to be able to take care of his every need. That is why our girls get the best of everything! We train you for all aspects of your duties! Now hush!"

Isabella was the most advanced of the girls. She had a spirit that could not be broken. She had the scars to prove it. Every one of them was administered at the hands of the Chancellor. Thinking about what she had seen, her thoughts began to race. *"My parents sold me! This school is designed to make you a high priced consort. It's not a real school at all!"* The screams in her head became so loud she could not stand it anymore.

Creeping over to Mary's bunk, she whispered "Can we talk?" "Sure." Quietly they crept into the lavatory. Mary asked, "Are you alright?" "No! I had my first class at the brothel! They are grooming us to become consorts!" "You're close, but not totally right." "I am risking beatings. I need to know what we are in for."   "When you graduate, you will be given a government job. Sometimes you will be asked to accompany diplomats." "Are we whores?" "No" said Mary. "Spies?" "I am not sure, but I am sure that we were sold to this school!" "What about the next batch of nine -year- olds that come in?" "We try to protect them as best we can. Now get back to your bunk, or we will all get it! If you're thinking about running, don't. No one has ever come back alive."

Agnes, Chancellor Harold, Max and Madam Chanel were having a late night meeting. "How do you expect me to teach these girls to handle a man when they are covered in bruises? They will not be attractive to our clientele! Stop beating them!" "You must be referring to Isabella. She is spirited but headstrong." "We need to purchase them proper undergarments. They will be sagging before they can be used as assets!" "Calm down, Chanel. Agnes can take them on a field trip." "No, I took the liberty of getting their measurements so we can order by catalog. I will need extra time with this group." Agnes announced "They are already questioning the need for these classes." "Smart ones are they?" Max smiled. "They will be our best assets yet."   "We will start instilling teamwork." "I want to give them makeup to practice with and some hair styling. These are tools they will need in the field." "I agree to all your requests. The minute their other work slips, the extra classes cease. Is that understood?" "Yes, Chancellor."

"Might I suggest a few other classes? We should also include childcare in case the need arises." Thinking quietly for a moment, Max voiced his agreement with Agnes' suggestions. "They have taken shop. Home economics classes would be beneficial as well." "Agreed."

Max cleared his throat. "What about driving lessons? My girls need to be capable of everything. We do not want them unprepared for the outside world." "Very well. If their grades slip, I take the extracurricular classes away." "Thank you, Chancellor." After the meeting, the Chancellor poured himself a Scotch. Rubbing his forehead, he muttered "These people give me a headache!"

In the morning, Headmistress Agnes announced, "There will be changes in your class schedule. We will cut the time in your normal classes to make room for new ones. Monday, Wednesday, and Friday evening classes will be with Madam Chanel. Tuesday, Thursday, and Saturday evenings will now be home and garden classes. Sunday afternoon will be a class on driving an automobile."

"If your grades drop, you will be removed from classes and given work detail. Do you understand?" "Yes, ma'am." "With shorter classes, the work will be concentrated. Be prepared to keep up!" Tuesday was their first home and garden class. It was taught by Headmistress Agnes. "You will learn to cook and set a table for a party of ten. You will learn proper etiquette, flower arrangement and how to entertain your guests. You will be taught how to make a proper drink and most important of all, how to be a gracious hostess. Once we cover this, you'll learn about childcare, first aid, how to grocery shop and keep a budget. We want you to be well rounded women capable of being everything a man needs."

Anastasia smiled. "Now these classes are necessary to land a rich man!" "So are the lessons from Madam Chanel. Trust me. A man needs you to be all things to everyone. At the end of our classes you will be given office/secretarial classes so you can own your spot in the work place. Shall we begin?" Agnes started explaining the art of setting a beautiful table.

Ingrid asked, "Why do you need so many pieces of silverware?" "That is an excellent question!" Agnes brought out charts. Each one showed a different piece of silverware and it's use. "Thursday you will learn how to read a recipe and prepare a meal. Do your assignments and ready yourselves for bed."

Rena admitted to the others that she was much more relaxed in this class. Isabella nodded, but she was not really listening. Her thoughts drifted back to her conversation with Mary. *"Could they be training us to be government spies? First, self-defense and building bombs. Now home economics and sex training? What the hell kind of school is this?* "Ladies, we will be receiving new students. Each of you will be asked to mentor them with their classes." "Yes, ma'am." "Bed, now ladies."

With an uncertain future and so many unanswered questions, sleep eluded Isabella. *"I am afraid for the new girls coming in, but I have no answers for them either"* she thought to herself.

The classes with Madam Chanel were the hardest to stomach. "Let us now discuss masturbation. It is referred to as self-pleasure. You can also manually pleasure another person. Whether it is male or female, the principle is the same. I will have one of my girls demonstrate how a woman pleasures herself. A male consort will demonstrate how a man can do this. The final demonstration will be how they can do this simultaneously."

"Shelly will show you where and how to touch yourselves. Then I would like you to try it. "Here? In front of everyone?" "Yes. Masturbation is a very natural thing." Shelly began caressing her neck and rubbing her nipples between her fingers. She let out a slight, breathy whimper. Her hand traced the inside of both her thighs, lightly touching the outside of her private place. Then she placed a finger inside. Scared, the girls screamed "I am not doing that!'' But once they saw a male consort named Jamie naked, curiosity got the better of them.   Their eyes were glued to the same dance Shelly had done. While their interest was piqued, Chanel nodded to Shelly and Jamie to manually pleasure each other to the point of climax. The students were pale and awestruck. Shelly and Jamie came around to each class member and explained the need for release. Chanel softly cooed, "I want you to practice this alone and with one another. It is a natural thing. There is nothing to be afraid of."

"Line up for the final fittings of the dresses you need to be wearing for class." Shelly found Rena crying in the corner. "What are all the tears about?" "I just cannot do this!" Rena exclaimed. "You can and you will! Someday your life may depend on what you have learned here with us."   Patting Rena's hand, Shelly gave her a knowing smile. Isabella told Rena "Tackle this like you would a hard math problem. Once you learn the steps it's just a process." "You are not helping! My parents gave me morals! Apparently, morals are optional at this school! I cannot believe she thinks we should practice on each other!" Rena huffed. "I think the point of this class was to teach us to be comfortable with ourselves" explained Ingrid.

"This makes me so homesick!" cried Ingrid. "Remember, our parents sold us to this school for a monthly stipend and a dowry when we get married! We are just white slaves!" complained Isabella.

"I wonder what our next class will entail." whined Anastasia. Mary walked up behind Ingrid whispering, "They are being gentle with you with girls. We just got thrown into a sexual encounter with a sink or swim ultimatum! Notice not many of my classmates made it this far? My best advice: shut off your feelings! This is your job. There is no room for personal feelings here!" "Damn, we ARE slaves!" cried Ursula. "Yes. Our parents sold us into this life so they could have it easy!" "Then we are prostitutes, are we not?" "Yes, except better educated." "Why would our parents do this to us?" "They are poor! They needed a way to feed the family" explained Isabella. "Do you think our parents knew what they sold us into?" asked Rena. "No. I listened to the speech Max gave my parents. They believed it would be a better life for me with a paycheck for them attached to it."

"I wonder if there is a boy's school like this?" Anastasia asked. "No. Boys are important because they can work the fields. We were just another mouth to feed". "Get to bed, or we will all be in for a whipping!" Isabella could hear other girls crying in their bunks. She whispered defiantly, *"I will not give these sons-of- bitches the satisfaction of bringing me to tears!"* The next morning brought an announcement. There would be a new twist to combat training: torture for information would be thrown into the mix for advanced students. Isabella was first on the list of participants. Unfortunately, being a top student only made the Chancellor demand excellence from Isabella. If her team did not excel, she took the punishment for the rest of them   . She never gave her teachers the pleasure of seeing her in tears. Tears were a sign of weakness. One these girls could not afford. Not now! There were more lessons at the brothel Friday evening. After classes, the girls were instructed to bathe and dress nicely for the evening's lesson. After assembling in the hall, the girls were marched to the brothel in silence. "Tonight's lessons will be on oral sex with male and female partners." Shelly and Jamie appeared with another girl, Sonya. The trio explained, "Your job as a consort will sometimes be to accompany males or females. Your job will involve intense listening skills, public dining and graceful dancing as well as sexual service." "We are learning self-defense and academic skills" Ingrid volunteered.

"A good consort must be well-rounded. You will be a lady for their guests and sometimes care for their children as well. You will be expected to have skills in seduction and sex." Channel began giving instructions about how to "French kiss" a woman to the point of climax. She explained that hands and tongue were used for this. When the demonstration had ended with Shelly and Sonya, Jamie was called in to demonstrate these skills by a woman on a man. Confusion and embarrassment turned the girls crimson. Ursula asked, "Do boys do that to other boys?" Chanel smiled. "Excellent question! Yes, they do!" Jamie brought out another male consort for the next demonstration. "Next week, we will discuss intercourse with a male and a female. You will be attending a formal dinner dressed in your finest gown to practice your social skills. Now line up to try on your dresses, please."

"Isabella, may I have a word, please?" "Yes, ma'am." "Why do you have bruises everywhere?" "Training, ma'am. If my team does not perform to the Chancellor's expectations, I take the punishment for all of my teammates." "I will speak with the Chancellor! You will not be very appealing with all of these bruises! This is unacceptable! You girls are much too thin to fill out these dresses properly! This will never do!" Chanel struggled to contain her anger.

"I will train you in the use of pain for pleasure. This takes a special kind of talent, which you obviously have."   The seamstress yelled, "Madam Chanel!" "Yes, Claudia?" "These girls have lost more weight! I will have to take their dresses in again! And the bruises ma'am. How am I to do my job? These girls look a fright! The hairdresser is having a fit of her own. Some of their hair is so tangled she will have to cut the knots out!" "I will take care of this!"

Chanel left for the Chancellor's office. She walked in without knocking. "I was not aware that you have an appointment" Harold said coldly. "Look Harold, I cannot do my job with these girls when you use them as punching bags! I cannot make them attractive and alluring to men with bruises covering their bodies! Furthermore, they keep losing weight! The dresses needed taken in again! These girls have hair that is so badly tangled that the tangles need to be cut out! They look like boys, not young women!" "I get your point. There will be no more corporal punishment."

"I would like to give Isabella specialized training" Chanel said. Smiling, Harold nodded. "In pain and pleasure. She is the perfect choice. She does wonderful with combat, weapons and torture training. They will be completing social graces training and beginning office work. When they are not in physical training, they need to dress as ladies!" "Understood." "I think Ingrid would make a good teacher. She is good with children."

"Sunday Max will start driving lessons. The girls need to be able to function in at least three inch heels." "Anything else, Chanel?" "They need something to wear besides those terrible looking uniforms!" "Fine. Cancel Saturday classes. You may take them to buy appropriate clothing." "They need new hair styles." "You're going to financially break me!" "Let me do my job Harold!" "Pick them up at 8:00 am Saturday morning after chores. You understand that they cannot be soft." "I understand, Harold but you get more with sugar than vinegar. Do you want to sleep with ugly women? No, you do not! They need to have class, beauty, social grace and great seduction skills. Their sexual skills need to be as good as their combat skills. Their lives many depend on it. Come see me Harold. I will personally relieve your tension" Chanel cooed, kissing him gently on the cheek. "I must get back to my girls."

Walking through the tunnels back from the school, Chanel was happy knowing she secured the girls some temporary relief. After the other girls had been walked back to school, Chanel took Isabella to a special room in the house. As they walked into the room, Isabella noticed how dark and heavy the room felt. She noticed that the bed and furniture had restraints attached to them. The walls had some sort of padding attached to them. It looked like a mattress.

Chanel opened some large wooden chests that contained what looked like torture implements. Isabella touched what looked like a medical device. The steel was cold. Isabella manipulated the opening and closing. It had teeth like a gear would. "What is this for, Madam Chanel?" "For those who don't cooperate. It holds the mouth open for things to come." Whips made with horse hair and leather and wooden paddles hung from one wall. "These look like tools for torture" Isabella remarked. "As I said, some people find pleasure in pain." Chanel called in female and male consorts to demonstrate. Jamie was tied to a padded board with his back facing outward. Using a whip, Shelly hit Jamie's back. The sounds that came from him were the same kind she heard during the demonstration of oral sex. Channel then explained, "Some people like to give pain and some like to receive it. Both provide sexual release. We will discuss this at length after your next class. I wanted you to get familiar with our special room. I have made you a booklet for training in these skills. I'll expect you to know these pages. You will be tested on the material. Understand?" "Yes, ma'am."

"I have permission to take you shopping on Saturday with my girls. Be ready to see a new and improved Isabella!" Smiling, Chanel patted her butt. "You'll enjoy this lesson" she said.   Running back to the school, Isabella made it to the dormitory in time to hear the Headmistress' announcement. "From now on, you will be required to wear female attire when not in physical training. This means dresses, heels, makeup and your hair done. On Saturday after morning chores, you will be going on a field trip with Madam Chanel. Each of you will get three dresses, three pairs of heeled shoes, makeup and new hair styles. Everyone will comply. Goodnight ladies. Remember, Sunday is your driving lessons" "My, this is going to be fun!"

Thursday evening's lessons on how to host a dinner party and making drinks was a well needed break for the girls. "The new girls will be arriving in two weeks. How do we pretend to like this place and not tell these girls to run for their lives? Their parents sent them here for the same reason ours did. To give us an education and a better life." "Our parents sent us here because they needed the money and we were not strong enough to work on the farm!"   "Ladies, pay close attention when learning how to make a good martini. It is a staple in any home. Tomorrow your lessons with Madam Chanel will be three hours long. Your afternoon classes will be fifteen minutes each. Goodnight, ladies!"

Full of apprehension about the evening's events, Isabella, Ursula and Rena were prepared for the class on sexual intercourse. Walking into class, the girls noticed mattresses on the carpeted floor. Anastasia whispered, "Are we sleeping here?" Isabella said sternly "No. This is where we will practice sexual intercourse." Rena whined "Oh God! She's really going to make us do that?" "I am afraid so. It is a part of our training!" whined Ursula. "We will just have to bear with this" commanded Isabella. "We have seen what happens to girls who do not make it to graduation!" All three girls shivered at the memories of what they had seen.

Madam Chanel gently invited them to join her. "I understand you are concerned about this lesson, but I assure you I will make this lesson as painless as possible. Have a seat along the red wall and we will begin." Shelly and Jamie entered the room, acting as if no one could see them and began to demonstrate the art of foreplay.   While Madam Chanel gave a verbal description of what was happening, Shelly and Jamie began kissing deeply, letting their tongues caress each other's mouths. Then they began touching each other's bodies. Jamie cupped Shelly's breasts. He squeezed her nipples, sucking, biting and pulling on them.   This gave Shelly a pulsating throb throughout her body. Shelly then leaned in, biting Jamie's nipples. Using her tongue, she traced a line to the top of his belly. Bending down further, she began licking the underside of his ball sack. Jamie moaned in pleasure as Madam Chanel explained how sensitive this area was on a man. Gasping in horror, the girls said nothing as Chanel talked. Shelly then took Jamie's penis into her mouth.   She fully enveloped his shaft as she suckled the head. This made his penis go from flaccid to hard in minutes. Jamie then used the tip of his tongue and pushed inside the folds of Shelly's womanhood, caressing the sides of her clitoris. This left her begging for more. Jamie then stood up and put on a condom.

Madam Chanel explained that condoms were used to prevent pregnancy and venereal diseases. The girls began crying. "I will never do that with a man!" Once Jamie was prepared, he and Shelly positioned themselves so everything could be seen. Once Jamie had mounted Shelly, he began slowly moving in and out of her. He kissed and caressed her. Moving faster and faster, he pounded her flesh. Moaning and screaming in pleasure, Jamie collapsed on Shelly. Madam Chanel smiled. "See girls? There's nothing to it."

"I have brought five of my best male consorts to help you through your first time." Ursula screamed, "You do not expect us to do such a disgusting thing, do you?" Cooing gently, Chanel said "Yes, Ursula I do." "But!" "This is why your first time needs to be with a professional. Someone who will be gentle with you. These men train all our virgins."

"Gentlemen!" called Chanel ,clapping her hands. In walked five of the most beautiful young men in the world. Their skin was as creamy as buttermilk; they had chiseled bodies and firm, round buttocks. With their manhood covered by silk robes, they stood perfectly still. "Ladies, these young men are: Chadwick, Bradley, Goddard "God" for short, Thatcher, and Sebastian."

"Let's match you with your counterpart."

"Isabella, you are with Goddard. Ursula, you are with Chadwick. Rena, you are with Bradley. Anastasia, you are with Thatcher. Ingrid, you are with Sebastian."

"Gentlemen, make the ladies comfortable. Before you start, I expect you to give your best performance. Take them gently, but firmly. They will be scared and resistant. No matter how much they protest, this must be done!" "Yes, ma'am."

"Just remember, you will be their teachers. Teach them what you would expect a woman to know. Understand?" "Yes, ma'am." "I will be here if you need anything.

Now it is time you joined your dates." "Why do we have to do this in front of everyone else?" whined Rena. "In case there are questions, of course" cooed Madam Chanel. "We cannot do this in front of anyone else!" shouted Ursula. "Perhaps you would feel more comfortable in a room with privacy?" "Yes, ma'am." Madam Channel assigned the pairs to private rooms.

She smiled at Isabella. "You and Goddard will go to the special room I showed you earlier." "Fine" said Isabella. Chadwick, Bradley, Thatcher and Sebastian had done this many times before. They knew how to handle a virgin. They always started out with kissing and hand holding to help girls relax. Then like clockwork, each man started the routine of gently caressing each girl. As the girls flushed crimson, a warming filled their insides. They quickly discovered how this could be enjoyable.

Now the real work started. Voices began rising with questions. "You want me to put that in my mouth? That is disgusting!"   Laughing, the men offered to show the girls how good it felt. "Oh, I could never let a man do that to me!" With a gentle lift, Ursula found herself flat on her back as Chadwick kissed and licked her breasts. Using his tongue, he circled her belly with a smile.   Gently moving her legs apart, he began pushing his tongue inside the folds of her womanhood. As he licked gently, she opened like a flower's petals welcoming the sun. As he nibbled at her clitoris, Ursula had a wonderful feeling of excitement and warmth. Breathing hard, Chadwick asked, "Are you ready?" "I am afraid!" "Do not worry. I will be gentle." As he mounted her, fear, excitement and pain hit her at once. Screaming in both ecstasy and terror, Ursula became a woman. The other girls had the same experience, except for Isabella.

As Isabella and Goddard entered the special room, Isabella looked deep into Goddard's eyes. With a cold, hard tone, she said "Let's get this done!" "In a hurry, are we Madam?" "Do you like to give or receive pain?" snapped Isabella. "A little of both, my dear."

"Take off your shirt!" demanded Goddard. Trying to act cold, Isabella removed her blouse. "Turn around slowly. I see you are no stranger to the Chancellor's whip" Goddard said. "No sir. I am not." "Why is that, Isabella?" "I do not take orders well, sir." "You will from me!" Goddard said with a sinister gaze. "I think you can take a little punishment. You're not like those soft, prissy girls you came in with. Have you been in here before?" "Yes. Madam Chanel brought me here and showed me around." "Where shall we start?" "Step over here." Grabbing Isabella's hand, Goddard marched her to what looked like a bed with restraints at the head and foot boards. "Let's get rid of that uniform skirt and see what we have. Nice, except for all those scars on your back." Giving Isabella a kiss, he smiled. "I see you need practice to open up those pink lips!"

Removing his robe, he pushed her head toward his manhood. He demanded oral sex. Isabella smiled, opening her mouth. Once his penis was inside, she closed her warm mouth around it, biting down hard. Screaming, Goddard picked Isabella up by her hair and punched her until she let go.

Composing himself, he said "That is not playing nice, now is it? "Going to the chest of drawers, he pulled out a metal dental device used to hold open the mouth of a patient. "Here, this will hold open that mouth of yours." Shoving in the dental device, he opened her mouth as wide as the gauge would go. He pushed his penis in and out of her mouth until he was ready to explode. Suddenly stopping, he looked into her terror- stricken face. "You do not get off that easy!" As he pulled the gauge from her mouth, she cried out in pain. Blood was dripping from her mouth. Goddard smiled, licking it from her lips. "Now will you play nice?" "Yes, sir." "Good girl." Goddard began the ritual he enjoyed: kissing the neck and biting Isabella's nipples hard. This caused both pleasure and pain. Smiling, he blindfolded her so she could not see what would come next. He began orally stimulating her, then slapping her ass. Just as Isabella had gotten used to his pace, he announced "This is both pleasure and pain!" Pushing her ass into the air, he rubbed his penis against her open folds. Then he slammed into her again and again. She screamed in pain. Goddard smiled. Looking into her face, he announced, "I am not finished yet!" Turning her around, he took her anus, screaming "I own you! I will always be your master!" After a few minutes, he untied her. "Get cleaned up! I may want more." Isabella stood up on wobbly legs. She was walking to the basin to clean up when she spotted the whip. She thought, *"I should to draw a little blood myself."* Grabbing the whip, she crept up behind Goddard. She pulled back the whip. *Snap!* Goddard received several more lashes. Isabella screamed, "Here is some pain and pleasure for you!" Dropping the whip, she cleaned herself up and reported back to the main parlor. Looking haggard and worn, Isabella looked into Chanel's eyes. Chanel cooed, "It does get better. I promise. After morning chores, I will be taking you on a field trip." "Where are we going, Madam Chanel?" "We will be shopping for new clothes, hairstyles, shoes and other things to help you transition into dressing like women. You are physically women. You must learn to dress and behave as women as well."

"Go back to school. Get some rest. Tomorrow we will have a fun day!" Smiling brightly, Madam Chanel escorted the girls through the tunnels back to the dormitory. After bathing, the girls discussed the lessons they had just received. As their fear and adrenaline levels dropped, they realized that they were now women. Physically anyway. Pride slowly began to fill their heads as well as their hearts. With sore and exhausted bodies and minds, sleep took them over. Saturday morning would come early.

After morning chores, Headmistress Agnes announced "It is time to dress for your field trip. Dress in street attire and join me in the front hall." After dressing, the girls scurried to the front hall. Madam Chanel was waiting for them. "Ladies, we will be riding a bus into town. I expect you to be on your best behavior. Understood?" "Yes, ma'am." The forty-five-minute ride was filled with excitement and anxiety. Walking into an exclusive clothing shop, the girls received scowls and whispers in their direction. "Yes? May I help you?" Madam Chanel smiled coolly. "Yes. I brought these young ladies in for a fitting of ladies attire." "Are you sure this shop will meet the needs of these girls?"   With an icy smile, Chanel whispered, "You know very well who I am. I know your husband intimately!" "I understand. Ladies, follow me!" After choosing several dresses, the girls lined up for the hair salon. Because of their matted, tangled hair, all five girls had been relegated to short or medium length hairstyles. They were styled to look as feminine as possible.

On the return trip to the school Isabella asked, "Why were those women so snide to you, Madam Chanel?" Clearing her throat, she cooed, "They are jealous because their husbands prefer the company of my girls to them. They have to keep up appearances. They never turned down our money, now did they? They believe it is acceptable to judge others when they have skeletons of their own."

" You ladies need to wear your new clothing whenever you are not in physical training class. I have included a pant suit which will be worn for outdoor activities. We will also teach you how to roll your hair with curlers to get the same result when you style your hair." "Do we carry purses?" "Yes. Women carry them to carry their personal items." Whispers among the girls were rising in decibel. "Do you have any other questions?" "Will we be expected to provide condoms for men?" "It is always a good idea to have a few on hand. Men are not always responsible when it comes to birth control. We will discuss this further in our next meeting." As the bus pulled up in front of the school, Chanel said "Ladies, take your things to your room. "Chanel headed directly to the Chancellor's office. "Harold, I thought you handled the shop owners?"

"Hello, Chanel!" "I took the girls to the dress shop. We were given a cold welcome." "I assume you handled it?" "Yes, but I should not have had to! I reminded them their husbands preferred the company of our girls to theirs!"   Laughing hard,

Harold said, "You told her!" "Those hypocritical, self-righteous women make me sick!" "Do the girls have driving lessons tomorrow?" "Yes. Max will teach the class. Then they will apply to take the driver's test."   Smiling, Channel cooed, "Our girls need to know how to drive. It will keep them out in the world. Some of our girls are not old enough for a license, but with a little greasing of the wheels, there will be no issues."

"What will they practice on?" "Their first lesson will be on the Renault Celtraquatre. It is large and well built. Once they have acquired the skills to handle speed and accuracy, we will move to the Gaz 61. It is four-wheel drive. You never know when you will need to drive through water or steep terrain."

"That sounds reasonable. "When do we graduate this batch?" "Soon. We will call a meeting to discuss which ones are ready!" "Agreed." "Harold, I feel Isabella would make a fine courtesan. She is not emotional. Everything is a job, nothing more. She will be a fine asset in the field."

"Emotions can be an asset" explained Harold. "I have chosen cover jobs that suit each girl's personality traits. This will help keep moral dilemmas down."

"Ingrid has a gentle, loving side. She is very nurturing. She will make a wonderful kindergarten teacher." Chanel smiled in agreement with the Chancellor's choice for Ingrid. "I hope your intuition about each girl's assets matches their jobs. When a woman enjoys her job, she takes pride in what she does" smiled Chanel. Leaving, she kissed Harold with a hot passion that he felt deep in his belly. Pulling away, Chanel smiled. "We both know how much I enjoy my job." "Yes, we do" breathed Harold.

The girls whispered about the new lessons on Sundays. "I heard we will have driving lessons!" squealed Ingrid. Scowling, Isabella shook her head. "Another set of skills to conquer. Like sex or hand- to -hand combat." Ursula whispered, "I wonder which car we will learn on?" "We have chores first, now get to sleep!" complained Rena.

With sunlight streaming through the dormitory windows, the girls stirred rubbing their eyes. Headmistress Agnes announced, "You have a busy day." Chores and breakfast went by quickly. "Report to the history classroom for your first lesson on the mechanics of the combustion engine!"   Isabella raised her hand and said, "I thought we were learning to drive?" Smiling, Headmistress Agnes said, "You must understand the inner workings of an engine before you can master it." After the class was seated, Max began his lesson on the history of the Renault Celtaquatre.

"The Renault was built in France between 1934 and 1938. It is considered a small family car. It was normally two toned in color."

Stats:

Eight liters of fuel will travel sixty-two miles per hour

Thirty horsepower (8cv) two power

Brakes: cable-drums. Front and rear.

Battery: Six volt

Cost: 16,900 to 20,500 Francs

$2,857.31 to $3,466.48 US currencies.

This car has a three speed manual transmission on the floor. A three speed car shifts in an "H" pattern. It also has a third pedal known as a clutch. Your left foot presses the clutch pedal while your right hand shifts the floor mounted gear shifter.

Reverse: Toward you and up

First gear: Toward you and down

Second Gear: Away from you and up

Third Gear: Away from you and down

"Does everyone understand so far?" "Will we learn how to put in fuel and oil?" asked Ursula. "Very good question" replied Max. "I will prepare you to take care of your automobile. You will be able to handle any situation that arises. Let's go outside." The girls followed Max to the car they would learn to drive. Max explained the reasons for needing wing mirrors. "The mirror on the side of the car is called a wing mirror. This mirror helps the driver see behind him or her and to the side of the car. Our heads cannot turn on a swivel to see, so we use mirrors. They are adjustable." Opening the car door, Max pointed to the rear view mirror. "The rear view mirror is used to see behind us though the rear windshield. This mirror is also adjustable." Max asked each of the girls to sit in the driver's seat. "Adjust your mirrors so you have maximum view of both sides and rear of the automobile." Max then showed how to open the gas tank for refueling.

Lifting the bonnet (hood) of the car, Max showed the class how to check the oil. "Your oil must be up to this line for maximum efficiency." Anastasia raised her hand. "Why does a car need antifreeze?" "Good question. A car needs antifreeze to help cool the engine in the summer time and prevent it from freezing up in the winter. Get in and let's take a ride. I will explain each thing I do. When I am done, you will start the car and adjust your mirrors. After everyone is comfortable with the first steps, we will start driving."After guiding the girls through the first steps, Headmistress Agnes rang the bell for lunch. Lining up, Isabella led the girls to wash up.

Agnes whispered to Max "How are they doing? " "They are nervous as expected, but listening well." After lunch, everyone returned. They were walked to the back field that was used for guest parking for the brothel. Marching single-file, they arrived to see Max setting up a road course. Whispering back and forth, confusion ran rampant between the students.   Stepping up, Max's voice raised several decibels. "Quiet!! Follow instructions closely. Isabella, step forward."

"Get into the driver's seat. Adjust your mirrors. Put on your seat belt. I will be in the passenger seat giving you instructions. Once you have checked your mirrors and are ready, we will begin."

"Turn the key in the ignition. We will start with moving the car forward. Press down on the gas pedal. When changing gears, use your left foot to press down on the clutch and your right hand to shift. Always watch your mirrors. Watch the road speed. Then we will slow to a stop and use your mirrors to reverse. This is all about timing."Each girl received the same instructions. Next, each girl had to go through Max's road course. At the end of the day, Max announced that they would practice twice during the week and every Sunday for the next six weeks.

Sending tearful students to dinner, Max looked exhausted. Agnes brought him three fingers of Scotch to settle his nerves. He shook his head as he looked at the Chancellor. "Harold, I am not sure I can have them ready in six weeks." "We have no choice. Chanel will take them out to test their other skills. Graduation is coming soon." "Ursula actually took her hands off the wheel and covered her face!" "It was the first day. It will get better." "I need another drink!" grumbled Max.

"How did Isabella handle this challenge?" "After three times around the field, she had her timing down. I would say it is time to make her team leader. What are your ideas, Harold?" "Let us put her to the test of teaching the other girls. If they fail, she fails." "Isabella does not handle failure well. She will make sure they are skilled in driving." "I see" smiled Max. "Have her report to my office." After evening chores, Isabella reported to the Chancellor's office.

"You wanted to see me, sir?" "Yes, Isabella. I have decided to make you team leader. Your classmates learning to drive are your responsibility. If they do not graduate, neither do you. Whatever they do wrong, you will be held accountable for. Do you understand?" "Yes, sir. They will rise to your expectations." "You are dismissed, Isabella."

Walking back to the dormitory Isabella fumed. "How do I get these girls through drivers training?" Harold's words screamed in her mind. *"I will not graduate if the other girls flunk driving class!"* Calming herself, she planned out how she would get everyone through driving class.

Isabella drew everyone a copy of the shifting pattern. Passing them out, Isabella announced, "I am now team leader. It is my job to get you through driving class. If you do not pass, I do not graduate. You WILL pass. We need to make a gear shift and pedals. Any free time we have will be spent practicing! Ursula, we never take our hands off the wheel. Our hands must be at ten and two o'clock!" Thinking out loud, Isabella said, "What can we use as a gear shift?" Running to the custodian's closet, Isabella returned with a plunger. She assembled blocks of wood to make a clutch, brake and gas pedal. She then stuck the plunger to floor.

Sticking her diagram to the wall, Isabella asked each girl to sit the chair using the plunger as the shifter and practiced . Each girl practiced shifting using the clutch. When she was satisfied with their progress, Isabella said "We will practice every night before bed so we will be ready for class." In between classes, the girls practiced shifting using the clutch, gas and brake pedals. By Wednesday, the girls had the shifting pattern down. Madam Chanel appeared at the final bell.

"We will be hosting a party for you to demonstrate all the skills you have acquired. Decorating, food preparation, drink making and other skills. You will each be assigned to create a small, informational summary to be completed by the end of party. Report to the Chancellor's office for debriefing. Any questions ladies?" "What do we wear to something like that?" "I have selected formal gowns for you . When you report and receive your assignments, you will get your dress. Each of you will report to me so our seamstress can do any alterations. Saturday after chores, report to my parlor. I will assign jobs for the party preparations. You're excused."

Anastasia exclaimed, "Geez! As if we don't have enough on our plate with classes, driving, and the new girls that will be arriving soon!" Isabella nodded. "They're testing us to see how much we can handle at one time." Ursula piped up, "It's a precursor to what our jobs will be like after graduation." "Report to the parking lot for driving class." "Yes, Headmistress Agnes." In the parking lot, Max was preparing the course. Isabella looked into the eyes of her frightened friends. Smiling, she said, "You know the shifting. Make me proud of you!"

Max asked each girl to go through the same steps as the last lesson. To his surprise, they handled the road course and shifting gears well. "Alright, ladies, Isabella has practiced with you. You have accomplished so much in three days. Now we will run the road course in reverse. Isabella, you will go first!"

Isabella adjusted the mirrors and buckled herself in. She shifted the car into the reverse position. Turning to look out her rear view mirror and putting her foot on the gas, she swerved through the obstacle course. After stalling a few times, she got to the end of the course. "Now, forward!" screamed Max "You will do this five times. Then, line up for dinner."

"A reminder, ladies. I will add another obstacle for our next class. You're dismissed!" Isabella took the girls to wash up. "Wash those faces! You cannot cry in the middle of driving! You are going to hit another car! What if children were in the car? Just like all of our skills, our lives may depend on our driving skills!" Frustrated, Isabella thought "*What are they going to do in a combat situation? Cry when someone shoots at them? We are going to need to practice driving backwards for speed and agility.*" She began making a lesson plan in her mind. Practice would start Thursday before classes.

Isabella snuck into the Chancellor's office and stole the keys to the Renault. She made her classmates join her outside. Complaining loudly, Rena was trembling from the cold. "It is four a.m. and damn cold!" "You need the practice!"Once the girls had run the backward driving drill twice, Isabella announced "You need to be able to do forty miles per hour forward and backward! Friday morning, we will try accelerating to a speed of sixty miles per hour! Ursula, get these keys back into the Chancellor's office without being seen! Classes start in an hour! Clean yourselves up!"

Friday morning, Rena was assigned to steal gas for the car. "Check the fluids, Ursula! Anastasia, you're first! Go backward at thirty-five miles per-hour through the course. Then, forward at sixty around the parking lot!" "Okay, each of us will run this drill three times!" At the end of the day, Headmistress Agnes announced, "The Chancellor has noticed that the Renault has been taken out twice. If you have any knowledge of this, come forward now!" When no one stood up, Agnes knew what had happened. "Isabella, report to the Chancellor's office after evening chores!" Knocking on the Chancellor's door, Isabella stepped inside his office. "Yes, sir?" "Do you know why I asked you here?" "Yes, sir. Someone took the Renault out without permission or supervision." "Do you have anything to say about this?" "Sir, you assigned me to be team leader. You told me if my classmates do not graduate, neither would I. You wanted me to teach them so they would pass driving class, did you not? I made an executive decision. We took the Renault out to practice under my supervision. They have accomplished all the goals I set for them. They even checked the cars fluids and put gas in. If there is to be any punishment, I should receive it on their behalf. They were under my supervision."The Chancellor's mouth broke into a smile. "You have done what any good leader would have done. You accomplished your goals and took responsibility for your subordinates. This proves your leadership skills. Stealing the keys and gas was sloppy, but otherwise well done."   Returning to the dormitory, Isabella smiled to herself. She was thinking she would be the best in command. Saturday morning brought chores and the appearance of Madam Chanel.

"You need to accompany me to my parlor to be assigned jobs for the party and try on your gowns. Everyone follow me." Walking single-file, the girls' apprehension mounted. Entering the brothel, Ingrid felt sick to her stomach. Anastasia felt a cold chill climbing up her spine. Ursula and Rena put a comforting arm around each other. They remembered their past visit to the brothel. Isabella felt calm and relaxed. She had stood her ground with Goddard. She feared nothing at Madam Chanel's. "Let's begin with job assignments. Isabella, you will be in charge of security. Our team covers exterior and interior exits and perimeter.

Anastasia, you are in charge of the bar. Make sure we have plenty of alcohol. There is a drink guide. Know all drinks by heart.

Ingrid, you are in charge of invitations. I have a guest list. Prepare the invitations for delivery.

Ursula, work on the menu with the kitchen staff. Appetizers through dessert.

Rena, you handle decorations. We have lights and other party decor. "Let us start the gown fittings. Ladies you remember our seamstress, Claudia. "After fittings began, Chanel started matching skin tone to color of the gowns.

"Ingrid, we use calligraphy for our invitations." "Miss Chanel?" "Yes?" "I am pleased to report no bruises. They have not lost any weight either. They are in much better condition this time. No rats' nests in their hair and a few have tried styling it. Their makeup application skills are better. There is hope for these girls."

"Separate to your job areas and begin preparations. I will meet with you individually to give you your special assignments. You have two hours to work on preparation for the party and report back to me. Is that understood?" "Yes, ma'am." After two hours, each girl reported to Chanel on the progress on party preparations. Once the girls went back to the school, Chanel called in her security, kitchen staff and bartender to the parlor. "How did our girls do?" "Isabella aggressively took charge. Ursula took our working menu apart and changed everything we decided on. Anastasia hated our drink choices. She said that women like drinks that are appealing to the eye and taste good. Our choices are appealing to men. Rena feels our decorations are old and need to be revitalized." "They know what they want" chuckled Chanel. "Ingrid does not agree with our style of calligraphy. She says it's too ornate. She feels simple and classic would be best." "Give the girls a wide berth in their choices." "Understood, ma'am."

Chanel whispered, "Our girls are almost ready to fly. They have come a long way.

We will have a meeting tomorrow evening to decide what their new assignments will be." After evening chores, the girls went to the dorm. "Isabella, did you get beat for taking the Renault?" "No. I defended our position. The Chancellor agreed. His only complaint was that the stealing of the keys and gas were sloppy. No one should have known we were there."

"We have party prep and driving lessons. What else do you think we will have before graduation?" "I am thinking some kind of war contest to prove our proficiency in our other skills. Weapons, hand-to-hand combat, use of a compass, living off the land. Things along those lines."

Rena asked, "Contest or combat? " "They are one in the same, I am sure "whined Ursula. "I look forward to this kind of contest "smiled Isabella. "We need to get some sleep. We have driving lessons in the morning "complained Anastasia. Chores and the usual Sunday breakfast of pancakes made this seem like every other Sunday.

Smiling, Max looked into the dining room. "Ladies, meet in the back lot in ten minutes. "I understand you have been practicing. Let's see how well you do. "After covering forward and reverse with a little added speed, each girl proved proficient with driving.

Smiling, Max announced, "It is time to test another skill set. Isabella, get in the driver's seat. I will be in the passenger seat. While you drive, I will shoot the targets I have set up. Each of you will drive and shoot." After three hours of practice, Max called it a day. Lining up the girls went to wash up for dinner. Max received three fingers of Scotch from Agnes as he walked through the front door. He headed straight for the Chancellor's office. "Hello, Max! How did they do today?" "Surprisingly well, Harold. Driving with speed and shooting targets seemed to come rather naturally to them." "What is next?" asked Harold. "Driving under fire." "That may take some extra practice. I counted on that" smiled Max. "Is Isabella doing well?" asked Harold "She is excelling." "Our annual war games/ combat competition should be exciting this year. Isabella will make it interesting." "I agree" smiled Max.

The girls were excitedly whispering about the day's events. "Are we going to practice this week?" "I believe we will need Max's supervision because of the guns." "We will keep practicing shifting and driving skills without Max." "I heard them talking" giggled Rena. "They are getting a new four wheel drive, heavy terrain truck!" "Will we learn to drive that one too?" asked Anastasia. "It will depend on our proficiency with the Renault" explained Isabella.

Working on the party preparations kept the girls busy. Then the new batch of girls arrived. They were scared little girls. They looked to the older students for comfort and support.

"What do we tell the new girls about life at this school?" "Nothing yet. They are too fragile for us to tell them about this place yet" explained Ursula. "Agreed. This place is scary enough without being told you will be trained as a consort and a spy." "Right now, we will be as helpful to them as we can. Try and sleep, ladies. Your day starts early in the morning!" announced Headmistress Agnes.

The girls were quietly sniffling and sobbing into their pillows. They thought no one heard them. The stringent school schedule helped keep new students busy. This kept them from missing their parents. Wednesday after classes, Max took the girls to an open field twenty miles away for driving class. Anastasia asked, "Why are we all the way out here?" "Our lesson today will be driving under hazardous conditions. Isabella you drive. Ursula, you shoot at the targets. I will be in charge of conditions."

Driving the course, Isabella saw smoke. The conditions started with smoke bombs and a barrage of fire directly at their vehicle. Isabella navigated the course twice then changed places with Ursula. The team completed both parts of the course as both driver and shooter. Although they were scared and excited at the same time, the team rose to the challenge. "We will do this again with more obstacles." There was a collective sigh of relief as they returned to the school. "I will see you Friday, ladies." As Max entered the front hall, Headmistress Agnes appeared with three fingers of Scotch. "He is waiting for you in his office. "How did they handle this trial?" "They were confused but rose to the occasion. Believe it or not, they are all crack shots even under tough conditions." "Pretty impressive." "They will be great assets in a war zone." "Excellent! I was hesitant to graduate these girls from our school this early. We will start the meeting when the others arrive." Just then, Chanel announced herself. "Good evening, Harold.

Max, how are you?" "Fine, Chanel and yourself? " "I am fine" smiled Chanel. "Would you call Agnes, Max?" Agnes was with the new students. "Excuse me, Headmistress Agnes. The Chancellor is waiting." "I will join you as soon as I settle our new girls in for the night."

After twenty minutes, Agnes joined the group in the Chancellor's office. "Trouble with our new girls Agnes?" "They are just homesick and missing their parents." "What shall we do about assignments for the party?" "Well, I feel we should set goals that are easy to understand."

"Ingrid will gather intel from the diplomat stationed at the consulate. She needs to find out where his children attend school. Ursula needs to pickpocket the Ambassador of France, photograph the contents and return the wallet before he notices. Rena will have to sneak into his office and copy his passport.

Anastasia will find out when he meets with the High Council. Isabella needs to break in to the Ambassador's office and photograph his itinerary of meetings for the following week. They will then provide us with proof of completion. They can work together to achieve their goals."

"Chanel, you will give each girl her assignment and all tools needed to complete them." Harold handed Chanel a bag containing cameras and locking-picking tools. The meeting dispersed and Chanel retreated to her solarium to plan the new lessons. She sent word to Agnes that the girls were to meet her at the brothel the next day. When they arrived, Chanel brought out a mannequin to practice picking pockets. She discussed how to gather information from your mark by plying them with alcohol. "Anastasia, men are willing to bare their souls after enjoying some pleasure." "You mean sex!" "A good blow job can make a man tell all. I will give you lessons on getting the job done and returning to the party before you are missed." "What if he wants regular sex too?" "The average man wants half and half." The girls looked confused. Chanel explained, "A half and half is when you start with oral sex until he becomes erect. Then you finish with vaginal intercourse. Most men do not last longer than fifteen to twenty minutes from start to finish. Then they want pillow talk. So, if you need to use one of our rooms, they will be available. We will practice before the party. Typically, you can pull information while planning another date."

Anastasia's face turned a bright crimson. She whispered, "I do not think I can go through with this assignment!" "Remember what happens to the girls that do not graduate. They end up here or in a hole some field! Weakness in any form is unacceptable!" "I do understand, ma'am." "Think of it as a chore you must do. It is a job, nothing more. You will practice with one of our male consorts. He will teach you technique and efficiency. Get some rest, classes start early."

Crying in bed, Anastasia could not fathom having to be a "whore "to complete this assignment. Taking her by the hand, Isabella dragged her to the lavatory. "What the hell is wrong with you?" Anastasia explained what her assignment was. Isabella nodded. "We are allowed to work together to complete our assignments. We will figure this out together. I will come up with a plan!" Smiling and winking, Isabella patted Anastasia's arm. "Now, get to bed!"

'Damn Chanel! She knew Anastasia could not handle a task like this! I will have to be her partner for this assignment. This is how they weed us out!' thought Isabella. Sleep eluded her. Plans danced in her mind about how to get everyone's assignments done working together. Isabella whispered, "We need to meet before starting work on party preparations." Ursula yawned. "What's this meeting about?" "I have a plan to get all of our assignments done together. Then we need to help Anastasia with hers. We can discuss this later. Go back to sleep."

After chores, everyone lined up for driving practice. Max passed out manuals. "There will be a written test as well as a driving proficiency test. You must memorize this manual to pass your written test. You must keep an "A" average in your studies to graduate. I am sure you ladies are painfully aware of the consequences to those who do not graduate." "Yes, sir. " "This will demonstrate how well you can handle pressure." Whispers between the girls grew louder. "Silence, ladies! We need to review all you have learned in driving class. Isabella, you're up first!"   After several run-throughs, the girls lined up for lunch. During clean up, Isabella whispers "We are going to work together!" "Always" replied Ursula.   Isabella explained Anastasia's assignment. "I will work up a plan so three of us can cover the tasks dealing with information, copies, and proof. Then I will assist Anastasia with her assignment. We all need to graduate from this hell!"

While working on bar preparations, Anastasia took notes on special drinks to help loosen the tongues of targets. "We will need to use one of those drinks for your task. I will bring you up to speed when I finish my plan. We need to spend time practicing with the mannequin. We should all be able to pick a pocket without being noticed. It's just as important to return the item to the target unnoticed. This party is a chance to prove that we excel at our job" explained Isabella. "Once we have our plan down, we will work on how long it should take to accomplish all tasks and return to the party unnoticed. Since I work security, I will know where the men will be posted."

After some practice with the mannequin, hidden talents came to light. Ursula was a natural at stealing from the mannequin. For the final test, the girls were taken into town to work a crowd. If they could pickpocket a crowd without being caught, they could handle their assignments.

When they returned to school, they were called into the Chancellor's office to show what they collected. There was an assortment of wallets, passports and jewelry. Max beamed with pride. "Our girls have learned well." "Well done ladies. You may return to your party planning." Walking back to the brothel, Isabella announced, "Meeting before bed! We will discuss my plan." Having completed tasks and after their evening meal, they were sent to the dormitory.

"I have figured out how to help Anastasia with her assignment. Since most of your assignments have to do with copying documents and turning them in, if we work together it can be done in half the time. Anastasia is uncomfortable with the idea of being a "whore" to get information. We are going to handle it. Anastasia, since you are bar tending, we need you to whip up a special drink with a special ingredient. Once the mark has consumed his drink, he will experience dizziness, blurred vision and a lack of coordination. It will also loosen his tongue a bit." "I cannot do what Chanel said." Isabella smiled. "We are going to give him the time of his life. He will think he is going to sleep with all of us. We will tie him up with these silk cords and tease and taunt him. We will get the information and he will pass out. You will have to practice like Channel said, in case we cannot get to you fast enough. We will be with you for the party." With preparations for the party in full swing, the girls had to pass their driver's tests. Each took the written exam and a test behind the wheel. Each girl passed with ninety-eight percent except for Isabella. She received a perfect score as expected. Their test results were sent to the Chancellor for his approval.

Next was the final gown fitting. With corsets and boning, they looked like ladies, not little girls. Chanel smiled sadly. "It is such a shame they had to grow up so soon. They will be great operatives."

The night of the party came with an influx of wait staff, cooks, bartenders and security staff. The girls could blend in unnoticed. As the guests started to arrive, Ursula, Ingrid and Rena set about completing their assignments. Isabella and the security team checked the perimeter. Once perimeter check was complete, Isabella dressed as quickly as she could. She then checked in with the others making sure that their assignments were completed. She then checked on Anastasia. She was busy making drinks for guests. While the string quartet played a soft waltz, Anastasia spotted her mark. With a smile, she started a flirtatious chat. She gently brushed up against him suggesting they go for a walk. Xavier happily agreed. "Let me get us a drink." "Sounds perfect. Anastasia is it?" "Yes, it is." Handing him a drink, Anastasia put her arm through his, leading him down the hall toward the brothel. Xavier whispered, "Let's go somewhere we can be alone." "Sounds nice" giggled Anastasia. Chanel had already chosen room four for her assignment. The room was beautiful with red velvet covered walls trimmed in gold. There was a four- poster bed and a settee at the foot of the bed. A large pitcher and basin. Setting his drink on the night stand, Xavier turned to Anastasia leering. "Come to me." "You should wash up while I get ready for you." "As you wish" Xavier said turning his back to her, facing the wash basin. Anastasia quickly opened the vial and poured the contents into his drink.

Turning around, Xavier licked his lips and smiled. "Where shall we start?" As he grabbed at her, she ducked away. She then handed Xavier his glass. He gulped down the golden liquid in one swallow. "Now that is done. Let us get down to business!" growled

Xavier. "I have something for you to wrap those pretty pink lips around!" "In time, Xavier. " Anastasia sat down on the bed, patting the pillow next to her. As he started walking to the bed, he staggered. This caused him to trip on the rug. "Oh, my! We had better get you on the bed!" smiled Anastasia. "My thoughts exactly!" growled Xavier. Climbing on the bed, he dropped to his back, grabbing at Anastasia again. She easily escaped his grasp. Frustrated, Xavier yelled "Do your job!"

A knock on the door quieted Xavier's lustful advances. Opening the door, Isabella smiled at Anastasia. "So, the party got moved in here? "Xavier howled, "Come join us! "There was another knock. "Oh, more surprises!" cackled Xavier.

"Ladies, let us inspect this merchandise." Tying his hands with pink silk cords, they begin undressing him. Having five women touch and caress him was a dream come true for Xavier. He did not mind all the silly questions about business meetings and his job.

Chanel taught them that you must always inspect a man's penis. He could be diseased. Xavier, losing his patience yelled, "When is our fun going to start? Stop teasing me!" The girls looked at one another whispering, "It does not look right! "Xavier's eyes started to flutter. Rena left the room to get Madam Chanel.

Returning, Rena pointed out what they deemed to be disfigured. After inspecting Xavier's malformed penis, Chanel said that he had a disease. "Did any of you girls have sex with him?" "No ma'am!" "Good, go back to the party. Finish your assignments. We will handle him."

Back at the party, things went well. There were no problems of any kind. After clean up detail was complete, Isabella, Anastasia, Ursula, Ingrid, and Rena reported to the Chancellor's office with proof of their completed assignments in hand. Verifying all proof, the Chancellor announced they had one assignment before graduation. Night maneuver exercises. "Report for instruction at five a.m. Well done, ladies!" Ursula looked to Isabella and mouthed "Night maneuvers?"   The team went back to the dorm. Their minds raced at the concept of what five a.m. would bring. Sleep came easy and fast, but five a.m. came much too soon, waking them from well-deserved sleep. They yawned while standing in the breakfast line. Max appeared in the doorway of the dining hall. "Ladies, come with me."   The team followed Max in cold silence. "This will be your last assignment before graduation. This final task will encompass all your combat and survival skills. You will need to work as a team to accomplish your mission.

You will be given a compass, a knife and a canteen of water. You will need to live off the land, collect clues and avoid pit falls. Make it back to the school in forty-eight hours. There will be obstacles and combatants in your way. You must collect the other team's flag and present it to our Chancellor."

"Remember, you have forty-eight hours. You will be blindfolded until you're dropped off. Good luck. Go prepare." The rest of the day was filled with dread and uncertainty. At nightfall, the girls had their last meal. They slept with their packs in hand.

Suddenly, a red light shone overhead. "Grab your packs! When they reached the parking lot, hoods were put over their heads and they were shoved into a large truck. They rode for several hours. A sudden stop startled them.   Landing hard on the ground, all they heard was "Find your own way back to the school. Good luck!" "They were scared, but they refused to show it. Isabella pulled off her hood. Then she pulled the hoods off her teammates. "It's so dark out here!" cried Ursula. "Who has the light? Who has the compass? "Rena announced, "I have the compass." "We need to figure out where we are and how far we are from the school". "I have a map in my pack!" cried Ingrid. "How many hours was that ride?" "It was four hours!" beamed Anastasia. "Which towns are that distance from the school?" "I found four towns on the map."

"Which direction do you think we drove in?" After several minutes of discussion, Isabella decided to head northwest.

"We have to stay off the main roads so we cannot be followed easily." Rena said there would be traps to keep them from getting home. "Agreed. Capturing that flag will be another problem!" exclaimed Isabella. Ingrid piped in. "We need weapons!" "I am hungry and tired!" whined Anastasia.   Rena spoke up. "Stop your crying! We are all in this together!" Trudging through the woods, the moon gave off a creepy glow. The body of swamp water gave off gasses. Anastasia screamed in a hushed voice "what is that?" Isabella explained that the combination of gasses coming off the water being hit with moonlight gave off the creepy glow.

"I need to stop and rest" Ingrid announced. "Ten minutes. Then we have to keep moving. We will be easier to track in daylight. We have to find the traps." "Agreed. These burlap sacks may be useful once we find their camp. We can use them to scare the other team!" smiled Isabella.

"Let's get moving again. It will be dawn soon." After walking for another hour, Rena said, "Shh! Look up ahead. Our first obstacle. We need his rifle." Isabella gave the orders. "Rena, flank around to the left. Ingrid to the right. I will sneak up behind him. Anastasia, it's time you put that whiny girl act to good use. Act lost. Cry! Make sure to keep his attention."   Stumbling into the camp, Anastasia cried that she was lost and had been left in the woods. "Are you not the gardener?" "Yes. Are you hungry?" "Yes, I am so hungry!" While the gardener tended to Anastasia, Isabella crept up behind him. Grabbing a log, she hit him on the head. Once he fell to the ground, Isabella grabbed his rifle. Rena tied him up. Ingrid grabbed his supplies. While eating the camp stew, Rena kicked the gardener. "Where are your friends? How many are there?" "I will not betray my comrades!" Anastasia smiled. "I listened to his radio chatter. There are four others." "Very good" cooed Isabella.

"To prove we are fair, we will leave the fire burning for warmth. We cannot have you screaming out for your comrades." Ursula took off her neckerchief and gagged the gardener. "Let us see what we have: compass, food, handgun, and rifle. Let's have a look at this map. There are red marks indicating where the other camps are." Isabella nodded. "This map is a decoy in case he was found. We will head this way. The terrain is rough but we will be ahead of them, so we can prepare to steal the flag. Move out, girls!"

"Why are we going the hard way?" cried Ursula. "They will not expect that. They assume because we are female, we will take the easy path. This radio will give us an advantage over them too."   After five miles into heavy terrain, complaints started coming again. "When are we going to rest?" Isabella explained that they needed to make it to the top of the ridge. "Why?" "It will give us a great view of the lower area. None of the members from the other team can sneak up on us. We need to stay ahead of them and set our trap to capture the flag and make it back to the school! Stop griping and start moving!"   Fifteen minutes into the march, Ursula stopped dead in her tracks and pointed upward. Isabella looked up into a tree stand and put her finger to her lips. Using hand signals, she told her team to flank both sides of the tree. Isabella pointed the rifle toward Headmistress Agnes, who was dressed in black and camouflage. Ingrid flanked pointing the handgun towards Isabella's back. "Come on down! We have you surrounded!"   The team dragged Agnes out of the tree stand. Isabella tied her up while her team mates grabbed her supplies. "Where is the next one?" Agnes cackled, "I will tell you nothing!"   Grabbing Agnes by the neck, Ursula pointed her knife at Agnes' throat. "Kill me! I will never reveal where the flag is!" "If I kill you, it would be a favor to all the new students so they cannot be ruined by this school!" "We have trained you well" smiled Agnes. "You would kill me to complete your objective."

Ursula smiled. "I will never stoop to your level."Tie her up. We will put her in the cave. Grab her radio! Let's move out! The top of the ridge will give us the best view and we can regroup!" Halfway to the top of the ridge, Ingrid tripped and sprained her ankle. "I cannot walk!" Isabella immediately took charge of the situation. "Ursula, make a splint for her ankle!" Taking turns, the girls worked together to carry Ursula. Once they reached the top of the ridge, Isabella said, "Break out the supplies. Let's see what we have." Anastasia whined. "There's not much food and I am hungry!"

"Rena, take the rifle and see if you can kill a rabbit or two for dinner. Ursula, you need to monitor the radio for chatter. Maybe you can figure out where they are camped out. Ingrid, let's see if we can locate the truck they brought us out here in. We will need it to transport Ursula back to the school. Anastasia, see what you can do with these supplies."

Following tire tracks, Ingrid found the truck camouflaged in the brush four miles from the ridge. She left markers so the team would be able to find the truck again. She circled back to find Isabella. "I found the truck. We should move everyone down here" announced Ingrid. "Ursula cannot walk! Her ankle is the size of a beach ball. We have to take the truck back to our camp." After thinking for a moment, Isabella decided to move the truck in daylight. It would be completely unexpected. "Let's move the truck. "Ingrid said, "No keys.'' "We will have to bypass the ignition." After carefully starting the truck, it loudly came to life. Easing the truck as close to camp as they could, the team parked and camouflaged it. Once they returned, Ursula said they would go out before dawn to check the perimeter. This would leave the flag unattended. "Guards are posted here and at a post three miles past camp. If we captured the flag, those guards could prevent us from getting back to school."

Rena returned with four rabbits. "Let's cook them. "Skinning the rabbits was difficult, but Anastasia threw together a decent meal of rabbits, wild onions, turnips and MRE's. Isabella made up a perimeter grid. Each girl took a turn patrolling so everyone got rest. At 3:00 a.m. Isabella, Ingrid, Anastasia, and Rena awoke. "Time to break camp and take our places around the other team's camp." Ursula whispered, "I cannot walk! How will we get back to the school?" Ingrid smiled while removing the branches that hid the truck she had stolen. Once everyone made it to the truck, Isabella drove cautiously down the dirt road. Ursula read the map. Rena said, "Camp is about ten miles down this road." Parking off the road, just before dawn all three guards walked off the perimeter. Isabella ran to the camp site to search for the flag. At the far corner of the camp was a large tree with what looked like a drooping branch. Upon closer examination, the flag hung from the branch. With fast fingers, Isabella untied the flag. She quickly realized it had been booby trapped. If she yanked on the flag, a small charge would set off black powder explosive. With Ingrid's help, Isabella cut the flag from the tree and quietly escaped back to the shelter of the truck.

Excited they had made it this far, Anastasia reminded her team there was still one more obstacle they needed to avoid and make it back to school on time. Starting the engine, the girls thought they may be home free. They made it four more miles, when shots rang out. Hitting the gas pedal, the truck launched forward. Isabella pulled off to the side of the road to check on her team. A dark figure skulked up to the driver's side window. "Well, it looks like you girls will not make it back in time!" chuckled Max. Isabella yelled, "I do not believe this! You would stop us from our objective? You're too soft!" Just then, a shot rang out from behind the front seat. Screaming in pain, Max cursed. "Damn you!" "I will graduate from this hell hole!" screamed Anastasia. "Drive, damn it!" Isabella took off, leaving Max on the side of the dirt road.

When the school came into view through the dirty windshield, Isabella asked, "What made you shoot Max, Anastasia?" "He was standing in the way of us getting back to school to graduate!" "Nice job!" "Thanks." Pulling into the courtyard in front of the school, Isabella and Ingrid helped Ursula from the truck. Anastasia held the flag in her hand. Arm in arm, the team marched into the Chancellor's office and presented him with the flag. Smiling, he said "You made it with four hours to spare." Rena said "We are ready to graduate, sir." After a deafening silence, Headmistress Agnes, the gardener, Max and the rest of the faculty arrived. Max was bleeding profusely from his shoulder. He announced that the girls had won. Excusing the girls, Harold smiled. "I will assume they are ready!" Agnes replied "Yes, they would have killed to achieve their objective. "That is what I needed to hear."

Preparations for graduation started immediately. Before receiving their assignments abroad, they attended a debutante ball. This was nothing more than a show that was put on for their parents. Isabella, Anastasia, Ingrid, Ursula and Rena were presented in the most beautiful gowns. Single rich men flocked all around them.

Max presented the parents with large dowries and proof that their daughters were going to marry well. The parents were ecstatic that their daughters had done well and were able to take care of their families. As all the parents left, the decorations were put away as they had been many times before. The girls were told to report to the Chancellor's office to receive their first official assignments as operatives. They were as follows:

Isabella – assistant at the American consulate.

Anastasia – file clerk at the local government office.

Ingrid – Kindergarten teacher

Ursula – Research assistant in the Prosecutors office

Research assistant in the Public Defender's office

Each girl was sent to town to start their careers. They would soon be sent to the United States where their training would be put to good use as operatives. They were put in community housing for single women. This would help them to blend in with the local women. This also gave them a chance to size up the men in powerful positions that would become easy prey to their charms. Their cover jobs gave the operatives plenty of time to accomplish their assignments.

Ingrid started her first day meeting the families of diplomats and learning the needs of the children she would teach. Foreign languages would be important to these families. They could be stationed in any country.

Ursula and Rena began learning who was who in the local criminal elements and which cases would be won or lost at the discretion of their bosses or judges. They began researching local crime families.

Anastasia was a file clerk in the same building with Ursula and Rena. This made it easy to pass along information and files as needed.

Isabella worked in the next building as an assistant. She processed all diplomatic paperwork. This gave her knowledge about where they were stationed, for how long and job statuses. Their work began with simple assignments.

Chapter Two: The Teaching of Manners

A diplomat had an indiscretion that came to light. All evidence was to be copied and removed so he could avoid prosecution. Mack had engaged in sex with a twelve-year-old girl. Her parents wanted him prosecuted. There was physical evidence along with a homemade movie for his personal collection.   After making copies of all the pertinent information and passing it along to Max, the girls were given the task of teaching him manners before he was sent back to his own country. Diplomatic immunity prohibited his prosecution.

Mack was enticed into what he thought would be an evening of sexual fun. He was tied up, which he did not mind until Isabella heated up a branding iron and burned a large, round mark into his chest. His flesh sizzled like bacon in a hot skillet. She burned him again on the left side of his face. This caused him to scream in agony. The burns were intended to serve as reminders of his crimes.

Isabella wanted him to know how the little' girl felt having her virginity taken so violently. She was considered soiled, dirty and ruined for any man. No man would marry her.

Isabella turned to Mack and a smile spread across her lips as she told him, "This is how that little girl felt when you violated her!" Isabella commanded the girls to roll him over and hold him down. Isabella shoved a long icicle up his ass. This caused him excruciating pain. The ice numbed him from the inside out. All evidence melted away.

After Mack regained consciousness, he was untied and left in a puddle of his own urine to contemplate what had just happened to him.

Isabella commanded, "Get up! You have three hours to pack! You're being sent back to your own country! You're a disgrace to your people!"

Isabella, Anastasia, Ursula, Ingrid and Rena were leaving and chatting about the day's work. It was not so bad at all!

They reported back to Max and presented proof of their completed assignment. Max expressed how pleased he was with how they handled their first assignment. "Did any of you have a problem with your assignment?" The operatives answered in unison, "No sir!" "That's good because you will have assignments where you will have to persuade people to do things our way. Alright, ladies! Back to your regular jobs."

Chapter Three: Beatrice

Once the girls acclimated to their jobs, they became actors in a play.

Ingrid was the teacher for the kindergarten class. She enjoyed working with children and developed bonds with their families. Beatrice was Ingrid's favorite pupil from her French class. She was a happy child and excited to learn all she could.

Ingrid was summoned by Max for a "special assignment." Beatrice's father was selling secrets. He had been watched for quite some time by Her Majesty's Secret Service. Any time they had enough information to take him down, he had a different objective. He always had Beatrice with him when he handed off a package.

Ingrid needed to get close enough to copy all the documents and switch them out. He would be charged with treason and killed no matter which way it played out.

Ingrid fished a dinner invitation out of Beatrice's father. While having dinner, they discussed the many places he had been stationed and how his wife died. The evening went well. It was followed by a goodnight kiss and another dinner invitation. The next day, Ingrid received a note saying he was running late at the office and they could start without him. This gave Ingrid the opportunity she needed. She asked Beatrice to wash up for dinner, Beatrice complied. This did not surprise Ingrid.

As Ingrid slipped into the office, she quickly located the files and switched out the papers. She slipped out before Beatrice noticed her missing. Ingrid again had a lovely evening. Before her class started the next day, Ingrid received a note from Max. He needed to see her at once. Max informed Ingrid that Beatrice's father needed to be interrogated about selling information. This was not something she could do. She had become attached to both Beatrice and her father. Ingrid asks, "What if I refuse?" "Then someone else will do it and Beatrice could get hurt. Do you want that?" "No, sir" replied Ingrid. "Then I suggest you do the interrogation."

Ingrid decided there would be a date without Beatrice present so she could do her job. After a drink or two, Ingrid started asking causal questions to see how loosened up he was. After dosing his drink, he should be ready.

"How long have you been selling information?" "About ten years." "How many countries?" "Many" he laughed. "Ingrid, you are so beautiful." "Thank you." "When is your next drop?" "Sunday, in the park where I take Beatrice to play."

"Why do you always bring your daughter with you? " "As a cover. No one will shoot a child!"   Grabbing at Ingrid, she moved to the side. Hitting the couch,   Mack passed out. Once she was sure he was unconscious, Ingrid called Max, giving him all the details. Max gave her a new directive. "At the drop, they are all to be killed." "I cannot do that!" "Both men are to be killed when they make the exchange." "What about Beatrice?" "She will be fine."

Full of sadness, Ingrid went home to plan the death of these two men. It should be something inconspicuous. After speaking with Ursula about how to pull this off, Ursula volunteered to help her.

Ursula dressed very seductively. Her cleavage was bounding over the top of her tight sweater. Dropping her purse, Ursula bent over to pick it up. Both men gallantly offered their services. While talking sweetly and holding the attention of both men at chest level, Ursula reached her arms around both men. Rena stood behind them, dropping poison in each man's drink bottle. Becoming excited at the sight of Ursula, both men gulped down their beverages and concluded their business. Both men were hoping to have a chance to win Ursula's favors. They departed in opposite directions. Heading home satisfied with business conducted, Beatrice's father decided to take a nap before his daughter arrived home. As he laid his head down to sleep, he never woke again.

His partner got in his car for the drive home. He never arrived. Falling asleep at the wheel, he drove off the side of the road, rolling down a steep embankment. Leaking fuel caused a large fire. He was unable to be identified.

When Beatrice arrived home, Ingrid was there to tell her about her father dying in his sleep. And that she would attend a special school. The same one her teacher had attended. After all was taken care of, the girls reported to Max for a final debriefing. "You ladies handled this very well and without leaving a mess. Little Beatrice is now able to join our family."

Ingrid shouted "You did not care about information! You just wanted Beatrice!" "Yes that was our true objective. She is so bright. Ladies, you are excused. Yes, Ingrid, I know what will happen to her at that school. "How could you wish that on a sweet child?" "We want the best and brightest. She is both."

Chapter Four: Pillow Talk

Business was booming at the brothel. Chanel was training a new batch of girls from the school. With a full house in the brothel, Chanel decided to help out by taking a date with one of her regular clients. After a long steamy hour, Chanel spent the next thirty minutes with pillow talk in case Devon had some secrets to unload. "What's troubling you, Devon my sweet?" "You know me so well, my favorite lady." "You know you can tell me anything, Devon." "Chanel, you know I'm a teacher at the prestigious private school." "Of course, darling. You are a wonderful teacher if I do say so myself!" cackled Chanel. "Our priests are teaching more than base subjects." "Tell me more" whispered Chanel. "Well, there has been talk about one boy that the priests have been passing around." "Was this boy a willing participant or were the priests being "bad boys?" "This is a secret." "I understand." "The boy is Max's nephew. His parents know, but they are concerned about making waves.   The

Catholic Church carries a significant weight with University applicants." "The parents are keeping quiet so that he can get a good recommendation?" "Yes! I know I should not have said anything, but I am concerned about the boy's welfare." "I see" consoled Chanel. "I will handle this matter with the utmost care. I promise."   Devon left the brothel with a clear conscience. Chanel returned to her office to contact Max. With a jovial laugh, Max strolled into Chanel's office. "So what can I do for the Madam of the House?" Laughing, Chanel poured Max three fingers of bourbon and asked him to sit. "I heard something during pillow talk that you need to hear." "Alright, I am listening." "You know I have a few regulars that teach in the private school." "Yes. I do remember that." "Some of the priests have been "very bad boys" and have been teaching the students more than the scholastic requirements needed for going on to University." "Do you have the names of these priests?" asked Max. "There's more. They have a favorite boy that's being passed around. Max, it's your nephew."   "Joseph?" "I am afraid so. His parents are concerned about making waves against the church. They are afraid that the Diocese will write a bad report and keep him from graduating to University." A storm cloud covered

Max's face. "I cannot believe they are afraid of the church! I give them money to afford the best education for Joseph and he gets abused?! I will come up with a plan!" screamed Max.

"Thank you for telling me, Chanel. This is not your fault." "Do you think Harold knew about this?" asked Chanel. "No. I do not believe Harold knew this. I will apprise him that I need to pull our girls off their day jobs for this operation." "As I assumed that you would." "Any word on how our little prize Beatrice is fairing at our school?" "She is very bright, but she questions everything just as we expected she would. Our teacher did not understand why we removed her father so that she could attend our school. Ingrid always had a tender heart. That is why she is a wonderful kindergarten teacher." "She challenged me because I told her Beatrice was coming here. She had grown attached to Beatrice and her father. A little humanity goes a long way in our jobs, Chanel." "So it does, Max. Another drink?" "Yes, please Chanel. How goes your work?" "We are filled to capacity every night, so we are doing well." "How are the new students fairing? " "They are scared, but functional. They will be fine." "I have noticed a decrease in the ones who wash out. You have a smaller kitchen staff." Laughing, Chanel said, "My loss is

Harold's gain!" "The new students seem to be sturdier stock."   "I need to catch Harold before he goes home for the night. Keep me informed of your nephew's well-being." "Thank you, Chanel." Walking the corridor with his back turned toward the school, Max stormed into Harold's office. "DID YOU KNOW?" he bellowed. "Why are you screaming at your superior?" "Did you know, Harold?" "Know what, exactly?" "About the priests sexually assaulting my nephew and other boys! That parents are afraid to speak out against the church because they are afraid their sons won't be admitted to University?"

"I have heard whispers, but nothing concrete. I did not know about Joseph." "You know I have to do something about those priests." "I understand. Just be warned. In the process, you may uncover more dirty secrets. The church did not become "all powerful" without money and knowing how to cover up secrets. Many of those secrets were covered up with the Pope's knowledge."   "What do you know, Harold?" "I know the girls will be away from their day jobs. You may uncover secrets you are not prepared for." "My girls can handle it." "This may be a long-term operation." "So, there's more going on than just perverted priests?" "I can only tell you that many things go on under the guise of charity and helping families." "I understand" sighed Max.

"I will contact Isabella." "Give her my regards" sniped Harold. Contacting Isabella, Max told her that everyone was to report to his office after work. The girls had their mid-day meal together and speculated on what the new assignment might be. "After Beatrice, I'm not sure I can handle another assignment!" cried Ingrid. Laughing, Isabella announced, "I had hoped for an op where we could use our fighting and physical training skills. I'm ready for a good fight!" "I heard from Chanel" quipped Anastasia.   "This mission is personal to Max. Maybe we will get to use all of our training on this one" Ursula smiled. "I have been hoping for something to get me out from behind this desk. My backside is getting so huge! Desk duty is not helping!"   "Back to work, ladies. We will meet at Max's office." Behind Max's office door, it was silent. There was no response to the knocking on his door. After fifteen minutes, the door opened. Max's eyes were bloodshot and tired. "Come in, ladies." "Max, you look like shite! What is wrong with you?"   "After some pillow talk, Chanel learned that our prestigious private school is housing pedophile priests. They have been abusing my nephew and other boys at the school. They have been passing Joseph around. His parents never said a word for fear that reprisals from the church will affect him going to University. Your operation is to get proof of the abuse so we can have the priests removed from their positions of authority. You will pose as nuns in training. If asked, you have not taken your profession of vows. Ursula gave Max a questioning look. "Profession of vows is when you marry God. As nuns in training, you will be teacher's assistants, office clerks and such at the school." "Will we wear full habits?" "No. As nuns in training, you wear a black pinafore jumper over a starched white shirt. Stockings, plain shoes and a head veil for a habit and of course, a crucifix. I need as much information as possible on this school along with anything else that would violate church regulations. We will make arrangements for you to start Monday. I will put together a file that contains the regulations for the school and church. I will include the guidelines for nuns in training. Pick up your files and study them over the weekend." "Do not worry, Max. We will help your nephew." "Thank you, ladies." "Wow, those priests are grotesque!" "I second those feelings! Nuns in training? Doesn't that go against our consort training?" "No. Now we use our listening skills." "Will Max remove Joseph from the school?" "I think he needs proof in order to have the school shut down." "Those boys deserve to go to University. They have been through so much at the hands of revered members of the church. These were people they should have been able to trust!" screamed Isabella. "Like our school?" asked Ursula. "Not exactly. Our training, no matter how brutal it was, we can help others who can't protect themselves." "So political of you. Towing the party line, Anastasia." "No, I have accepted my destiny." "I guess it's our shared destiny. "Salute!" Isabella raised her glass as they all had a shot of vodka. Staring off into space, Isabella was lost in flashbacks of the beatings she had endured at Chancellor Harold's hand for not towing the party line. "I will repay his favor!" growled Isabella. Her mind was clear with cold-blooded detachment. "A spy I am" she smirked. Sleep eluded her as she prepared for work. Over the next few days, each girl received a large folder with all the details about nuns in training, academic curriculum as well as school regulations. Once they had memorized all the information, they destroyed the files. As they took in this new information, they realized that they needed to walk and talk like real nuns. Eventually they would be given their nun names and backstories. Each of them would be given an assignment to gain access to information at the school. Now their training would begin again.   They met to destroy their files. "Nuns are supposed to be meek and soft-spoken. They do not curse, drink or have sex. Their commitment to God is what they hold most dear. Chastity, purity and virtue are the standards they live by" announced Ingrid. "They live together in a commune style house. They eat together and pray together. Their bedrooms are sparse. Curtains are a luxury item. Poverty is expected. Money has no value to them except to provide the bare essentials." "Isabella's new name is Sister Mary Katherine. Her job is as a physical trainer. Anastasia is Sister Thomasina. Tom for short. She is a lab assistant. Ingrid is Sister Mary Pat. She is a teacher's assistant. Ursula is Sister Mary Dawn, the new assistant principal. Rena is Sister Mary Agnes. She is now the school receptionist." As the team arrived at the school, a cold chill crawled up Isabella's spine. This place was not a joyous place of learning. It was the same feeling she felt when she arrived at the school years ago. "Ladies, keep your eyes open. We need enough proof to shut down this shit hole! Never discuss anything in these corridors!" The chill that followed them through the corridors felt like pure evil. As they reported to the principal's office, their soft knock on the door received a loud response. "Yes?" Walking through a large doorway, Anastasia spoke up. "We were told to report here, sir." The scowl on the man's face told the story. He was forced to take them on. Holding his scowl, he said, "I am Father Patrick Francisco." "Are there any female students?" asked Ursula/Sister Mary Dawn. "Not at our school. We do have a home for wayward girls on our other campus. I do not feel that you will be needed in that part of the school." "Yes, Father Patrick." "I will show you to your postings and the faculty room. You may store your belongings there. We will assemble in the corridor in fifteen minutes." Isabella mouthed, "These priests are into other things. I can feel it! There are no locks, no privacy." Returning to the hall, Father Patrick was annoyed. He kept pointing to his watch. "We need to be punctual, ladies! Sister Mary Agnes, return to the main office. My secretary will instruct you of your duties. Sister Mary Dawn, you may join Sister Mary Agnes at the office. You will begin by cleaning up my files. Sister Mary Pat, you will work with Father Francis. You will clean up the lab, grade papers and anything else that he assigns you. Sister Mary Katherine, you will join our physical education teacher for the self- defense training of our boys. Any questions? I will be available before classes begin and at the end of each school day. I will leave you to commence your duties." Knocking on the door to Lab Room 101, a jovial Father Francis bellowed, "Come in! You must be my new assistant. Our mornings are spent cleaning up the lab and preparing for the day's experiments. I teach biology, anatomy and physiology and sexual education. I have prepared some material for you to familiarize yourself with. We can talk as we clean up the lab." Father Francis had a pleasant disposition. Chatting with him was not a horrid chore. Preparing the day's experiments was sort of fun. "What do you think of our campus?" Father Francis asked. "I have not been able to see much of it" replied Ingrid/Sister Mary Pat. "I will give you a list of the rooms that are off limits." "Why would you have rooms that are off limits?" Ingrid asked innocently. "They are the male changing rooms, showers and disciplinary rooms. The shop is off limits because of the machinery." "I see" blushed Ingrid/Sister Mary Pat. "Are there any female students?" "We feel that female students would cause a distraction that our boys do not need. We host co-ed dances three times per year. That is the only time females are allowed at our school." "You teach sexual education?"   "Yes. I teach abstinence and that masturbation is sinful. Prayer helps combat those urges. I teach the students about the changes to their bodies and personal hygiene." "I understand" blushed Sister Mary Pat. "Father Patrick mentioned a home for wayward girls at the other end of the campus. How did that start?" "We have a sister school for girls. That brought about the need for a place for wayward girls." "Are you referring to a home for unwed mothers?" questioned Sister Mary Pat. "Yes. Many girls find themselves in delicate situations. Their parents send them to our nuns for guidance and education. They place the babies for adoption."   "Oh, my!" "Yes, we do our best for all of our children. Here comes our first class!"

"Gentlemen, this is Sister Mary Pat. She will be my new lab assistant. Show her the utmost respect. Let's begin with a review of yesterday's material. Then we will perform our first dissection." Ingrid's mind was turning with questions. Ursula/Sister Mary Dawn found herself in a stuffy, closet-like room with files in stacks taller than she was. Father Patrick dropped in to brief her on what needed to be done. "Alphabetize the folders. Divide them into stacks. Medical files are red. The blue are family/student files. The green are student financial records. Organize them so that each file contains the financial, medical and family information on each student." "Yes, sir." "I will have more filing cabinets brought in for you to store files as you clear them. Please include any teacher's notes. Once these tasks are completed, you will do the same with correspondence about each student. If you need assistance, Sister Mary Agnes may help you once the school day is done. You are mine until 5:00 pm Monday through Friday." "Yes, sir." After Father Patrick left, Ursula screamed obscenities in her head. "Prick!" Isabella looked around at what appeared to be a gymnasium. "So, you're my new assistant?" chuckled Father Paul Masino. Isabella turned around with lightning speed and brought him to his knees. "Wow! I see why you teach self-defense. So, who just handed me my ass?" "I am Sister Mary Katherine." "The boys will get a big surprise to find out you're their teacher." Smiling, Isabella/ Mary Katherine said, "Yes, they will." "You are not dressed appropriately. I believe I have some clean gym clothes in my office." "Thank you." "So, how did you get lucky enough to become my assistant?" "I was assigned to you." "How about we spar before the boys arrive?" "That sounds great! I have never sparred with a nun." Laughing, Isabella said, "I am sure that they do not condone violence." "Your assumption is correct, Father Paul." "You may use my office to change." Dressed for combat, Isabella/Sister Mary Katherine emerged from the office. "Join me in the ring" smiled Father Paul.

With no habit to inhibit her movements, Isabella was ready for combat. An evil grin spread across her face as she sized up Father Paul. He asked, "Do I treat you with kid gloves because you are female and a nun?" With a laugh, she replied, "Bring your best, Father. I intend to do the same."

"Boxing or full on contact?" cracked Isabella/Sister Mary Katherine. Father Paul went into a boxer's defense position. Swinging but making no contact, Father Paul shook his head. A right cross smacked his cheek. Then a left. After a few flying kicks, Father Paul hit the mat.

"That's the best you can do? Get up! Now I understand why I was brought in to teach self-defense!" Standing up, visibly shaken Father Paul turned to face the boys that filled the room. "Class, this is Sister Mary Katherine. She is my assistant. She will be teaching your self-defense class." "Should we be gentle? She's a nun." Smiling,

Isabella looked at the class and said, "In the ring, I expect your best. Your opponent will not go easy on you because of your gender. Neither will I."

"Get changed and line up!" "Yes, Father Paul." After an hour of full contact training, Isabella/Sister Mary Katherine announced, "Twenty laps, boys!" "But…" "I'll run them with you! Father Paul needs a rest." As Isabella ran laps, she started planning her lessons for the class. The mid-day meal had been staggered so the girls could not meet to compare notes. Dinner at six p.m. would give them time to discuss what they had learned. Ursula/Mary Dawn was covered in dust and grime. She had noticed similarities in certain files.   Scholarship students were isolated. It was almost as if the priests knew they wouldn't be able to abuse those students. There were students whose parents paid exorbitant amounts of money in tuition. There were also the poor kids whose parents never came to see them. The isolation made them perfect targets for the priests!   Rena/Mary Agnes had come in to join her at 3:30 pm "Find anything useful in here?" As Ursula explained the filing system, Rena showed her personal notes concerning students that were poor and isolated with no familial support. "Max's nephew's parents are paying for him to be here, right?" "Yes, but for him to go on to University, these priests have to give him a recommendation." "So the priests literally hold the futures of these kids in their hands? Play along. Don't say a word and you get to go on to University and make your parents proud?"   "That's horrible!" "Hopefully the rest of the team has more information for us." "I hear the boss. Back to work." Anastasia/Sister Thomasina looked at the pile of mid-term reports she was to grade. *This is sub-standard incoherent babble! These reports were completed by thirteen year olds! We never had work like this!* "Father, how do you want these graded?"   "These are special kids. They need tutoring. I thought you could start working with them. Choose the ten worst reports. Those students will be your charges. Bring their academics up to passable." "Yes, sir. Father Clarence, is there a quiet room available for tutoring?" "Yes. I will have it set up in the morning." At 5:00 p.m, the girls met in the front corridor as they headed home for the evening. "God, this was brutal!" cracked Anastasia. As they sat down, Mary Pat explained about the wayward girls' branch of the school. She told the team that the school held three dances per year. Other than that, boys and girls were kept completely separate.   Ursula and Rena explained what they found in the files. "These priests are targeting the poor kids and the ones who want to make their parents proud. These students are less likely to complain." Isabella said she enjoyed her assignment. "But these kids are too soft for their ages. Ursula, once the files have been assembled, take pictures and make copies of everything. We need to start talking to the boys. Since you have them for tutoring, Anastasia start prodding them. We need names. The church will close ranks if they catch us snooping. We need more information on the branch for wayward girls. Once we give Max the information on the priests, maybe we will get permission to find out more about the wayward girl's school. Do your homework and turn in early! I will write Max a report and drop it at his office." As Isabella wrote her report, her thoughts drifted to the wayward girls' school. Ingrid explained it was a home for unwed mothers. A gnawing in her soul told Isabella that Max needed to know about this. Walking along the deserted streets, Isabella arrived at Max's office. Slipping the report under his door, she turned to walk away. She could feel a presence behind her. She was ready to fight. Max reached for her shoulder. Instinctively, Isabella rang out with a right cross. "Damn it, girl! I'm on your side!" "Sorry, Max." "I read your report. What does your gut tell you?" "My gut says that the wayward girls' school is a home for unwed mothers/unruly girls. I'd bet my soul that the church is selling those babies!"   "We will deal with your gut suspicions after we deal with the priests." "Did you get in touch with Joseph's parents?" "Yes. They confirmed what Chanel said." "The school needs to be shut down!" "Let's teach the priests some manners!" "I agree with you. That would not hurt the higher ranking officials in the church. They would only silence the accusations and transfer the priests to other areas. I will decide what to do next. You keep the information coming". "Yes, sir." "You are dismissed, Isabella! I will check in with your superiors about the wayward girls' school. If you are right, you may choose it as your next op. Fair?" "Yes, sir." "Get some sleep. School starts early. Goodnight."   Pleased that Max had taken her seriously, Isabella had to admit she enjoyed teaching self-defense class. Arriving home, Isabella trudged upstairs to the third floor and flopped on her bed. "What did Max say?" Anastasia asked. "He is going to check out my theories on the wayward girls' home. And if I am right, that will be our next op." Rena mentioned the main office was buzzing about a laundry where "bad "girls were sent. "Looks like we may have quite a bit of work to do within the walls of the church. Tell Rena to have a listen to the chatter. We may need to use the information." Ingrid mentioned the lab teacher. "He teaches sexual education, abstinence, that masturbation is sinful. No sex before marriage." "They will be some boring boys! Maybe they need a few lessons from Madam Chanel!" Laughing, Anastasia cracked "Her consorts would have fun with them." "I'd like to take those priests to the "fun "room and give them a few lessons on submission!" "I agree!" cracked Ursula as she walked through the door. "We need pictures and copies of those files. Pay special attention to the ones that have teacher's notes. Max will give us the orders, but I need you to look for anything pertaining to the wayward girls' branch of the school. Birth records, payment schedules. Lists of perspective parents." "I get it." "Check for girls who were suspended from St. Anne's school."   "Why?" I think girls are sent to the wayward girls' branch after they are suspended." "I see."   "I will look for those records. Since it's a sister school, I am sure the same priests are involved in both schools. I just had a thought, but I will keep it to myself." "No, I want to hear it." "What if they are doing a 'purity' thing? Deliberately breeding blonde haired, blue eyed babies?" "You mean like a 'master race?' "In a way, yes. They could sell those babies to wealthy families." "Not a bad theory, Ursula. I'll tell Max. "These priests are not straight or honest."

Returning to school, Ursula reported to the file room as Father Patrick stuck his head around the corner. "Excuse me, Sister Mary Dawn. I was wondering if you and the other sisters could stay late this evening." "I have no plans. I cannot speak for the other sisters." "You have done such a wonderful job with the filing. Maybe this evening you could help with the files at St. Anne's school as well as the branch for wayward girls? The Archbishops on our school boards would like to review our files for their annual meeting in two weeks. This room is so organized. You can finish organizing the other one by this afternoon." "But Father, I still have several hours of work to organize these files." "If you are willing to spend two to three hours every evening at our sister schools, we should be ready for the Archbishops to review our files in two weeks." "But.. I" "I have cleared it with Mother Superior. There is no reason to decline the extra work. I would like to see you permanently stationed at one of our sister schools.

Your evening meal will be provided." "Yes, sir."
By eleven a.m, Ursula/Sister Mary Dawn's back
was throbbing. *"Damn, this hurts!"* she thought.

During lunch, Ursula/Sister Mary Dawn and
Rena/Sister Mary Agnes were discussing Father
Patrick's demands. "I guess this will be our chance
to find evidence." Rena scowled. "He is cleaning
house. I am sure Anastasia will find out plenty of
things during her tutoring sessions." "Ingrid,
Father Francisco was really chatty. This will be a
long two weeks." "Twelve hour days are not what
I signed on for!" "Did Father Patrick say who
would go where?" "No. Just that we "have "to
organize the files at both sister schools."

Heading back to their assigned duties,
Ursula/Sister Mary Dawn noticed several janitors
coming from her work area. Confused, she peeked
in the file room to find four new wooden filing
cabinets. There was a letter of instruction taped to
the top of each cabinet. It detailed which files went
into which cabinet. When each file was complete,
it contained student's name, parent information,
health and financial information and teacher notes.
As Ursula/Sister Mary Dawn started assembling
each file, she noticed that all or most of the poor
kids' files contained teacher's notes.   Only ten
percent of the students whose parents paid tuition

had teacher's notes in their files. After reading the teacher's notes, she knew which boys were being molested. They were either poor, academically inadequate or had very little parental involvement. Ursula quickly made notes to herself about which files to copy. At 3:30 p.m. Rena/Sister Mary Agnes found Ursula in the file room. She was finished with her work as a receptionist for the day. Ursula quickly handed Rena the list of student files to copy. "We need to get this done before Father Patrick drops in on us!" Isabella/Sister Mary Katherine had asked Father Paul which boys were struggling academically. "Here is my list. There are six boys who are underweight and smaller in stature." "I should begin working with them immediately!" Retrieving the list, Sister Mary Katherine recognized Joseph's name. "I would like to start with this young man." Father Paul nodded. "He truly needs some extra help. He gets thrown around by the bigger boys."   In full workout attire, Joseph reported to Isabella/Sister Mary Katherine. "I hear you are having trouble with physical education training. What is upsetting you, Joseph?" Joseph avoided eye contact. He stared at his shoes. "I know your Uncle Max. He trained me in self-defense." Joseph's expression relaxed. "When I have something that I need to work out, I hit the heavy bag. Let's warm up."

Their exercises were slow going. "I have been told that the other boys push you around." "Yes, ma'am. Some do." "How about joining me in the ring? "Mary Katherine started Joseph out with some sparring?" He just went through the motions. "Do you enjoy being a patsy?" "No ma'am!"   "Then get pissed! I know about the priests, Joseph." His eyes widened. "How?" "A teacher confided in an associate of your Uncle Max. Let's talk while we work on improving your lack of self-defense skills. We are here to rectify the abuse by these priests. You need to trust me. I have earned my place working with men like your uncle. I have the scars on my back to prove it. There will be no judgment from me, Joseph."

"You are not a nun, are you?" smiled Joseph. "Whatever gave you that idea?" "You fight like a man!" "Sometimes you need to fight the devil with your fists. Now, hit me!" "But, you're a nun!" Isabella's fist smashed into Joseph's cheek. "Do I hit like a nun?" Crying hard, Joseph yelled "NO!" "THEN HIT ME!" She brought his face closer to hers. "The way you want to hit those priests when they pass you around and hurt you." Joseph brought up a right hook. He smashed Isabella in the face with every ounce of strength he had. "That a boy! Harness all that anger and hurt. Focus and make those punches count! You need to be on a high protein diet. You're scrawny." Hearing the door rattle, Isabella announced, "Father Paul, this boy is malnourished. He needs more protein and extra food." "We have limited resources, Sister." "He is too small for his age. I will bring this to the Bishop's attention." "No need for that. I will see that Joseph gets larger portions." "The boys need to be weighed in. I need to see improvements!"   Excusing herself, Isabella/Sister Mary Katherine made her way to the female changing room. Pouring water into the wash basin, she started to undress. A cold chill ran down her spine. Hearing a gasp, she knew by the terrified, whisper of a voice that it was Joseph. "Yes? What do you need?" "My God! You really do have scars covering your entire back!" Isabella washed up quickly and adjusted her habit. "I told you. I earned my place working for your uncle Max."   She made her way down the long corridor to the place designated for her to take her afternoon meal. It had been a draining morning. "How goes it, ladies?" "Father Patrick has decided that since we did a great job organizing the files here, we are going to spend two to three hours per evening doing the same for the files at both branches of the sister schools." "That's our entrance to the other schools. But an extra two to three hours a night is going to kill me!" "Some of us have papers to grade!" "I think we will be here for a while." "Why?" "Because even Max thinks there is more going on here than just priests molesting the boys." "I believe Ursula may be correct about them breeding and selling perfect babies." "I had a thought on that" chirped Ingrid/Sister Mary Pat. "Stalin implemented a breeding program. But what if it goes further? Virgin mothers would guarantee purity. What if the priests were deflowering girls to bring the highest price for those infants? Priests already think they are doing God's work. What if the boys are just toys for them until they get to the prize? This is so twisted, but very possible." "I need to know what Max has learned about my suspicions" quipped Isabella. "Keep your eyes open. Make copies of all the files, ladies. We will discuss everything at bedtime." "What about Chanel? Maybe she can give us her expertise on the purity issue." "Not a bad idea, Anastasia/Sister Thomasina. I'll tell Max we need to speak with Chanel." "Back to work, ladies! Father Patrick wants to meet with us at the end of the school day." "Understood." Sister Mary Katherine's next student was waiting for her. "Let me see what I have to work with here. You look pretty healthy. Good muscle tone. Are you ready to spar?" "Yes, ma'am. Joseph told me you are not an average nun." "He is correct. Let me see your self-defense position. Good. Now defend yourself after throwing several punches. Why are you holding back?" Mary Katherine grilled him. "You are a female and a nun." "HIT ME!" "I cannot, ma'am."   "I know about the priests. Joseph told me. Do you enjoy that?" Nicholas cried, "No, ma'am!" "THEN HIT ME OR I WILL THINK YOU ENJOY IT!" Mary Katherine got an inch from Nicholas' face and said in a hushed tone, "I bet you like sucking dick and being fucked in the ass!" A low growl came up from Nicholas' belly. "NO!" "THEN HIT ME!" He swung with all his might. Right, left, another right. He knocked Mary Katherine on the mat.   "That a boy! Bring all your hurt and anger to your fists. Make your punches count!" Nicholas could see the scars that showed through Isabella's undershirt. "If you're wondering, those scars are from beatings administered by a vicious Chancellor. They remind me never to let my guard down. We will practice three times a week so that no one will take from you what you do not allow them to again."

"Understood." "Ma'am?" "Yes, Nicholas?" "We all keep secret journals about what has been done to us." "I would like to read them. I will borrow them and return them. They are your personal property. Is this acceptable? You can trust me. May I take notes and make copies for my records?" "Will it be used as evidence against them?" "Yes, Nicholas. It will be used to help ensure that this never happens again. Priests are not supposed to abuse the authority given to them as teachers or priests." "Yes, ma'am." "Get cleaned up and go on to your next class." Shaking her head, Isabella/Sister Mary Katherine felt that if she could help these boys find their self-worth, they would do better in school and have less fear and anxiety. It was time to report to Father Paul to discuss her work with his students. Walking through the hall to his office, the whispers were deafening. Gossip was buzzing about her scars. "Hello, Father Paul." Shutting the door, he voiced his concerns about her showing her scars and not staying covered.   "I am not ashamed of my scars. It shows the students that I have been hurt and I am here because I survived. They will too. It teaches them to use their fear of the unknown as strength. No one has the right to demean them or take their self-respect. Sometimes you have to physically fight the devil incarnate. Bullies only win if you allow them to!" "We preach forgiveness, passive resistance and prayer." "Being someone's prey is not acceptable! I will not teach them to accept being assaulted! Good afternoon, Father Paul!" Walking briskly through the halls, Isabella/Sister Mary Katherine made her way to the front corridor. Pushing the front doors open, she inhaled cold air. Anger seeped from every one of her pores. The only place she needed to be was with Max. Only he could understand how much it hurt to swallow the church's line of bullshit. Ignoring Father Paul's screaming voice in her head, she ran through the building and found Max's office door open. "I was expecting you, Isabella. Or should I call you Sister Mary Katherine?" "I'm not in the mood for your sanctimonious bullshit!" "I heard you stood on your soap box." "Forgiveness, passive resistance and prayer! Forgive being forced to suck dick! And being fucked in the ass! Sorry, I do not accept that rhetoric!" Smiling, Max said "Looks like you could use a drink! How about three fingers of Irish whiskey?" "The girls are organizing the files for both branches of sister schools. The board is made up of Bishops that review each student's file. We also need to talk to

Chanel about the purity angle." "Your instincts were right, Isabella. Breaking up the church's baby ring will be your next op. First, we put an end to the molestation." "They will just be transferred! I vote we hurt them just like they did those boys!"

Smiling, Max replied "In due time, Isabella. We need those files. I will contact Chanel for you. You should visit her this weekend. There are only three days left of the school week. Go back and get your assignment for the sister schools. Brush your teeth. Nuns do not drink during the day" instructed Max. "I'm surprised they are not all closet drinkers" cracked Isabella. Walking back to the school, she tried to gather her thoughts. Father Patrick was waiting for her when she returned. He escorted her briskly back to his office. Closing the door, he explained how displeased he was with her behavior. "Father, I am passionate about preventing abuse of power. Children are a gift from God!" "I understand the need for self-defense training but I will not tolerate another disruption like this! Understood?" "Yes, Father." "I will not tolerate insubordination from you!" "Yes, Father." He dismissed her as if she were less than dirt. She vowed to herself that he would get what he deserved. She walked back to Father Paul's office to make amends. "Father Paul, may I speak with you?" "Yes, Sister Mary Katherine?" "I am sorry for giving my unsolicited opinion." "I truly understand. I take comfort in speaking with a truly "gifted "listener. I hope you have a close friend that you can talk to." "Yes. I am close to the other nuns in my order. We are trained to listen to each other and pray together." "I am pleased to hear that, Sister Mary Katherine. I believe Father Patrick is waiting to speak with you and the other nuns about an additional work detail. You are dismissed." As Isabella walked to Father Patrick's office, their prior conversation played on a loop in her mind.   Was his "good "friend Madam Chanel? It seemed highly likely. Arriving at the reception area, Isabella saw her fellow nuns awaiting their new work assignments. They were whispering among themselves about the new work detail. A gruff and gravelly voice announced, "Ladies, will you join me in my office?" They followed in a single-file line as Father Patrick motioned them into his office and closed the door. "As I have told Sister Mary Dawn, I am very pleased with the organization of the file room. I have requested of Mother Superior that you ladies organize the files at our sister schools as well. We are due for our annual review. I will divide you between St. Anne's campus and the school for wayward girls. Sister Mary Agnes and Mary Dawn will be at St. Anne's. Mary Pat and Thomasina will be at the school for wayward girls. Mary Katherine will teach physical training/exercise for the girls at the wayward school. They will require modified exercise. You will have your evening meal with the students from the school. Any questions?" "A ten to eleven hour day, five days a week?" Thomasina protested. "Only until the files are straightened out" smiled Father Patrick. "Let me bring you over to the sister schools and introduce you to the faculty. Gather your belongings."   Looking at the others, Isabella/Sister Mary Katherine gave them a knowing nod. As they gathered their belongings, Father Patrick announced, "If there's anything you need to make your duties easier or faster, bring it directly to my attention. Understood?" "Yes, Father Patrick." "First stop, St. Anne's." The three mile drive seemed endless. In a secluded area, a large stone building came into view. Coming to a stop, Father Patrick announced, "We're here."

As he opened the car door, Mary Katherine felt a chill run down her spine. Father Patrick directed Mary Pat and Thomasina into the main office. "I have brought you some help for the file room. This is Sister Mary Ann. She runs the campus here. Sister Mary Katherine is here to help with physical training. You will meet everyone at the evening meal. Good evening, ladies."

Looking around, Isabella/Mary Katherine asked where the students met for physical training. "Let's give you a tour of our facility." Father Patrick broke out into a huge smile. "This is an all-female school. We strive for academic excellence. Mary Agnes, Mary Dawn this is the main office. The file room is just off the reception area. Sister Maureen is our Headmistress. These ladies have done wonders with our files. They have agreed to help clean up and organize yours for the annual review. Our teachers will introduce themselves at your evening meal. Have a good evening, Sisters."

Sister Mary Ann smiled. "Ladies, if you will follow me. The first floor is classrooms for girls under the age of twelve. Parents often cannot handle their daughters as they start to mature physically. Hormones make them incorrigible. With our guidance and a strict regimen, they fall in line nicely. The second floor is classrooms for ages thirteen to sixteen. They study sciences, chemistry and biology.   We emphasize these courses. Most women are trained from birth to be wives and mothers. We need nurses to help with our growing population. They also need clerical skills to be able to earn a living. Many of our girls are, shall we say, homely and unattractive but academically exceptional. The third floor is for girls that are preparing to go on to University. We teach them to cook, keep house and to care for children. We also have a full kitchen and medical facility. We can handle most medical issues. The students who suffer head injuries require medical attention. They are sent to the local hospital. We have a separate wing that is the dormitory. Sister Thomasina, Mary Pat let me get you set up in the file room. Mary Katherine, our training facility is on the other side of the dining hall. I will join you there shortly." Sister Mary Ann unlocked the file room. "Here it is. It's a bit dusty, but all the files are here. Father Patrick is working on getting new filing cabinets. I will leave you to get started. Here is the bell light if you need anything."   As Isabella explored her surroundings, she noticed that there was a building behind the main campus. Curiosity was getting the best of her. "What is that building behind the campus?" "One is an infirmary. The other is an office where our doctor sees students." "I understand. May I ask about your physical education regimen?" "The girls need exercise for muscle tone and rebuilding muscle mass. They need to be eased back into exercising."

"Do any of the girls have physical issues?" "Yes, some do. We use mats for stretching, but calisthenics aren't really done." "I need more information. I teach self-defense to the boys. "The younger students will do fine. Exercise helps them focus. We have some girls who come to us in a delicate condition. Their parents are ashamed." "Unwed mothers?" "Yes. Parents have us help place the infants for adoption into good Catholic families. The mothers go on to have good lives. No one has to ever know about their indiscretions. Can you design an exercise program for them?" "Yes, Sister Mary Ann, but they will not be ready for exercise for a few weeks after giving birth." "Here are the guidelines from our doctor." Reading them over carefully, Isabella/Sister Mary Katherine smiled. "We can start with stretching. Then some light calisthenics. We can use bags of flour as weights. How about a self-defense class to improve tone?"   "I do not feel that would be appropriate. They need to become proper ladies." "Let me show you what I have in mind. A proper punch will tighten the muscles from your back to the middle of your abdomen. I want you to throw a punch." "I cannot." "Let me show you. Now, you try. You should feel it throughout your midsection and back. Can you feel it when you throw a punch?" Sister Mary Ann blushed. "Yes, I can." "Exercise helps with poise, self-confidence and academics. If you look good, you feel good and it shows in all areas of your life." "I will agree to let you implement this with the girls." "We will need weekly weigh-ins to keep track of our results." "Now I understand why Father Paul is so pleased with your results. I will try it your way." "I'm pleased we can agree" smiled Isabella/Sister Mary Katherine. "Let us head to the dining hall. It's time for evening meal." While at St. Anne's, the nuns were given a tour and a welcome speech prepared by the Diocese. Eight p.m. could not come soon enough. Isabella was already planning a trip to the infirmary. All the students at this school looked like petrified rabbits. The trip back to the convent was eerily silent. Isabella could sense the death of all these young souls at the hands of the church. It was slow extermination under the guise of education and enrichment. Isabella slipped away and went to Max's office while the others made the trek up three flights of stairs to their cots. They weren't real beds by any stretch of the imagination. As their cots sunk deep into the hardwood floor, Anastasia cracked, "These schools are just fancy prisons!" When Isabella reached Max's office, she was riddled with anxiety and emotionally drained. "I have been expecting you. How did your tour of the sister schools go?" "The school for wayward girls *is* a baby factory. Sister Mary Ann admitted that they get girls who are in delicate condition. The school takes in girls so they are not an embarrassment to their parents and arranges that the babies are adopted. They have a physician on staff and their own infirmary. There are very young girls there too. I suspect there's a breeding program. The unattractive girls are pushed to excel academically. The records should help figuring all this out." "What about the boys?" "They kept journals. Between those and the records, we should have enough evidence to have the priests removed." "Get me copies of everything. I'll handle the rest. I have a surprise for you." With a questioning look, Isabella turned to see Chanel behind her. "Nice to see you, dear. I have information for you. When the girls have been bred for purity, they end up working for me or dead. Some go on to University and return to work in the hospital or other offices affiliated with the Diocese. This loop keeps the girls quiet and palms greased. This weekend, I will arrange for you to meet some of the girls who came to me from the school." "Does the church get paid for the babies?" "Yes. We will discuss that on

Saturday or Sunday. Another thing to be aware of, Isabella is mothers and babies are shuffled from place to place by a tunnel system that runs beneath all three campuses. I will see if I can wrangle you a set of blueprints. I know everyone dear; There are skeletons in all the closets of the dignitaries and government officials. Be safe, Isabella. Good hunting." Chanel disappeared without a sound. Screaming with a mixture of anger and pride, Isabella bellowed, "I KNEW IT!"   A calm smile spread across Max's face. "Your instincts serve you well." "Can we hurt the priests?" "You need to know which ones to exact revenge on. The boys' journals will tell us what we need to know. Get back to the convent." This new knowledge gave Isabella a purpose: to bring down the schools. Her return brought a barrage of questions. "We will see Chanel this weekend. We will meet some of the girls that have come to her from the schools." Sleep eluded Isabella. She was thinking about the tunnels as she mulled over what questions to ask Chanel's girls. The nun's bells started tolling at six a.m.   It had been a sleepless night, Isabella/ Sister Mary Katherine was in for an excruciatingly long day. Looking forward to strong coffee and a lukewarm shower, Isabella rose, put her bare feet on the cold floor and stretched her arms wide. She looked at the itchy woolen habit she would have to wear with disdain. Smiling at the other nuns, Isabella grabbed her training clothes. She nodded to the others.   "Ready, ladies?" "Did you sleep?" asked Anastasia. "No. My mind wouldn't shut off." "This will be over soon. What do you think of St. Anne's?" "Those girls have been abused. They are terrified of the nuns. Anyone who complains gets sent to the other school. We need to figure out who is doing what at St. Anne's." "What's the plan?" "I need to get the boys' journals and the school records to Max so he can deal with the priests." "Someone should abuse them in the same way they abused the boys!" quipped Rena.   "How long until we have complete files?" Ursula shrugged her shoulders. "Maybe a week and that would be a stretch." Isabella smiled. "That will give us enough time to put an end to this shit!" Arriving on campus, Isabella/Sister Mary Katherine headed for Father Paul's office. Ursula and Rena reported to the main office. Father Patrick called Ursula/Sister Mary Dawn into his office. "It appears that you ladies will have our files in order by the end of the week. You will spend the day here. The rest of the week will be spent between St. Anne's and the school for wayward girls." "Yes, sir." "On

Monday, you will report to your new assignments." "Are you displeased with the work we have done here, Father Patrick?" "No, Sister. You have done a wonderful job. Once our files are in order, we can have you work on your other assignments. We have never had nuns work so diligently. I will be away in meetings until four o'clock. If you have any questions, our secretary Margaret will answer them. Good day, ladies!" Ursula and Rena smiled at one another. "This will be great." While they prepared for their new assignments, Isabella/ Sister Mary Katherine smiled as she opened the door. "Hello, Father Paul." "Joseph left this box for you, Sister." "Thank you, Father!" "You must have been able to get through to the boys you've been working with." "I told them they needed to channel all their negative feelings and use that energy when they are fighting. Focusing their rage and energies is important. When you swallow your emotions, they eat away at you." "The boys seem fond of you. Joseph asked when you would be in!" "I need a few minutes to change. Joseph can meet me in the ring." Father Paul had Joseph brought to the physical training room. "Let's get in the ring. Have you been practicing?" "Yes. Nicholas and I have been sparring together." "Good" smiled

Isabella/Sister Mary Katherine. "Did you get the box?" Joseph asked nervously. "Yes. I will read the journals at lunch." "I got one from everyone who has been having problems." "We need to spar. Father Paul is watching. Put your hands up!" After swinging a few times, Isabella/Sister Mary Katherine said, "Your defense is improving, Joseph. Now I will show you how to defend against more than one assailant. Twenty more minutes and you can head back to class." Father Paul patted Joseph on the back. "Your teachers have noticed that you have more confidence."

Isabella/Sister Mary Katherine eyed Father Paul carefully. She noted where he placed his hands. She wondered if he was one of the pedophile priests. After sparring with four more students, it was time for lunch. Sister Mary Katherine snuck away to a quiet place and began reading the boys' journals. Their accounts of the abuses they suffered brought tears to her eyes. "I cannot believe that a 'man of God' could do this to a child!" After reading Nicholas's journal, Isabella/Sister Mary Katherine was enraged. "I hope Max gives me a chance to beat the hell out of these perverted priests!" Closing the box, Isabella made her way to the main office. She whizzed past reception and into the file room. Looking up,

Ursula/Sister Mary Dawn asked, "Who's going to die?" "I've been reading the boys' journals." "I see. Did you make copies for Max?" "Yes. Is there anyone else out there?" "No." "The files and journals are all Max needs. I have to get them to his office and get back to my assignment." "We will cover for you." Running in a full habit was a difficult task. She was drenched in sweat by the time she climbed the stairs. As she reached for the doorknob, Max greeted her. "It's about time, Isabella!" "Look, Max. Trying to run in this God forsaken habit is hard enough. Stop breaking my balls!" Max smiled. "What do you have for me?" "Here are the boys' journals and copies of their school files. The journals are heartbreaking, Max. I want to inflict the pain on them that they deserve for crushing these children's souls!" "I would like nothing more than to see you unleash vengeance on them. But first, we need to take this information to the Archbishop." "I am positive that the girls at St. Anne's are receiving the same treatment." "Ursula will have to go through their files with a fine-toothed comb. You need to prove a correlation between the abuses and the girls ending up at the wayward school. The purity breeding program has been going on for years via the Catholic Church. They truly believe they are doing this for GOD!"

Laughing, Isabella said, "And I thought it was plain old-fashioned greed!" "That too" sneered Max. "Keep your eyes open." "We will" sighed Isabella. "I am actually looking forward to visiting Chanel at the brothel so I can get out of this habit. " "You are still undercover, Isabella." "How can I forget, Max? I think the boys should dish out a lesson to those priests. I suspect that the principal, Father Patrick set the abuse in motion" said Isabella. "We have to have proof! Black and white proof!" "You will get it." "This is not the best use of my skills" smirked Isabella.   Max cleared his throat and smiled. "I need to get back to the school, Max." "Come back after your shift at the sister school." Walking back, Isabella had a thought on how to satisfy her need for retribution and give the boys a self-esteem boost.   Max sat down in his leather chair after pouring himself a Scotch. He opened the box and looked over the school files. He immediately found a pattern. As he gingerly removed each journal, Max prepared himself for what he would be reading. He brought the bottle of Scotch within arm's length as he steeled his heart and mind to read the journals. Filling his glass, Max opened Joseph's journal first. The first few pages seemed normal. Joseph wrote of adjusting to the new school. Around page six, Joseph started discussing a few priests who would ask him to stay after class. This made him nervous and he wondered if he had done something wrong.   Asking Joseph to shut the door, Father Francisco, the lab instructor had questions for him. *"You seemed uncomfortable in Human Biology/Sexual Education class. Have your parents talked to you about what happens to your body as you're becoming a young man?" "No. My father said that he and I would discuss it when he feels I am old enough." Rubbing Joseph's back and shoulders, Father Francisco told him "Tension is bad for your academics. To be at the top of your class, you have to focus on your studies. I can teach you about relaxation. I will tutor you privately."*   Joseph knew something wasn't right about this situation. That was the beginning of the nightmare. Father Francisco smiled. *"I see by your school file that you are a scholarship student. "No. My parents pay tuition for me to attend here!" "According to records, someone named Max pays your tuition." "That's my uncle." "So your father is a farmer" "Yes. We have animals and grow crops"* smiled Joseph. *"Bad grades could push back your standing to go on to University." "I want to make my parents proud of me!" "I will help you to get and maintain* good grades. *We will meet three times per week and focus on any subject where you have less than an A. Now, go on to your next class."*

Unlocking the door, Joseph bolted to his next class. Later that night, Joseph wrote*: Journal, I was held after class by Father Francisco. He made comments about my family. Said we were poor. My parents worked very hard and went without new winter coats and shoes to save for me to be able to attend this school! He made me uneasy. He kept rubbing my shoulders and back. I have to meet with him three times a week for tutoring. I want to make my parents proud and go on to University! I will write again tomorrow.*

Max opened the other journals to read more entries. Each priest gave almost the exact same speech to each of the boys. Emphasizing that they came from poor families and bad grades would displease their parents. That tutoring would help ensure the best grades. After the third entries, Joseph and Nicholas started to divulge details of all the disgusting sexual acts that the priests demanded they perform. This included bringing in other random men. After Joseph's fifth journal entry, the tone became dark. *Journal: The tutoring isn't for my academics at all! Father Francisco had me suck on his penis! If I choked or gagged, he hit me with a strap and demanded that I do it correctly. He quoted scriptures as he ejaculated. Then, three other priests came in. They all took turns with me. Sometimes it would be oral sex. Sometimes it would be anal sex. A few of them liked to watch. I would rather be thrown out of school than to have to endure this! Father Francisco said Mom and Dad would lose the farm if I ever said a word to anyone about any of this. I have brothers and a baby sister. They need a place to live! I wish I were dead!* As Max read his nephew's words, he could not stop the sad, angry tears that flowed from his eyes. Anger boiled in his belly and hellfire burned in his soul. He swore vengeance on the priests that hurt these children. Isabella made it back to campus thirty minutes before Father Patrick. "Cutting it close, weren't you?" cracked Ursula/Sister Mary Dawn. "We need access to the files for St. Anne's! I am certain that what is happening to the boys here is also happening to the female students. We need to find out if the girls are also keeping journals!" "Agreed." "What about the school for wayward girls?" "I think the physical exercise is to help the girls get back to their pre-pregnancy weight." "Do you really think the church is condoning a baby factory?" "I do. "There were two minutes of eerie silence before they heard   "Ladies, you have completed the organization of our files. This is wonderful news! We will only need your assistance once a week to maintain order. You will now be able to spend your time at the sister schools. I know they will benefit from your help." "Yes, Father Patrick." The girls met at the front entrance. They pulled up the hoods on their heavy woolen capes. As they walked to St. Anne's, Isabella/Mary Katherine discussed with her comrades questions they may be asked. "I am guessing the files here will show the same pattern. Concentration on the students who are there on scholarship, ones whose parents do not visit and students who are below average academically with extensive teacher notes. I will ask around about the girls at the sister campus. Remember, we visit Chanel tomorrow."   Separating at the fork, each girl made her way to the school. Ursula and Rena went directly to the file room where they began alphabetizing student files. Isabella decided that while Anastasia/Sister Thomasina made her way to the file room, she needed the files for the girls who would be in her exercise class. Sister Mary Ann seemed disturbed by Isabella/ Sister Mary Katherine's request. "Why do you need these files?" demanded Sister Mary Ann. "I usually review student files to gain an understanding of their physical health and academic performance. This helps me to design a fitness program that encompasses all of the students' needs. I need to see the infirmary in case a student is injured. I can stabilize them until your nurse and doctor arrive." "Very well. I will have the files pulled. I can show you the infirmary. If you would come with me, please." As Sister Mary Ann showed her where supplies were kept, Isabella began drawing a floor plan of the infirmary, gym and operating room. "Why are you doing that?" asked Sister Mary Ann. "This is just for me so I can memorize where all the medical supplies are kept. You must always be prepared when dealing with children. You never know when there will be an injury." "It sounds like you have done this before" quipped Sister Mary Ann. "There were many injuries at the school I attended and the campus was ill prepared for that. Toughing it out doesn't always work. Injuries require medical attention. I am a practical person. The students are my only concern." "I completely agree with you, Sister Mary Katherine." "I taught the boys at your sister campus self-defense. I believe the girls should also learn self-defense. Women are now in the labor force and walk home at night. There are far too many drunken men who believe they can take whatever they please." "I have ministered in the larger cities. I completely agree. I would like it if you would consider teaching the other nuns here as well as the students." "Yes, of course! I would be delighted" smiled Isabella/ Sister Mary Katherine. "Whoever is available is always welcome to join the exercise classes!"   "I feel that self-defense should be a separate class for the nuns that are interested." "That would be fine" smiled Isabella/Sister Mary Katherine. "I would like to take the student files with me for the weekend to familiarize myself with them if that's possible." "No more than ten at a time" said Sister Mary Ann. "That will be fine" smiled Isabella. She gave Sister Mary Ann a look. "I promise to start with stretching and ease the students into an hour of exercises." "Let's head back to my office and I will get you the files. Of course, I will have to approve all of your curriculum." "Yes, Sister Mary Ann." "Oh, my! Look at the time! It's time for evening prayer and meal!"   As the bells chimed six times, the students formed single-file lines and headed for the cafeteria. Anastasia/ Sister Thomasina appeared in the doorway of the file room. "Ready for dinner?" "Yes. "The room was silent as the girls finished reporting for their chore assignments. These rotated so that each student did each chore and was treated equally. "This school is different. It functions with much more military precision. The boys have a lot more free time."   "Agreed." "One more hour and we're out of here!" "I have already started on the pile of files to be copied." "Excellent! Keep looking" cringed Isabella. The last hour passed like sands through an hourglass.

Standing and stretching, Isabella and Anastasia headed toward the front corridor. As they pushed open the doors, a cold gust of wind hit their faces. Pulling their hooded capes tight, they went to meet Ursula and Rena at the fork in the road. Trudging on to the convent, Isabella said she needed to see Max. "I will fill you in when I return!"   As they walked to the stairwell, a shy girl said, "Mother Superior would like to speak with you ladies." They climbed the stairs and walked the corridor to her office. The door was standing open. "Yes, Mother Superior?"

"Tomorrow is Saturday. We will be cleaning our home from top to bottom. I expect you to be in attendance and to assist." "Mother Superior, we have plans with Mary Katherine to minister to the ladies of Madam Chanel's house. She felt that because we are young, we might be able to establish a connection with her younger employees." "Alright. But next time you make plans, you need to consult with me beforehand. We do not normally venture into town without an escort."   "Yes, ma'am." "You are excused!"

They grumbled as they walked up the three flights of stairs. Dropping to the floor, Ingrid announced, "I need twenty-four hours of sleep!" "That won't happen here. It's not just the priests who have "happy "hands. Some of our nuns have demonstrated some questionable behavior. I overheard some of the students talking. We'll discuss it when Isabella returns." "I wonder how Max will handle this?" said Rena.   "Even if he presents the proof to the Archbishop, they will just relocate the problem priests to a different parish. The boys deserve their 'pound of flesh." "We totally agree with that sentiment!" Isabella walked through the dark corridor and reached for the door to Max's office. As she crept toward the light on Max's desk, she could hear heavy sobbing. "Max? Are you alright?" "I have read all the journals and the copied files." "I see" whispered Isabella. "I will talk to Joseph's parents, but I'm sure that the priests will only receive slaps on the wrists. How could I not know this was going on?!" cried Max. "They have been doing this shit for years! They knew that the "poor "kids would never report it. Those kids just want to make their parents proud! I have a meeting with the Archbishop to discuss the boys' allegations in five days. Hopefully they will be re-assigned to positions that are far away from children." "These boys deserve to get some revenge!" "You are undercover. You cannot throw the priests a beating!" Max scolded. "No, I can't. But the boys can!" "No, you cannot. You need to gather evidence from St. Anne's and the other campus." "I'll handle this, Max. You deal with the Archbishop and the school board. I will handle dishing out revenge!" Giving Max a hug, Isabella smiled. "On a happier note, I will be teaching a self-defense class for the girls." A mischievous smile crossed Max's face. "Boy, those perverted priests are in for a big surprise!" laughed Max. "I'm counting on it!" cackled Isabella. "We will be at Chanel's tomorrow." "I will be joining you there" smiled Max. "See you about noon. Bye." Walking back to the convent, the wheels began turning. Isabella was planning a special treat for the abusive priests. The bitter cold bit into her cheeks. Opening the door to the convent, she quickly ducked inside. Mother Superior was waiting for her. "My office, Sister Mary Katherine!" They walked briskly down the corridor to the office. Isabella closed the door behind herself before taking a seat. "As you know, on Saturdays we clean the convent! You made other plans to minister to young girls at the brothel without consulting me! We do not go into town without an escort!"   "We have an escort. Max will accompany us." "I will permit you to go this time! But when making plans in the future, you must consult me! Do you understand?" "Yes, ma'am." "Dismissed!"   The third floor seemed miles away, just out of reach. Opening the door, Isabella dropped to the floor. She was exhausted. "I guess she read you the riot act too." "Yes, she did! Max goes before the Archbishop in five days. We need to be ready!" "Do the boys get some revenge?" asked Ingrid. "Yes. We are in charge of that!" "I have discovered that some of the nuns have "happy "hands as well." "Abuse from men and women, how equally disgusting!"   "Let's discuss this at Chanel's. We need to be there at noon! Hit the hay, ladies. We have morning prayers before breakfast and chores before we leave for the brothel." With a look of disapproval on her face, Mother Superior wished them good luck with their ministering. The temperature had warmed up to a balmy fifty degrees. The ice sparkled in the sunlight as it slowly melted from the tree branches. The girls discussed their plans for the priests and bounced ideas around on the walk into town.   "I miss our place" cracked Ursula. "I even miss our school. These habits are itchy." Ringing the doorbell was a strange feeling. Chanel answered with a sickeningly sweet "Hello, ladies" They knew that they were home, in a manner of speaking.   Goddard looked at Isabella and smirked. "I love the habit. Did you come to play with me?" he cooed, stirring Isabella's competitive streak. Returning his cocky smirk, Isabella gave him a wink. "Later."   "Come with me, ladies. Change into more comfortable clothes. Let my laundry attendants see if they can soften up those habits. Once you're changed, join me in my private office. We can talk there. I will have the kitchen staff prepare snacks and drinks." Anastasia was the first to comment on how nice the silk felt against her skin. Ursula was enamored with the shades of purple in her dressing gown. Ingrid announced that she could lounge there all day. Sebastian escorted the ladies to Chanel's private office. On a gold inlay platter was a large assortment of finger sandwiches, pastries, fruit and an assortment of cheeses.   Sitting on a velvet settee against the far wall, Max was enjoying three fingers of Scotch. "Good afternoon, ladies" he smiled. Chanel looked deep into Isabella's eyes. "Max allowed me to read the journals and copied files. I understand how angry you are. This goes deeper than anyone knows. Let's get comfortable and I'll explain what I know. Then you can meet the girls here from St. Anne's. Some came from the wayward girl's school as well."

Bringing out a large folder, Chanel began to explain. "The nuns are just as bad as the priests. The poor girls are ridiculed, sexually assaulted and sodomized with foreign objects. I'm not talking about sex toys. I mean rulers, dowels, broom handles, whips, straps and horse riding crops. The ones that have concerned parents, money or decent grades are spared these indignities. The poor girls are used in the purity/ breeding program. Any infraction gets them sent to the school for wayward girls. Some of them have been sexually assaulted by their father or brothers. Most of them are impregnated by priests. The babies are sold to rich infertile couples. Blonde-haired, blue eyed babies fetch the highest prices. The priests feel that they are doing God's work. The church makes approximately ten thousand dollars per infant after expenses. Each girl can be bred until they turn sixteen. After that, they are considered too old for the breeding program. After that, one of three things happens:

A) They are sent to me

B) They are sent to the laundries. Their parents can have them committed there

C) Death

The girls that end up at the wayward school are considered to be "throwaways." Parents have too many kids to worry about all of them. The church offers assistance by getting them into the schools, paying their tuition and counseling them. One common thing in all the stories is that both priests and nuns quoted scriptures during the abuse." The ladies struggled to absorb all this new information. Chanel continued. "Unfortunately, there's more. The nuns brow beat, intimidate, threaten and coerce the pregnant girls to place their babies for adoption. I have also heard about things going on in the laundries." Ursula piped in "There are whispers that the laundry is equally twisted. It's a place where parents can commit their physically or mentally disabled children. Depending on appearance and IQ, these girls can be sent to wealthy families to work as nannies, servants or personal sex slaves." "As you can see, this has been going on for a long time. I will admit that I had to re-train these girls. We worked on improving their self-esteem, education, how to be good listeners. If they aren't up to par here, I send them to work in the kitchen or cleaning. I could never toss them out in the cold for things that aren't their fault. Would you like to meet some of the girls from the school?" "Yes, but I need a drink first!" screamed Isabella. "We all do!" said Ingrid. Max spoke up quietly. "We need to shut all this twisted shit down! First, we deal with the priests. The next op will be the unwed mothers and the baby ring. Lastly will be the laundry." "Will we have to dress in habits for all of these ops?" "I truly do not know." "Someone should go in as an unwed mother!" screamed Anastasia. "Let me work on that!"   Max scowled. "Chanel, did you get us copies of the blueprints?" "Yes. I can show you the tunnel system that connects the campuses."   Looking over the blueprints, the girls saw that each campus was marked along with all of the sidewalks and outer buildings. "The tunnels show a maze that runs from the infirmary to the lower floor of a small hospital where the on-call physician has his office. There is also a church funeral home and a crematorium along with a cemetery." "I will assume that this is for stillbirths, girls who die in childbirth or runaways. This is just the church's way of covering all their bases." "Let's talk numbers. How many babies are born per year? How many of those are stillborn?" "About one in every nine births. Deaths in childbirth happen because the mothers are young. At twenty healthy infants born per year, that equals about a hundred thousand dollars profit for the Catholic Church." "Not a bad payday." "These tunnels actually run all the way to the train station." "Interesting" smiled Max.   "Are you ready to meet the girls?" smiled Chanel. "This is Silvia, Theresa, Ruth, Katherine and Lucretia." Silvia stepped forward timidly. "Are you really nuns?" Max smiled. "They are undercover from another school. They are here to prove the abuse that you have suffered at the schools. Can you tell us your stories?" "I always questioned everything. My IQ score was high, so I was given a scholarship to St. Anne's. At first, classes went well. The nuns seemed nice. I was maybe twelve years old and naturally questioned everything I was told. The more I questioned, the meaner the nuns became. Girls disappeared. The nuns told us they were sent to the sister schools. At one point, I bent down to pick up a pencil I dropped and Sister Agnes had taken the pull rod used for unrolling maps and put it between my legs, rubbing it across my crotch on the outside of my bloomers. I asked what she was doing. She slapped my face. Told me I was incorrigible and that I needed discipline. After three more of these advances, I was sent to the sister campus because I had "behavior problems". Once I settled in, I was called into the principal's office for disciplinary guidance. He fondled me. I pushed him away. He asked about my heritage. I thought these were odd questions. Then he locked the door and said that I had to pay penance for being a whore. Stripping off my uniform, he bent me over the chair and hit me with a strap across my back. He then pressed against me. His penis was fully hard. He thrust himself into me again and again screaming scriptures. This happened several times a week. Before I knew it, I was pregnant! He told me that if I gave my baby up to be adopted, God would forgive me. I had three live births and one stillborn. No one ever saw me fat. I was kept in a wing for unwed mothers. I wasn't allowed to hold my babies once they were born. At sixteen, I was considered too old for purity. All of my friends that are here were treated this same way." Ruth had the same experience. Theresa was sent to the wayward school for disobeying her mother. Katherine had given birth to two sets of twins after four priests had taken turns with her. Lucretia had run away and was on bed rest until she gave birth. "I have tried to locate her parents. They moved away." "Why did you run from the school?" "Because those nuns are going to take my baby!" Anastasia tried to comfort her. "You will not tell the nuns where I am?" "No. But we need to ask you some questions." "Alright. I will try to answer what I can." "How old are you?" "Thirteen, I think." "You think?" "I have been isolated from the other students. I know I had a birthday." "How old were you when you started school at St. Anne's?" "I was ten. I came from my aunt's house after my Mama died. We lived with her. I was offered a scholarship to come to this fancy school for free. I got a nice new uniform. I got to stay at school all year, even during the holidays. When my teachers and the priests said I was "special", I believed them!" "Is this your first baby?" "No. My first one died. We said prayers for it in church." Isabella left the room. She was brimming with anger and rage. Chanel asked what the problem was. "Is she slow?" Isabella demanded. "I believe she is mentally challenged" Chanel replied. "What will happen to her?" "I am not sure yet." "Could she work in the kitchen or laundry room here?" "She doesn't have what it takes to live on her own. You need to unwind, love. Spend some time with Goddard to vent some of your frustrations. Spend some time in the red room." "I'd love to throw those priests a beating!" Chanel smiled. "Their time will come, dear." "Not soon enough for me! The boys I've been teaching self-defense to have a score to settle!" Cooing, Chanel said, "The church has woven itself into the lives of the people here for centuries. They will not go quietly or stop what they are doing. They truly believe it is God's work." "Their belief system is flawed beyond repair!" scowled Isabella. "You are good at your job because things are black and white for you. There are no gray areas to confuse you" soothed Chanel. "Lucretia believes the rhetoric she's been told!" "That is why I will care for her. She is terrified of the nuns." "Please do not allow them to take her back!" "She is not the first wayward soul to end up here. You must concentrate on the task before you." "Nothing gets to me. But this has crawled into my soul and sent seething rage into my fists!" "You need to relax " smiled Chanel. "The massage room is open." "First I need to speak with Max!"

Bursting through his office door, Isabella exclaimed, "Max, we need to end this!" "I have a meeting with the board in four days." "They will have cleaned house by then!" screeched Isabella. "We can use Chanel's information to deal with the sister schools, but those priests need to be punished!" "I will allow you to let the boys get some revenge. No killing the priests!" "Is that an order, Max?" "Yes, it is. I need you for the other ops. I will not tolerate you going rogue! Take Chanel up on her hospitality. You girls deserve some relaxation." Anastasia squealed. "Which room is open?" "I believe Thor is the masseuse today." "Ursula?" "Is Sebastian on duty?" "Of course!" "Isabella, Goddard is waiting for you in the Red Room. Rena, Ingrid, I believe we have your rooms ready!" Isabella opened the door to the Red Room and found Goddard fully prepared to be placed on the rack. "I see you have not forgotten stress relief play!" Isabella gave him a devilish smile as she tied him to the rack with leather straps. Once Goddard was secure, Isabella opened the large wooden chest that was filled with implements of both pleasure and pain. "Let's start with a flogger" she said, as she flicked her wrist and the leather tassels made contact with Goddard's bare chest. He let out a low, guttural moan of pleasure. "I think the flogger is too subtle" Isabella whispered. "How about the cat-of-nine-tails? Let's see if I can draw a little blood!" With every crack of the whip, Goddard's back oozed the red, delicious liquid. His release came again and again. After several more minutes, he spoke. "Now let's see what I can do for you, Isabella." Grabbing her by the hair, he spun her around to face him. Goddard found himself on the receiving end of a right cross that rang his bell. Wiping the blood from his split lip, Goddard bellowed "I see you still haven't learned manners!" Dragging Isabella to the rack, he opened up his favorite wooden chest full of toys. "Here it is!" Goddard said with a wicked smile. "I guess you need a refresher course on just what those pretty pink lips are for! " He pulled out a dental gauge and approached Isabella with an evil grin. "Open up!" As he grabbed her face, he pried her mouth open just enough to insert the gauge. Once it was in place, he used the lever to open her mouth as wide as it would go. This caused Isabella excruciating pain. Smiling, he said "Perfect! Now let's fill that pretty mouth with a man steak!" He forced his erect penis in and out of Isabella's mouth until he was ready to burst. Quickly pulling his penis out of the gauge, he ripped the contraption out of her mouth. Isabella spit blood in his face. "THERE'S my girl!" Letting her down from the rack, Goddard threw her across the bench, penetrating her with groans of mounting pleasure. Before she could reach the point of orgasm, he pulled out screaming "No release for you! Now I'm going to treat you like the bitch you are!" He rammed his penis into her anus. "That's how I do a bitch!" Catching her breath and regaining her composure, Isabella grabbed a whip. "You wanna play, God?" She brought him down with a full crack of the whip and tied him to the rack. Isabella alternated delivering blows to him with a horse whip and a cat of nine tails. After she was completely exhausted, Isabella cut Goddard down from the rack. She handed him a cold compress for his face. He tried to smile. It made him wince. "Feel better, Isabella?" "No. I'd like to introduce those priests to the rack!" "Maybe we can help the boys exact some revenge. Are you ready to don the nun robe again?" "I have no choice!" cracked Isabella. "What about the other schools?" "We will fix their wagons." "The only way in is to send a pregnant girl in undercover."

"Maybe, but for now we need to shut down those priests!" screeched Isabella. "One op at a time. I will make the church sorry!" "That's a tall order for girls. You were able to take me down because I allowed you to, Isabella."

Livid, Isabella glared at him. "I bet Chanel knows which priests enjoy a little pain! I am starving!" Isabella got up and made her way to Chanel's office. Chanel greeted her warmly. "The other girls are dining. I will have fresh food brought in for you." "Chanel, do you have ideas which of the priests need to administer pain to get release?" "We keep records on all our guests." "I would like to read the records regarding preferences." "My staff is a bit too old for them. I would like "my" boys to give them a special send-off. We both know that when Max presents our findings to the Archbishop, the pedophile priests will just be moved to another parish or school." "They ought to be removed from duty" cooed Chanel. "The Diocese would never do that, nor will they serve jail time." "I would say we put the priests in the ring one at a time with the boys they abused. Some of them are petrified of these priests. They have told the boys that they deserve the abuses because they are inadequate students and it's the only way to make the grades to please their parents. These priests hold University over the boys' heads!" Thinking for a moment, Chanel smiled. "I think we should host a party." "We live in a convent! Mother Superior is already livid about us coming here today." "You go eat. Let me talk to Max." Isabella took her seat at the table where a feast had been laid out. As they stuffed themselves, it started to get dark.   "We better get back to the convent. Mother Superior will be angry." Smiling, Max announced that he would drive them back to the convent. As they put on their habits, Anastasia complained about how itchy the wool was. Chanel cooed, "We added some lavender to soften up the fabric." "Thank you, Chanel. And thank you to everyone here." "Here is your set of blueprints." "We have Mass in the morning. Goodbye." Pulling up to the convent, Max escorted the women to the entrance. Mother Superior was waiting to greet them. Max spoke to her with reverence. He explained how well the younger consorts responded to the nuns. The scowl melted from Mother Superior's face. "We will have a busy Sunday. There will be morning Mass and in the afternoon, you will all attend a "Profession of Vows."

Anastasia looked genuinely confused. Rena put a firm hand on Anastasia's shoulder. Smiling, she said, "I believe it's the ceremony where a nun "marries"God." Swallowing hard, Isabella said "It sounds like a beautiful ceremony." "I would like you girls to see all the preparations for this event. It will soon be time for you to profess your vows." Nodding in unison, they asked to be excused to pray about the day's events. Max bid them all a good night and drove back to his office. He took the blueprint with him to study it. Mother Superior announced "Everyone is to be dressed in their best attire! Habits are to be pressed with perfect pleats and crucifixes polished to shining for this joyous event!"

Isabella started to think aloud. "I would rather go back and endure the hell of attending our school than to "marry"God!" It was another sleepless night for her, as she worried about how to get the boys their pound of flesh. As the sun rose, the girls readied themselves for Mass. After a light breakfast, with Bibles and rosaries in hand they headed for Mass. Father Paul led the announcements.   "Sister Francine Joyce will take her Profession of Vows. I expect you all to attend. We shall commence at three o'clock. The ceremony will be followed by a reception at the rectory hall." Mother Superior assigned Isabella/Sister Mary Katherine and Anastasia/Sister Thomasina to help the "bride". Sisters Mary Pat, Mary Dawn and Sister Agnes were assigned to decorate the rectory. Reporting to rooms under the chapel, Anastasia looked at Isabella with fear. "What is your concern?" Isabella questioned. "How do you "marry "God?" "I believe the ceremony is just a symbol of your devotion. You receive a silver band with a cross as a symbol of your devotion" explained Isabella.   Nodding, Anastasia seemed to accept this explanation. As Isabella entered a small carpeted room, she noticed crying nuns scurrying about. Hanging on a tall garment rack was a long, white wedding gown. It was a symbol of virginity and purity. There was a simple white veil to adorn Sister Francine Joyce's head.   In a velvet box was a silver band with a cross in the center. Anastasia asked Francine Joyce, "What can we do to help you?" "Can you make sure my shoes have been polished?" "Yes, ma'am." Returning with shoes in hand, Anastasia/Sister Thomasina asked, "How do you know if you're ready for this commitment?" "I studied for four years and prayed for guidance. I feel I am ready to devote my heart, soul and total being to God." "But that means forsaking all Earthly pleasures." "Yes. I will abstain from sex and all vices. I am ready" smiled Sister Francine Joyce. "You too will take this journey and you will be joined to God."   Nodding, Isabella/Mary Katherine asked, "Do you need help with your dress?" "Could you check on the food and decorations? I want everything to be perfect." "Yes, ma'am." Closing the door, Isabella and Anastasia said no in unison. The kitchen was filled with catering staff. Appetizers filled silver platters. As they walked into the rectory, it was a wonderland of white flowers, fine linen table cloths and a fully stocked bar.   There was Irish whiskey, Scotch and a large assortment of other alcoholic beverages. Large punch bowls were filled with champagne punch. Whispers of the Archbishop's arrival were on the lips of nuns and priests alike. Rena, Ursula and Ingrid were arranging center pieces. Isabella smiled and spoke quietly. "How do you feel about this?" "Truth be told, it's an idea the church forces women to follow. It's archaic at best." "That's why the priests are having sex with children. Nuns are virgins and priests are celibate. I guess children are fair game!" scoffed Isabella.   "Well, that rules us out as becoming nuns. You have to be a virgin!" cracked Rena. "I would rather be a harlot! At least they get paid!" smirked Anastasia. "I hear the chimes "announced Ingrid. "That means the chapel will be filling with guests."   Sneaking off, the girls watched as Francine Joyce was zipped into her long white gown. The veil was placed gingerly on her head covering her face. Two small girls dressed in First Communion dresses carried her train. Everyone took their places for the ceremony as the choir began to sing. Sister Francine Joyce began her procession down the aisle, led by other nuns. White rose petals adorned the aisle floor. As they got closer to the pulpit, tears of love and devotion began to flow. The girls looked at each other. They were all wishing Francine Joyce would run before it was too late. As she took vows of purity and chastity and gave herself to God, the priest blessed her ring and placed it on her ring finger. At the end of the service there was an announcement. "Now we may celebrate and rejoice. We are proud to add Sister Francine Joyce to our fold. Any gifts are to be donated to the church." The reception was just like a real wedding. Music filled the air. There was an abundance of food and love. Max tipped his hat to Isabella. "What do you think?" "Never will I allow myself to succumb to this antiquated bullshit!"   "Does that mean you do not wish to change vocations?" Max said teasingly. Isabella gave him a glare. "Hell no!" Laughing, Max smiled. "I'll see you tomorrow evening." "Yes." I want to end this!" On the walk back to the convent, Isabella snickered, "How does she spend her wedding night? Reading the Good Book?" She felt the sting of a hard slap across her face. Mother Superior denounced her blasphemy. "Ten Hail Mary's and five recitations of The Lord's Prayer, with a few extra hours to be spent in reflection in the chapel!" Isabella used every ounce of restraint she had to suppress her first instinct of returning the slap to Mother Superior. "Maybe some more time with the whores you minister to will remind you why we make this our life's mission!" "Yes, ma'am" Isabella said shortly. The other girls looked at her in shock. "Are you okay?" "Yeah, she just caught me by surprise." "Let's get upstairs. I think Chanel's idea about throwing a party might be the best way to go after all." "When does Max present the evidence to the Archbishop?" "Wednesday." "How about a party to teach the boys manners and proper etiquette?" "We will arrange that for Tuesday evening" replied Isabella. "I want to finish this!" "Agreed." "But we still have the selling of babies to deal with. See what you can find out about the laundries, Rena." "We will tell the boys and priests the party is to help the boys improve their social skills now that their academics are much better." "I vote that each of our 'favorite' priests get to spend some time on the rack!" cracked Isabella. "Let Joseph be the first one to crack the horse whip! I will ask Goddard to help with the special events" Isabella said with a smile. "Rena, since you're surrounded by the busybody, gossiping women in the office, it's on you to find out as much as you can about the laundries. If I am correct, the church has been profiting from the labor of the poor and disabled for years. We will have this place shut down!" "Agreed!" they exclaimed in unison. "I will have Max contact Chanel about the party. I think we may have to send someone in undercover at the school for wayward girls to see how the selling of babies is actually carried out." Ursula blurted, "I cannot wait to get out of these damn habits and go back to our regular day jobs!" "Amen!" piped Ingrid. "Remember, we still have to get the filing organized at both of the sister schools." "Yes. I need to meet with Max to look over the blueprints to the tunnels that run under the campuses. The way Chanel explained it, pregnant girls and babies were transported to the hospital via the tunnels so that the infants were never seen. This way there were no questions asked. After giving birth, they either return to school, are sent to the laundries or to Chanel."A doctor is on staff with a fully functional infirmary. The girls are never left unattended. "How much do you think the church makes off these girls and their babies?" "A hundred thousand or more per year. That doesn't include tuition or the fun they have fucking the students. Plus all the free labor!" I poked around in the office. Did you know there's a campus garage? What does a nun or a priest need with a Mercedes-Benz stretch limousine?" cracked Ursula. "It's got a built-in bar and plush carpeting. They hide it under a tarp." "Hidden assets?" Isabella scowled. "I guarantee there are more. Let's get some sleep. We have a lot to accomplish in two days." Isabella snuck out the back door in the kitchen. She slipped a piece of metal in the door jamb so she could sneak back in. The scouting expedition showed more cars. She put away her camera and hurried to Max's office. She was drained as she reached the top of the stairs. Pushing hard on the door, Isabella walked through the darkened outer office. Max smiled and held out a glass to her.   "Whiskey, neat." "Thank you. I need you to get in contact with Chanel. We are putting on a party Tuesday evening to teach the boys proper etiquette and social graces. I will need Goddard's assistance to teach the priests a little something about manners." "You get one or two priests. No more." Max scolded. She gave him a heavy sigh and rolled her eyes. "I have checked the figures. The church is clearing approximately a hundred thousand dollars on just the babies."   She tossed the camera to Max "For priests and people who have taken vows of poverty, they sure have some expensive cars. We will have enough information about the laundries and selling of babies to shut this whole campus down! I'm looking forward to our day jobs again. These ops dealing with the church are emotionally draining. Give me a straight up fight any day!" scoffed Isabella.   "I have to agree. When it comes to church and state, the lines blur easily. I will have Chanel and Goddard here at nine o'clock tomorrow night. I made you a smaller duplicate of the blueprints. I need all of your evidence by Wednesday morning so I can present it to the Archbishop and the Board of Trustees. You're in the home stretch, Isabella. Relax!"   "That's easy for you to say, Max. Mother Superior slapped me! It was all I could do not to return the slap!" "Are you okay?" Max asked, concern furrowing his brow. "I'm fine, but I am done with those nuns!" "Get back to the convent before you are missed!"

"They said their goodbyes and Isabella trudged back filled with dread. As she opened the kitchen door and quietly slipped inside, she was greeted by Mother Superior. "Where have you been?" Mother Superior demanded. "I took a walk to clear my head. The ceremony we witnessed today caused me to reflect on some things that were weighing heavily on my heart" Isabella said calmly. Mother Superior smiled.   "That is why we ask our new nuns to spend a minimum of two years in study and prayer before making the "Profession of Vows. It is a lifetime commitment and should not be taken lightly" smiled Mother Superior. "I would have to agree "smiled Isabella/Sister Mary Katherine. "I should get to bed. School starts early. I did want to discuss with you about taking a small field trip Tuesday evening. My fellow sisters and I have been tutoring a few of the boys. Their grades are now impeccable. We need to teach them some social skills. I have arranged the use of a private room in town." "Normally, such things require a discussion with the Board. You will need an escort for yourselves and to be accompanied by a priest!" snarled Mother Superior.   "Max has agreed to be our escort and I will ask one of the priests at school to accompany us." "I see that you take well to your duties with the children. I see no harm in this. We will need to depart early from the sister campuses. I will make the necessary arrangements. DO NOT disappoint me, Sister Mary Katherine." There was an ominous tone of warning in Mother Superior's voice. "Yes, ma'am "replied Isabella. Creeping up the stairs, Isabella turned the handle to the dormitory. *Squeak!* "Damn these old buildings!" she said to herself.   "Did Mother Superior catch you sneaking back in?" "Yes. We had a discussion. We will talk in the morning. Goodnight." Plans for revenge danced in Isabella's dreams. The boys would get their pound of flesh. Which priest was the worst? As she drifted off to sleep, a smile crept across Isabella's face. Morning came much too soon for Isabella/ Sister Mary Katherine. As the girls said the morning prayers, Isabella made mental notes on the priests. *If I can only invite one or two priests, the punishment should fit the crimes that have been perpetrated by the rest of them! Joseph should get to take the first swings. Maybe he should use the gauge on them that Goddard is so fond of! Perhaps that will satisfy his oral fetish! I'm sure that since our priests enjoyed forcing our boys into anal and oral sex, they should enjoy receiving the same from Goddard. He's so gentle!*

Ursula/Sister Mary Dawn whispered, "Boy that was a long prayer! "Just had some things on my mind" Isabella answered. On the way into breakfast, Rena looked into the large cauldron on the stove. "Oatmeal again? What I wouldn't give for a full breakfast. Pancakes, eggs and bacon!" "Remember, they took a vow of poverty!" said Ingrid/Sister Mary Pat. "That doesn't mean we should starve!" whined Rena/Sister Mary Agnes. "Hell, I would settle for a large cup of actual coffee, not this tea" said Anastasia/Sister Thomasina.   "This part is almost over" smiled Isabella/Sister Mary Katherine. "It seems like it's been forever since we've been at our normal day jobs" commented Ingrid/Sister Mary Pat. "I cannot wait to get back to normal clothes, decent food and not being forced to pray six times a day" smiled Rena/ Sister Mary Agnes.   "Eat and we will make our way to school" Isabella smiled. Pulling on long, woolen capes they started the long walk to campus. The air was cold and chilly. There was a blue and gray blanket of snowflakes that filled the sky for as far as the eye could see. Their hooded capes were no match for the snowy weather. The miles to campus seemed endless. "My hands are frozen!" exclaimed Rena. "I will not be able to type!" Bursting through the campus front door, Rena scrambled to find a radiator to warm her hands by. The school began to bustle to life as the office staff began to arrive. Isabella spoke in a hushed whisper, "Remember, Rena we need to find out about the laundries. How they get the girls and money." "Got it, Isabella." "I am off to a meeting with Father Paul" smiled Isabella. "Which priests are we inviting to the party?" joked Ursula/Sister Mary Dawn.   "I will discuss that with Joseph and Nicholas today. We have self-defense practice." Walking down the corridor, Isabella was filled with pride in her accomplishments with the boys. Opening the door to Father Paul's office, Isabella/Sister Mary Katherine noticed that he had his back to her. As she quietly approached his desk, she heard a quiet, muffled cry. As she got closer, she heard buttons snapping.   Then she heard Father Paul say, "This is your penance for talking to Sister Mary Katherine! Go clean your face! You disgust me!" Isabella/Sister Mary Katherine tapped Father Paul's shoulder and punched him square in the jaw. As she dragged the unconscious priest into the boxing ring, she saw Joseph run from Father Paul's office. Isabella/Mary Katherine screamed at the dazed priest. "Stand up!" "But Sister Mary Katherine, you don't understand!" "Oh, but I do!" she scoffed at Father Paul.   "I was ordered to do that!" Father Paul stammered. "Excuse me, Father Paul?" "We take orders from the principal, Father Patrick Francisco. He said that we needed to teach the boy humility!" "By sexually assaulting him?" Mary Katherine questioned angrily. "It is meant as a teaching tool! I admit that we do have some priests here that really do enjoy this aspect of the job." "Put your fists up and defend your position!" Sister Mary Katherine shouted at Father Paul. "You are a woman and a nun " he stammered. "So? Show me how big of a man you are! Since you get off on hurting kids! Defend yourself because I will not miss!" Sister Mary Kathrine screamed as she landed a punch to Father Paul's right eye. "Fight! Defend yourself! Just pretend I am an eight-year-old boy or maybe you prefer ten year olds!" Father Paul pushed Mary Katherine away from him. "Oh, is that all you got?" Mary Katherine taunted him. Father Paul received a round house kick. A right, a left a right and another left. "Show these boys what a man you are! Look at yourself! Afraid of a demure woman!" Landing a punch on Mary Katherine's right cheek, Father Paul surprised himself. "Please! My great-grandmother hit harder than that!" A crowd of boys had gathered around the ring. They were cheering for Sister Mary Katherine. "Punch that son-of-a-bitch!" shouted Nicholas. Joseph jumped in the ring. "I want a shot at Father Paul!" "Me too!" screamed Nicholas. The boys joined Mary Katherine in the ring, forming a circle around her. They took turns punching and kicking Father Paul. They were enjoying their moment of revenge. Heavy footsteps outside the gym door told Mary Katherine to send the boys out through the side door. She then helped Father Paul to his office and poured cool water into his wash basin. As she cleaned his wounds, the principal Father Patrick came into his office shaking his head. "Today's self-defense class was a bit intense" smiled Sister Mary Katherine. "I see. Perhaps I should be the one to accompany the boys to their lessons on etiquette and social graces. If things get out of hand, I can reign them back in." "Father Paul, you should go to the infirmary. I am sure that Sister Mary Katherine can handle teaching your classes for today." Mary Katherine shot Father Paul a look that told him to keep quiet about the beating he had endured. Handling the classes with ease, Sister Mary Katherine called the boys into the office. She explained the upcoming field trip to them. "This will only make things worse for us" Joseph whispered. "No, it won't. I have a little surprise for Father Patrick Francisco. I guarantee it's something he won't forget. Trust me. My friend Goddard will show him how it feels to be someone's bitch! Wear your best clothes and use your best manners!" "Yes, ma'am." As she sprinted toward the main corridor to join her sister nuns, Mary Katherine was summoned to Father Patrick's office. As principal of the school, he was given a wide berth to run the school his way. "Close the door!" barked Father Patrick. "I do not know what happened to Father Paul" Mary Katherine said. "Heed my warning. You will not push me around!" Father Patrick said in a low growl. "I can make your posts here very uncomfortable! Do you understand?" Sister Mary Katherine nodded. "Do you plan on teaching me humility? Like you do the boys? The difference between me and those boys is I don't take shit from any man! Give it your best shot! My Chancellor when I was in school tried to break me. I have the scars to prove it!" "I run this campus! Just remember who you answer to!" barked Father Patrick. "I answer only to God and so do you!" "Unlike you, I know my place in this world! You think you are king! God would not approve! " Mary Katherine said angrily. "Report to the campus for wayward girls! I cannot stand the sight of you!" Mary Katherine slammed the heavy wooden door on her way out. Whispers were flying around the office as Mary Katherine walked through the outer office. "Sister Mary Katherine! You need time to reflect on your behavior! Report to Mother Superior. She is waiting for you at the convent!" On her long walk back, Isabella noticed a large black car following closely behind her. As the car pulled to a stop beside her, Isabella's pulse quickened. She was mentally preparing herself for a fight. Chanel cooed out the window, "You are hard to keep track of, Isabella. Get in. I will take you to Max. You are the talk of the town!" smiled Chanel. "Father Paul has been admitted to the Intensive Care Unit at the hospital. He was brought there via the tunnels to keep him out of public view. The little ones now consider you a hero!" "No one asked what Father Paul did?" "Joseph told Max everything!" "That prick Father Patrick tells the priests to assault the boys to teach them 'humility!" "No, it's to keep quiet!"   Slamming through the door to Max's office, Isabella ripped off her habit and donned pants and a long-sleeved shirt. "That's better!" she said as she walked over to the bar. She poured herself three fingers of bourbon and downed it with ease. She poured herself another. "I spoke to the doctor who is treating Father Paul. He says the priest took a bad beating" Max said. "He deserved it! I caught him red-handed! He was forcing Joseph to perform oral sex on him as penance for talking to me!" Isabella screamed as she fought to hold back the tears that stung her eyes.   "I agree with you, Isabella." "I taught him a lesson about "humility!" "Yes, you did! And so did the boys! They had a good teacher!" Max said with a smile. "I understand Father Patrick will be accompanying the boys to Chanel's." "Yes. I have plans for him." Chanel cooed, "Goddard is preparing the pain/pleasure room. My girls and I will teach the boys social graces. Pulling out chairs, table manners, proper etiquette and how to ask a girl to dance. I will leave Father Patrick for you and Goddard to deal with. My kitchen staff will prepare snacks, finger sandwiches and drinks."

"Will the boys witness the "entertainment?" "Maybe they deserve a shot at Father Patrick for ordering the abuse." "If I were a gambler, I would lay odds that this prick has abused these boys too!" cringed Chanel.   "I did not get the chance to talk to the other girls about the laundry. "You can talk to them tonight" reassured Max. "To be honest, Isabella we were all taking bets on how long you would hold your temper. I never doubted your ability to give those priests a beating. I just thought it would happen sooner. This proves that you've matured. You've become more lady-like." "Gee, thanks Max!" she said sarcastically. "Will the others be joining us for the entertainment portion of our little soiree?" "Of course! They will enjoy seeing some justice served."   "Shit! I will have to deal with Mother Superior! She knows you are here with me "working out your anger issues." "Ha! If she only knew! Saying ten Hail Mary's and ten of the Lord's Prayer isn't going to do jack shit toward resolving my anger!" "I agree" chuckled Chanel. "Unfortunately, you need to placate Mother Superior for a little while longer. The party is tomorrow night. I go in front of the Archbishop and the Board on Wednesday. This op is almost over, Isabella." "I never knew how emotionally draining this could be. It's more difficult when it involves the abuse of children. When the church profits off the backs of indigent women and children under the guise of religion. It makes it very hard to remain silent about all of it." "Just remember, with each op, you grow as a person and an operative. These growing pains are what make you ladies the best at what you do" smiled Max.

Chanel piped in, "All of you girls have potential. You are wonderfully well-rounded women who can handle anyone and any situation. I am very pleased with your accomplishments and very proud of you, my girls. Believe me when I say you were always a challenge." Isabella leaned in and accepted a hug from Chanel. "I am ready to finish this" Isabella said determinedly. "Let's study the blueprints for your next ops. Take notes on how the tunnel systems work. These tunnel systems were designed to operate beneath cities and towns during World War II. They needed alternate routes to bomb shelters. The church utilizes this system to move the mothers and their babies from one place to another. As the church's profits increased, the campuses needed to be enlarged in order for the church to maximize the profits they made off the books. These schemes have been operating for more than two centuries." As Isabella read the historical documents about the tunnel system, she shook her head. The only way to stop this was to air the Catholic Church's dirty laundry. Max derailed Isabella's train of thought with a plate of sandwiches. "I thought you might be hungry" Max said.

"I'm famished! Thanks Max! I will need to get back to the convent soon.

Nightfall is already here." "Just eat" smiled Max. Feeling better, Isabella made her way back to the convent with a spring in her step. Reaching for the handle on the large oak door, it was pulled open before Isabella touched the handle. Sister Mary Ann looked frightened as she said, "Mother Superior is angry and demands to see you at once!"   Sister Mary Katherine made her way down the corridor to Mother Superior's office as cold chills ran down her spine. She knocked on the office door with a trembling hand. "Enter!" came a shrill reply. "I see you finally decided to return to your post!" Mother Superior barked. "When I left campus, I started walking and ended up at Max's office" Isabella answered. "What do you have to say for yourself?" "I lost my temper when I witnessed Father Paul sexually abusing Joseph" Isabella said.   "It was a lesson in humility!" "No! It was sexual assault! Obviously no one knows the difference here!" "Due to your insubordination, I do not feel that this convent is the right place for you. I will have a new assignment for you at the end of the week. I am disheartened to admit I do not believe you are fit to be a nun! You do not take orders or heed instruction. You fly off the cuff. That will not be tolerated here! I expect you to be on your best behavior until you receive your new assignment. Understood?" "Yes, Mother Superior!"   As Sister Mary Katherine turned to leave, Mother Superior said, "You are a disappointment to the church!" Trudging up the three flights of stairs, Isabella entered the dormitory looking defeated. Anastasia looked over at Isabella with a twinkle in her eye. "Did it feel good to throw that sick freak a beating?" "It would have felt better if he would have fought back. But the boys got their pound of flesh!" "We heard all about it" Ursula smiled. "That should make you happy." "No, because I learned that it's the principal, Father Patrick who is giving the orders to abuse the boys. He decided that he will be the one to escort the boys to the "Social Graces "event at Chanel's." "That works perfectly for us!" giggled Ursula. "Let's just say Goddard is preparing for Father Patrick's visit."   "Will we be attending this event?" asked Rena. "Of course. We will change out of our habits when we arrive at Chanel's." "Since you're getting reassigned, does that mean we will too?" "Probably not. I was the one who beat up a priest. They like you!" cracked Isabella. "I am still compiling all the information about the laundries "said Ursula. "This church should be burnt to the ground!" she exclaimed. "It's not just an individual Diocese that is bad. This has been happening for over two decades. The entire Catholic church needs an overhaul" complained Isabella. "I agree. Pedophile priests, selling babies and slave labor. This is some seriously twisted shit!" "The nuns are no better" Rena added. "It's time we shine a light on all these skeletons within the church closets! Prepare for tomorrow, ladies!" Mother Superior woke Isabella and the other girls at half past four in the morning for prayer. "Why?" asked Anastasia/Sister Thomasina. "I need to be sure that Sister Mary Katherine's actions have not poisoned the rest of you!" Ingrid/Sister Mary Pat spoke up. "So, we are being punished for Sister Mary Katherine's bad judgment?" "Yes. To show you the error of her ways" Mother Superior answered coldly. "So, if we want to stay on your good side, we need to show Sister Mary Katherine the error of her ways?" asked Ursula/Sister Mary Dawn. Turning to face Mother Superior, Mary Katherine said, "If you have an issue with me, take it up with me. Don't punish them." "Very well. All of you, report to my office!" Once they had filed into Mother Superior's office, Mary Katherine was directed to stand at the easel. "Turn and face your sisters! Remove your habit!" Mother Superior barked. "This is an effort to teach you humility. To think of others before thinking of yourself!" Mother Superior struck Isabella twenty times with a cane. This caused deep gashes on her back. The others watched in horrified silence. Isabella endured every blow without making a sound. Her back already bore the scars from a previous Chancellor's cruelty. Looking at Mary Katherine with a blank stare, Mother Superior said, "I did not enjoy this. It was a lesson you needed to learn. Get cleaned up! Ladies, no one breaks the rules!"

Isabella vowed then and there that she would bring this bitch to her knees. Sister Francine Joyce brought in salve to apply to Mary Katherine's gashes. She whispered, "I heard Father Patrick instructing Mother Superior to do this to break you!" "Thank you for the ointment. You should go. I do not want you to bear my same fate. Tonight he will get what he deserves!" Isabella said through clenched teeth. The other nuns were told to carry on with their duties. Mary Katherine was to be left alone to reflect on her behavior and the lesson on "humility. "Isolation was another punishment commonly doled out by the nuns. *Caning, isolation, sexual abuse and forced labor were all forms of torture used by Stalin and Hitler* thought Isabella. *The church is a dictatorship using the guise of religion to control people.* Wincing in pain as she walked, Isabella/Sister Mary Katherine knew she could block out the pain in her back to get through the night. As she walked through the front doors of the campus, all the bustling in the office became hushed whispers. People pointed and looked at her with pity in their eyes. Mary Dawn and Agnes acknowledged Mary Katherine and quickly lowered their eyes. Mother Superior had warned them. They were to shun her until they were told differently. Father Patrick motioned Mary Katherine into his office. "I will understand if you need to use today's self-defense class as a silent study hall" he said. "That will not be necessary. I can do my job. A good workout with my students should help to ease the pain and stiffness in my back" "I applaud your dedication to the students. Is everything ready for the "social graces" class tonight?" "Yes, sir. I would like to dress as if this is a formal affair to show the boys proper attire for such an occasion. "We will wear our habits and change when we arrive so that we blend in." "That seems acceptable." "I would like to begin the course with teaching the boys the proper way to tie a necktie and proper table etiquette." "I can see that you have put a considerable amount of thought into this. They were so far behind academically; there wasn't time for things like this. I am pleased with the change in your attitude. Get to class now. Ladies, Sister Mary Katherine will fill you in about tonight's events." "Yes, Father."   Mary Katherine nodded to the office staff as she made her way to Father Paul's office. Changing into sweatpants and a man's muscle shirt, she prepared for class. She was doing a slow warm-up as the boys filed in and began to change for class. Joseph cried out to her. "Did they hurt you because of me?" As Joseph sobbed, Nicholas whispered, "We will tell Father Patrick that we hurt Father Paul." "No! That isn't necessary. I can handle a little pain. I stand behind you both. No one has the right to hurt you. Even if they are following orders. Get changed. We have work to do!"   "Joseph smiled, "You are tougher than a man!" Laughing, Sister Mary Katherine said, "Hardly! I have felt the Chancellor's whip a time or two myself! I fear nothing. Nothing will stop me from protecting you!" "We love you, Sister Mary Katherine!" "And I love you! Now get to work!" By lunch, Isabella was exhausted but counting down the hours until that night's events. Rena asked if she was alright." "Yes. I'm just tired, stiff and sore. Tonight, we wear our habits and change at Chanel's. "Is this really a class on social graces?" asked Anastasia. "Yes. We will teach them about opening car doors, pulling out chairs, table manners, dancing and proper etiquette. This is our final night! Tomorrow Max presents evidence to the Archbishop and the Board of Education. How are the files coming at the other schools?" "You were right. The same system is used there, except that some girls are sent to the wayward campus. These girls are poor, scholarship students. Their parents are not actively involved in their academics. These girls are blonde and blue-eyed. They all have high IQ's and very low self-esteem. They are ideal breeding material. It seems Father Patrick is very active at the wayward school. "I spent an hour teaching the boys how to tie a tie" smiled Isabella. There were three hours left of the school day. "How did you explain my absence last night?" asked Isabella. "I told the truth. You found a priest abusing a child under the guise of humility. We told them that he ended up in the Intensive Care Unit. Father Patrick was angry. The nun actually cracked a smile! Back to work." As the day crept by, chatter buzzed in the air. The school day ended with squeals of delight as the nuns tried and failed to shush the boys. "Ladies, I will see you in a few hours. I'm looking forward to getting to know you outside of school." "Yes, sir. "Would you like to meet at the convent?" "Max will escort us to the house." "I know Madam Chanel and that you have been ministering to her consorts. They really responded to you because of your youth and exuberance. It seems you have a real gift." "Thank you, Father Patrick. We will see you later." Walking through the snow that danced in the air, Ursula announced "That principal makes my skin crawl! I bet he's one of the priests who "father children for God!" Yuck!" "Let's concentrate on tonight's events!" Opening the large oak door, they ran up the stairs as they heard "Ladies!" "Yes, Mother Superior?" "Evening prayers begin in ten minutes!" They removed their capes and boots and headed to the chapel. An hour of prayer put Isabella to sleep. An elbow to the chest reminded her what she should have been doing. With bags in hand, the girls were ready to go to Chanel's. Max arrived at exactly seven o'clock that evening. Mother Superior asked, "Are you waiting for Father Patrick?" "We need to arrive at the party before the students." "I expect exemplary behavior, ladies!" "Yes, ma'am." "Max?" "Yes, Mother Superior?" "I expect perfection from these ladies." "Yes, ma'am." Max opened the door for them, as a gentleman should. "How are you, Isabella? I heard about this morning." "It wasn't my first beating and I doubt it will be my last." "Have Chanel take a look at your back before the festivities start" "Yes, Boss." As they arrived, Chanel was ushering in the guests. "Ladies, you can use my personal chambers to change out of those clothes. Isabella, I need to see you" cooed Chanel. "Let me have a look at your back, dear." "It's not my first beating" Isabella replied. "The cane had serrated metal inlay, which can cause infection." Removing the bandages, Chanel gasped. "That must be excruciating!" "It does hurt" Isabella grimaced. "Let me ring my private physician. He is here to give physical exams to my new consorts." The ringing of a bell let the doctor know he was needed. "Yes, Chanel?" "My Isabella was injured." Looking at the gashes on Isabella's back, Doctor Burton shook his head. "I need to clean and irrigate these wounds. You will need to take an antibiotic regimen twice a day for two weeks. Apply this salve and change the bandages three times a day for two weeks." "I am being thrown out of the convent on Friday" Isabella said. "You will stay here!" Chanel exclaimed. "Let's get these gashes taken care of. The boys should be arriving shortly."

Helping her dress, Chanel smiled, "You have grown into a beautiful woman. Goddard is prepared for tonight. No worries. All will go as planned." "If the boys saw what we have planned for Father Patrick, it could cause them irreparable damage. But they deserve their pound of flesh too." "Having a moral dilemma, Isabella?" "I have grown fond of the boys." "Is he named in the journals as a perpetrator?" asked Chanel. "No, but Father Paul admitted that Patrick gives the orders and instructions about which punishments should be administered." "So, he tells the other priests to sexually abuse these boys and they blindly obey him" "Yes, Chanel." "Return the favor to him. I let Goddard read the journals. Now you give Goddard the orders" Chanel smiled. "The boys don't need to see that. They are going to need psychiatric help as it is" cringed Chanel. "I hear a car. Sounds like the boys have arrived. Finish dressing, dear. I must go and greet our guests." A ringing bell announced the arrival of guests. "Ladies!" clapped Chanel. In a single-file line in the foyer stood a line of consorts no older than fifteen. "Good evening, gentlemen!" Joseph smiled and kissed Chanel's hand. The other boys did the same. "Ladies, please show our guests to the ballroom" instructed Chanel. Nicholas held the door for the ladies and led the boys to follow them in single-file.   A large table had been set for a four-course meal. "Sister Thomasina, you are here too." "Tonight you may call me Anastasia" she replied. As Isabella, Rena, Ingrid and Ursula emerged, the boys stood with their jaws hanging open. Joseph smiled and asked, "Where are your habits?"   Smiling, Isabella whispered, "We dressed up just for you." Nicholas whispered, "You're beautiful!" "Thank you, Nicholas!" "Let's talk about proper dance etiquette."

Putting on music, Isabella announced, "Ask one of the girls to dance." Each boy walked forward timidly.   "Ask her "may I have this dance? When she says yes, lead her by the hand to the dance floor. When you want to change partners, you approach and ask "may I have this dance? Keep changing partners until you end up back where you started. Next, escort the ladies to the table. Pull out their chairs, wait for them to be seated then gently push their chairs up to the table. Ask them about their day. This is called small talk. Let's discuss the order that food is brought out: Appetizers, salad, main course and dessert. There will always be water glasses on the table along with wine glasses and a drinking glass. If a meal is buffet style, the lady always goes first. Are there any questions?"

"Why are there so many forks?" Laughing, Rena explained, "For appetizers like shrimp, you use the three-pronged fork. The short, wider fork is for salad. The longer fork is for the main course. Coffee is served with dessert. Now ring that silver bell on the table, Nicholas." At the sound of the bell, servers brought out appetizers and finger sandwiches. "Now we practice!" Father Patrick smiled at the younger girls. Max nodded to Chanel. It was the signal to take Father Patrick to a private room.   "Patrick, how about a tour?" Chanel asked sweetly. Putting her arm through his, she led him down the corridor. "This room is requested by patrons with 'special' tastes."   Admiring the dark wood, Father Patrick touched the oak bedpost. He noticed the leather headboard. "What do you offer in this room?" "Let us find out "smiled Chanel. "What's your pleasure?" she asked Patrick. "I like to command" he said with a wink. "Have you ever tried being Submissive?" "To a woman?" "Yes" smiled Chanel. "Never! I am always in control."   "Well, I like my men restrained" Chanel replied. With a forceful shove backward, Father Patrick stumbled. Chanel grabbed his left arm and pinned it above his head. As she kissed him, he heard a click. "Now, let's try this again." Pinning his other hand above his head, she kissed him deeply. *Click.* With both hands secure, Chanel smiled. "That's much better! Now tell me, what would you command, Patrick? Or do you prefer Father? I think you enjoy the power you have over your students. It's time you learn what it feels like to be on the receiving end of your "command!" I bet you like to watch while your priests molest, sodomize and fuck the students!"

Chanel stood back quietly for a second. Goddard had been standing in the opposite corner. He was sizing up his prey. Chanel spoke sweetly. "This is Goddard. We call him God. He is going to teach you a lesson in the true meaning of humility."   Father Patrick's eyes were as wide as baseballs as he began to realize what was in store for him. Goddard spoke in a guttural monotone. "Let's start with those pretty, pink lips. I have the perfect place for them!" Going over to the chest of pain, Goddard retrieved the mouth gauge. "This was originally designed for dentists to keep mouths open while they were pulling teeth." Goddard shoved the gauge into Father Patrick's mouth and opened it as wide as it would go. "Do you remember ordering the priests to force those boys to perform oral sex? Now I will fill your mouth and fuck it hard!" Goddard growled. Standing on the platform, he forced his erect penis into Father Patrick's mouth and thrust in and out. Behind him, Isabella screamed, "Make him bleed!" Goddard smiled and sliced Father Patrick's cheeks. "That's better. There's more room now!" After several more minutes, Goddard ripped the gauge from the priest's mouth. Blood dripped from his mouth onto the floor. Spinning the rack, Goddard exposed Father Patrick's back. "Let's start with my whip! Forty lashes to start!" As the whip hit his skin, Father Patrick groaned. It was a strange combination of agony and ecstasy. As his skin was torn open, blood gushed from each gash. "This is how you made those young boys feel! Do you have any remorse for what you've done to them?! Now it's time for YOU to learn a lesson in humility!" Ripping down the priest's pants, Goddard penetrated him with so much force that his anus ripped and his perineum tore. "I guess we need something larger to inflict maximum pain!" Goddard thought for a moment. "I know!" he said as he went into the kitchen. He returned with a rolling pin. "This will do nicely!" Goddard sodomized Father Patrick again and again. Taking him off the rack, Goddard tossed him on the bed. As he poured salt into the priest's open wounds, he said with a laugh, "Clean yourself up! You disgust me!" Dressing was excruciating for Father Patrick. "That's a pound of flesh!" smiled Isabella. "I guarantee he will remember this!" "How did our boys do?" "They were perfect gentlemen with impeccable manners. I would say they all earned passing marks in social graces" Chanel beamed.

Max drove the boys back to campus while the girls changed back into their habits. "Where is Father Patrick?" Rena asked. "Licking his wounds" Chanel laughed. "He will need a doctor to patch him up." Doctor Burton announced, "Father Patrick needs to be admitted to a hospital." "Couldn't have happened to a nicer guy!" smiled Isabella. "I will escort him to the hospital. You need to get back to the convent." "Thank you, Chanel." "Max is back. He will drive you to the convent." As the night wound down, Isabella went straight to bed. She was asleep before her head hit her pillow. Max completed his report and was ready to present it in his meeting with the Archbishop at nine a.m. As the girls lay in bed, Anastasia asked, "Did you help Goddard with Father Patrick's lesson, Isabella?" Stirring from sleep, she answered, "No. I have no personal knowledge. I need plausible deniability. We have other ops to execute here. I can't be deemed a threat to the children." "You did a great job keeping the boys on task. Is Mother Superior really making you leave?" asked Ursula. "Yes. She said I will be reassigned. In her eyes, I am solely responsible for what happened to Father Paul." "He deserves a lot more than a beating for what he did to Joseph!" exclaimed Rena. "Mother Superior knows "all "that happens here, but still I am to blame "scoffed Isabella. "How can she know what goes on and do nothing?" questioned Ingrid. "The church is her "master". She dares not question church sanctioned abuse and molestation" replied Isabella.   Sleep eluded her. She was concerned about how Mother Superior would chastise and punish her comrades once she left the convent. These thoughts plagued her mind. She decided to go for a run to clear her mind. Slipping on pants and a long-sleeved shirt, Isabella snuck out through the kitchen door. Her first few steps were at an average pace. Each step after that quickened until she was at a full run. The sweat froze on her face as Isabella kept up her maddening pace. Five miles was enough distance to clear her mind. Feeling relieved, Isabella/Sister Mary Katherine quietly slipped back into the kitchen door. She found Mother Superior waiting for her. "Morning prayers are about to start!" "I needed to clear my head" Mary Katherine explained. "You look like you've been running" Mother Superior accused.   "I have. I ran five miles. It helps me to clear my heart, mind and soul." "Exercise is a good vice, but prayer is more important! Obviously your priorities are not aligned with the church! Get changed and report to the chapel for prayers!" Sister Mary Katherine cleaned up and donned her habit. She arrived four minutes late. The looks from her comrades told her she was in for another caning from Mother Superior.   As prayers ended, they walked single-file, heads bowed toward the dining hall. The silence was deafening. Breakfast did little to break the mounting tension. Finally, as they prepared to walk to campus, Mother Superior clapped her hands and spoke with a cold tone. "Sister Mary Katherine, it is obvious that you do not belong here. Our convent is too confining for you. I feel that splitting you up is the best course of action. Sister Mary Agnes and Sister Mary

Dawn, you will be moved to St. Anne's campus. Sister Thomasina and Sister Mary Pat, you will be assigned to the wayward school. Sister Mary Katherine, you will be given a room at Madam Chanel's to continue your work with the consorts so that they can find peace with the Holy Spirit. Please pack your things and report to your new postings. You are dismissed!"   "I am covering Father Paul's class until he is released from the hospital" Mary Katherine replied. "After today, you will no longer be needed. I split your team up, Mary Katherine so that they would not be unduly influenced by your disrespect of the church. You are not welcome back on this campus. Say your goodbyes, Mary Katherine!" Donning her street clothes and smiling, Isabella handed Mother Superior her habit. Nodding, she walked out the convent doors forever. Walking to campus, Anastasia looked at Isabella for reassurance. "Nothing changes except that you will need to gather information and feed it back to me in precise notes for the ops. Stick together. Keep constant contact. I am trusting you to handle this!" Isabella exclaimed. "You may actually have more freedom now that you are not living at the convent. This is good for us but I will miss our students." Opening the doors and walking into the front office, they could hear whispers about last night's events. "What is all the excitement about?" questioned Mary Katherine. "The Archbishop is here for a board meeting. That is why we were brought here to organize the filing system" replied Mary Katherine. "We heard they are reassigning staff. We can only wait and see what happens. Father Patrick is in the hospital." Mary Katherine smiled. "I hope he feels better soon. I need to see my students!"   On the walk to Father Paul's office, Mary Katherine prepared her speech. The students were quiet as they filed into the classroom. "Hello! I wanted to tell you that today will be my last day as your teacher. I have enjoyed teaching you self-defense. You have done exceptional work." Joseph spoke, his voice barely a whisper. "You have to leave because of me." "No. Mother Superior gave me a new posting." "They fired you!"

"No, Joseph. Everything will be fine. With Father Paul and Father Patrick in the hospital, they will be switching some teachers around" smiled Sister Mary Katherine. "You may call me Isabella. If you ever need me, just tell one of my other sisters here." Nicholas ran up to Isabella and hugged her tightly. "I love you!" "I know. No backsliding. Practice with a sparring partner." While Isabella said her goodbyes, Max and a Justice presented irrefutable proof to the Archbishop and Board of Education intimidation and abuse. Max demanded that the priests be brought up on criminal charges. The Archbishop said that the Diocese would handle the situation. "NO!" demanded Max. "You will just reassign them elsewhere! Those journals describe unspeakable torture at the hands of these priests!" "They will be removed from the school." "That's not good enough. They preyed on poor children who only wanted to make their parents proud!"

Archbishop Hubbard announced that all classes would be canceled until they could find replacements for the offending priests. "We are done here." Collecting the files, Hubbard said, "Thank you for bringing this to our attention." "We have duplicate copies of all the evidence files in case any of yours get lost" smiled Max.

Archbishop Hubbard closed himself in Father Patrick's office. Over the public address system came the announcement that classes were canceled. Isabella informed Max of their new postings. "I am banned from campus." "Well then, I guess you need a ride to Chanel's." On their way out the door, Rena and Ursula handed off the report about the laundry to Isabella.

Chapter Four: Dirty Laundry

Bringing her bags to Max's car, Isabella stared off into space. Her thoughts were scattered. Max smiled. "What are you thinking about?" "Mother Superior separating us." Max said soothingly, "Well, you did throw Father Paul a beating and allowed the boys to get a few shots. You are the strong-willed leader of the group. Separating you allows Mother Superior and the nuns to keep control of the campus. You do not follow rules. That's a sore spot for nuns." "She made it sound as though ministering to Chanel's consorts was a bad thing." "The nuns are very judgmental toward them." "Any sexual activity outside of a marriage is forbidden in the eyes of the church. On a lighter subject, you don't have to wear the habit anymore. At Chanel's you will have better food, clothing and a softer bed." Pulling up to the front gate, Max pressed the button on the intercom. A voice responded "Yes, Max?" Then the gate opened and a man opened the car door and carried Isabella's bags into the house. Chanel greeted her with a hug and kiss. "Welcome, Darling! Oh my dear, you look so pale. Let me show you to your room. Then we will have brunch and I am taking you on a much needed shopping trip!"

Chanel led Isabella down a hallway with red velvet wallpaper and gold trim. Opening the door, Chanel showed Isabella the layout of the room. "Here is your sitting area, bedroom and washing area. Is this acceptable?" Chanel questioned. "Oh, yes!" exclaimed Isabella. "Wash up, dear. We will have lunch in the conservatory." Isabella looked in the mirror at her ashen reflection. "*I need some sleep*" she thought to herself. As she made her way to the conservatory, Isabella felt a sense of peace. It was almost as if she belonged here. "Max has been filling me in." "Yes. The pedophile priests are gone. Mother Superior separated my team." "They resent that you have more authority over your girls than they do. That is the true reason you were banned from campus." Isabella let out a long, deep sigh. "I need to look over Rena and Ursula's report on the laundry/asylum." "There is plenty of time for that, dear. Let's have some lunch and a little shopping trip before you begin your next op." Chanel's words were firm but gentle. "You must take time to relax so you don't get burned out." Max smiled and said, "I fully agree with Chanel." "I have the report to review before we begin the next op." Isabella said.　　　Max looked into her eyes. "You need twenty-four hours off. Go shopping with Chanel. Buy gifts for the girls. Visit a salon. I don't care what you do, but no work!" "Understood" smiled Isabella. "I know you are concerned about your comrades. They are doing fine" soothed Max. "I caused the anger among the priests and nuns" Isabella said wearily. "Worry in twenty-four hours. I'm ordering you to go out and have fun!" Max scolded lightly. With a hearty laugh, Isabella scoffed, "You order me to have fun?" "We will start fresh on Friday morning. Chanel, I am leaving her in your capable hands!" Chanel giggled. "You know just how capable these hands are, Max!" "Enough, Chanel!" smirked Max. "Finish your lunch, dear. We have shopping to do!" "I haven't received a paycheck since we started working at the school" Isabella said shyly. With a sly smile, Chanel said, "This is on the church! I left a heavy coat on your bed along with a purse. It's time for you to dress like a refined lady again." Running back to her room, Isabella found a knee-length fur coat and matching bag. Grinning like a Cheshire cat, Isabella said, "I could get used to this kind of luxury!" Isabella could hear Chanel calling, "Move along, dear!"　　　Having a footman holding open doors and a driver was nice! Lucretia came running out the front door to the car door. "Here are the chef's lists and lists of the girls' personal needs." Lucretia panted as she handed the lists to Chanel. "Very well. Thank you, dear" Chanel replied. Lucretia waved goodbye as the car pulled away. Chanel filled Isabella in on the newest fashion trends. "Women have begun wearing pants in the workforce." "This sounds much better than dresses and heels." Laughing, Chanel said, "They do get in the way of kicking ass! I am just not a dress and heels type of woman."

　　　As they pulled up to the boutique, Chanel handed her driver, Leo the chef's lists. She then took Isabella's hand. "Shall we?" Walking through the doors, the staff greeted them warmly. "What can we do for you today, ladies?" "Have you got any pant suits? I prefer pants over dresses" quipped Isabella. "And low-heeled or flat shoes" she added.   "Right this way." After trying on several pairs of shoes, Isabella chose four. "Next, the salon!" Chanel chimed. "No worries, dear. I have ordered the same items in the sizes and favorite colors of your comrades. Now, let's do something about your hair!" "Why? It's fine." "A mid-length style will be easier for you to manage. And, of course you will need a new hat" Chanel said. "Maybe you're right" Isabella exhaled. "I need to fill this list for the girls at the house" Chanel said. "I will return shortly."   Isabella was given instructions on how to keep her style fresh. She was given a facial and some light makeup was applied to her face. Chanel returned carrying multiple packages. "You look lovely, dear!" Chanel smiled. After loading up the car, they returned to the brothel. "Dinner is in an hour. Go get some rest. I will assign Lucretia as your handmaid. Do not lift a finger." A few moments later, there was a small knock on the door. "Come in" Isabella called out. "Miss Isabella? I am here to help you. What do you need?" "Why don't you pour me a drink, Lucretia? Three fingers of bourbon, please." "Yes, ma'am." As Isabella took a long sip, she grinned. "That's perfect, Lucretia! Thank you." "You're welcome, ma'am. Mistress Chanel would like you to join her in the formal dining room."   "Tell me, Lucretia, how did you end up here?" "It's a long story, ma'am." "Well, if you'd like, we can talk in the evening when things calm down here."   The dining room was filled with fresh flowers, the best china and shimmering silverware. Isabella enjoyed appetizers and a large salad before the main course. It was homemade beef stew that was served with fresh baked bread. Dessert was served with coffee and brandy. The peach cobbler melted in her mouth.   "Chanel, dinner was exquisite!" "Do you need any male companionship tonight?" "No thanks, love. I am looking forward to sleeping in a soft bed." "How about a massage?" "That would be nice." As Isabella settled in to read Ursula and Rena's report, there was a soft knock at the door and a familiar face stood in her doorway with a jar of warm oil. Goddard smiled. "I was told you needed a massage and a hot bath." "Come, lie on your stomach after you remove your robe."   Goddard warmed his hands with oil. Starting at her neck, Goddard used his magical hands to massage her spine, thighs, calves and feet. Isabella sighed deeply. Goddard smiled. "I will draw you a hot bubble bath." As Goddard turned his back, Isabella slipped into the tub. She exhaled deeply as the hot water relaxed the soreness in her back. "Let me wash your back" Goddard said.

"I hear you succeeded in unseating the pedophile priests." "Yes. I am sure they will be reassigned. But the students will be safe now. That's what matters most." "I will leave now so that you may rest. My previous offer still stands." "After this next op, I promise." Nodding in approval, Goddard kissed the top of Isabella's head. "Get a good night's rest." Isabella sank back in the tub. Her eyelids fluttered slowly. She was almost asleep when she jolted awake. Pulling herself out of the tub, she slipped into a nightgown and crawled under her blankets before falling fast asleep. Lucretia slipped in to clean the tub. As she closed the door, Lucretia whispered, "Sweet dreams, Missy." After closing the brothel doors at midnight, Chanel asked, "How is our girl?" "She's fast asleep, Madam." "This is good. Life in that convent was hell on her!" The night maids began cleaning up the visitor areas. At eight a.m. the cooks started preparing breakfast. At nine a.m. Lucretia slipped into Isabella's sleeping chamber with a fresh cup of coffee and a plate of fruit and biscuits.

"Good morning, my lady" she said sweetly. Stretching, Isabella asked, "What time is it?" "It's after nine." "Oh goodness! I really slept in!" "Here, slip into your dressing gown and have some breakfast, ma'am. I laid out your navy blue pant suit and had a writing desk brought in for you to read your reports. Miss Chanel would like to meet with you at eleven in the conservatory." "Thank you, Lucretia." After a leisurely breakfast, Isabella dressed for her meeting with Chanel. Walking to the conservatory, Isabella's thoughts drifted to how she could get used to the comforts that were provided to her here.   As she entered the brightly lit conservatory, Chanel greeted her with a warm "Good morning, dear! Did you sleep well?" "Wonderfully!" exclaimed Isabella. "We have a girl from the laundry here that you can speak with. Lunch is at one o'clock and tea is at three p.m. Max will join us for dinner this evening."

Report on the Divinity Laundries/Asylums

These facilities began operating over two hundred years ago by order of the Catholic Church. They were known as Institutes of Confinement. They housed primarily Protestant and "fallen "women. Most were prostitutes but some of these women had never engaged in sex.   Catholic missionaries were required to approach prostitutes and distribute religious tracts to them, which usually lead to them being sent to the laundries. This did very little to decrease the number of street prostitutes. Anyone who challenged the norms or the moral code was labeled as "fallen". Anyone who had a child out of wedlock was labeled "fallen and criminal." These facilities grew from a need to control appearances and profit from free labor.   Under the guise of saving the souls of women and children, many families were forced to give up their children. These laundry facilities housed "hopeless "children. These were typically children who had mental deficits, disabilities and those accused of transgressions against the moral code.   The church prefers to have "punishment" occupants. None of these people are abusive, violent or cruel. None of them have been convicted or tried for crimes but they are all locked in. This includes petty criminals, mentally disabled women and abused girls. Parents can also commit their daughters if they are sassy, questioning their bodies or going through puberty. Federal subsidies for asylums are larger than for orphanages, so the church started diagnosing orphans with mental illnesses they do not have.

Children of unwed mothers were forcibly taken. They were beaten, lobotomized and used in pharmaceutical testing. Children were seen as sinners and criminals. Promiscuity in view of the public could also land you here. These facilities made massive profit from free labor. A hundred and fifty-five bodies have been found in mass graves.

Shaking her head, Isabella shuddered at the knowledge that the church was behind this. She was quiet through lunch. By the time tea was served, she was incensed by the arrogance of the Catholic Church. "When you are up to it, you can talk to Lucretia." After tea, Chanel asked if Isabella would like Max to sit in during her talk with Lucretia. "No, but is there anyone here who knows shorthand? Max can have them transcribed. Susie worked in an office before joining us. She can take notes for you. Would you prefer to do this in the conservatory for privacy?" "Yes. Let me grab the report from my desk" said Isabella. "Already done" smiled Chanel.   "I will join you with Lucretia in about ten minutes." Isabella made herself comfortable while she waited for Lucretia. Suzy sat in the back right corner, out of Lucretia's view. Lucretia approached timidly. "You would like to speak with me?" "Yes. Do you know what is in this folder?" "No, ma'am." "My comrades gave me a report about the laundries/asylums. I am very angry at how people were treated. I would like to stop this from happening to other girls. I would like to know how you ended up there."   "Well, I was a bad girl. That's what my mamma said. I had trouble at St. Anne's. I could not keep up with my school work. The nuns beat me for being stupid. Finally, Father Patrick said I belonged at the wayward girl's school. I started there a year ago. Mamma and Papa could not come visit me because I have five brothers and a baby sister. I got a scholarship to St. Anne's. I lived on the campus year-round with the nuns and priests. Father Patrick said I had a fresh mouth and that I needed to learn respect. I was twelve when the nuns told me I was a sinner. Father Christopher told me I could give a special gift to God. He said God wanted him to give me a baby and that it would be a gift to another mamma and daddy who could not have their own baby. I was helping people. I got pregnant, but my baby died. We lit candles and said prayers for him. Sister Aggie said I was too small to have a baby. When I got pregnant again, I ran away so they couldn't hurt me anymore. Now I live here with Chanel. She is so nice to me. She never yells or hits me."   Lucretia lifted her blouse to reveal a small, round belly. "People used to come to my school and look at us like we were prize cows. I saw some of them give the nuns monies." "Is there anything else you remember?" "Lots of girls go into the tunnels with big bellies. They don't have a belly when they come back. If you are too dumb to have pretty little babies, they send you to work hard in the laundries 'cause you're useless for anything else."   "How many days do you work in the laundry?" asked Isabella. "All seven days and fourteen hours per day. Sunday church is two hours. One girl got sick at the laundry. The nuns said they were taking her to see a doctor. She never came back. I heard gunshots that night. When I asked about that, the nuns said I made it up to get attention." "How many girls are at the laundry?" "I can't count that high, but there's more than fifty. Girls go there 'cause they can't make no more pretty little babies." "What makes a pretty baby?" Isabella questioned. "Oh, you know. Blue eyes and blonde curls" Lucretia said sadly. Lucretia looked over at Chanel. "I did good, right? I can stay here?"   "Yes, dear" Chanel reassured her. "My baby too?" "Of course, dear. Go and help the cook with dinner" Chanel instructed. "Yes, Mistress."

Isabella looked horrified as Lucretia skipped down the hall. "Jesus Christ, Chanel! Those poor girls! The government pays the church to say these girls are mentally ill to collect more money along with profits from slave labor!" "I put word out to other brothel owners and got this list of laundries" growled Chanel. "I handed the list over to Max so he can have them shut down. Suzy, can you please transcribe notes from this conversation?" asked Chanel.   Isabella asked, "What about Lucretia?" "She will stay here with me" said Chanel. "Not to question your maternal instincts, but she's what, twelve or thirteen and obviously a bit slow mentally." "I will not return her to that school. They are using children to breed a "pure "race of babies! Go and rest before dinner. We can give Max the notes and reports to have those places condemned. Parents had their own children committed. Max will have each of those girls properly evaluated before finding suitable placements for them." Isabella screamed, "They are breeding young girls and selling their babies!" "I understand the anger you feel, Isabella. But these things have been going on for two hundred years. That means that the church's tracks are very well hidden. Wash up for dinner. Max will be here soon." Upon Max's arrival, Chanel brought him three fingers of Scotch. Looking into her face, Max knew this was no social call. "Let me guess? Isabella has read the reports?" "Yes, Max. I have." Isabella said. Suzy handed Isabella the transcribed notes. Putting everything in a folder, Isabella handed it to Max. After several minutes, Max looked up into Isabella's face. "We have lawyers, judges and peace officers to handle this. We will close these laundries/asylums and re-staff them with paid employees. Most of these girls and women will need to be placed in new jobs." "What about the ones who have been lobotomized? They are no longer functional. They will be sent to a hospital. Your job is done. Now let me do mine! Your next op will center on the wayward school. You will stay here until that op is complete. Then your comrades will rejoin you." "Max, are you sure?" Isabella questioned. "That's an order!" Max said flatly. "Let's go have a nice dinner with Chanel. End of story!"

Chapter Five: Church & State

Max rubbed his head as he read through Ursula and Rena's report along with the notes from Isabella's interview with Lucretia. Thinking aloud, he said, "Christ, the Catholic church has been dirty from day one!" Just then, Anastasia, Ursula, Ingrid and Rena burst through his office door. "I see you made it!" Max joked. "Those crazy nuns tore our filing system apart! The Archbishop is cleaning house! I guess Isabella shook up the entire Diocese." "Here is the information we gathered about the laundries and an interview Isabella did with one of the girls from there." Anastasia gasped after reading it. "I have people in place to dismantle the laundries and restructure them to provide gainful employment. The women will need years to heal. Those who were lobotomized will be placed in a sanatorium. The nuns will be brought up on charges. They committed fraud by taking money from the government and claiming that the laundries were asylums. Now it's time to close down the baby factory set-up!" Max explained. "The nuns still want Isabella to teach self-defense." "She is no longer a nun!" Max said sternly. "Without the habit, maybe the girls will feel more comfortable telling Isabella their stories." "Hello, ladies" cooed Chanel. "Where's Isabella?" "Over here" came a familiar voice. Isabella was standing in an alcove, packages in hand. "Did you really think I would forget you?" As they grabbed at the packages and ripped off the pretty wrapping paper, the girls squealed with delight as they pulled out pant suits, silk undergarments and real shoes. "Oh, hell! We still have to wear the habits!" cried Rena. "I have arranged for you to be permitted to don office attire. I told Mother Superior you are now questioning your decision to become nuns and you are taking a sabbatical from your duties." "Thanks Max! You're wonderful!" "Mother Superior blames this on Isabella's willful behavior." Laughing, Isabella said, "I'll accept the blame for that, Max!" "I never believed you wouldn't. All of you will be taking up residence here with Chanel starting Saturday. You will carry on with your duties at the school during the week. You will sleep in the dormitory with the students two or three nights a week. This will give the other nuns a break" said Max. "That sounds fair to me!" Ursula squealed clapping her hands. "You still need to use your nun names and your attire will keep to the school's dress code" Max warned. "Yes sir!" the girls said in unison. "This way, Isabella will be able to spend a few nights at the campus as well." "If I may be bold, I believe Mother Superior is also involved in all of this. She followed the order from Father Patrick to cane Isabella" sniped Anastasia. "Sister Francine Joyce told us." "Understood" Max said, shaking his head. "We need to stop the selling of babies! After checking out the story Lucretia told me, I did overhear that the priests were breeding babies in the hopes of creating a "master race. " Blonde haired, blue-eyed babies sell for the highest prices. After bearing two or three children, the mothers are discarded and sent to either the laundry or other brothels. If they're sickly, they are of no use so they are killed. The ones that excel academically are sent to University on the church dime to become teaching nuns. This protects all the church secrets." Isabella piped up, "We need to follow the tunnel system so we can understand how the mothers and babies are moved between the campuses." "Get through the rest of the school week. We will start on that plan this weekend at Chanel's. Return to campus. Leonardo will drive you" cooed Chanel.   Hugs were passed between the comrades before they returned to campus. "Holiday is over, Isabella. You will start your self-defense/exercise classes for the wayward campus tomorrow at eight a.m." "Yes, sir" grinned Isabella. "I'm going to enjoy this!" Isabella said smugly. "Without the habit, I might have an easier time getting through to the girls." Anastasia ecstatically yelped, "No more habit!" "You are re-evaluating your decision to become nuns" Max reminded them.   Leo appeared in the doorway. "May I take you home, ladies?" "Back to campus, Leo!" smirked Ursula. After loading the girls and their belongings into the car, Isabella looked into Chanel's eyes. "We need to end this for Lucretia and all the other girls that this farce of a religion has ruined!" Seeing the anger and frustration that stormed in Isabella's eyes, Chanel whispered, "There are many churches, religions and entities that sacrifice children in God's name. We cannot save them all but we can slow the process down. The heart you so vehemently hide hurts for those children that will one day become you. You will always prevail."   Max interrupted them. "Ladies, are you planning world domination without me?" "Never, Max" cooed Chanel. "That's my girl!" smirked Max. "Always" said Chanel, giving Max a wink. "Do I need to give you two some privacy?" Isabella scoffed.   Chanel laughed. "If Max had me, he would never need another woman! Get some rest, Isabella. You will need to perform at your best." "I always perform at my best! Anything less is unacceptable!" "Good night, Chanel" he said as he kissed her hand. "My pleasure, as always." Closing the door, Chanel turned to Isabella. "How about a snack? Cakes and tea?" "That would be nice" said Isabella. She exhaled a deep sigh of relief as she sank down into the comfortable over-sized chair in Chanel's parlor room.   The afternoon sun cast a kaleidoscope of colors along the walls as it shone through the stained glass windows. Lucretia appeared in the doorway and proceeded to serve them their snacks. Her hands trembled slightly as she poured the tea into tiny, gold-rimmed cups. "What's troubling you, dear?" Chanel asked. Lucretia shifted her posture slightly. "It's getting close to time for my baby to get born. What happens to me after that? How will I be able to care for my baby?" she asked with worry clouding her ice blue eyes.   "Will we pray for him if he dies like his brother did?" Lucretia asked turning her back to them so they wouldn't see the tears rolling down her cheeks.   "Your baby will be fine, dear" Chanel soothed. "Should anything happen, we will say a prayer and light candles for his soul." Lucretia turned and gave Chanel a sad smile as she left the parlor and returned to the kitchen. Isabella took a slow sip of her tea before she spoke. "Chanel, what is the plan once Lucretia gives birth? I know we told her that no one was going to take the baby away from her, but is it really a good idea to raise a baby in a brothel?" Chanel paused. "I have a solution for that. I am in the process of arranging for Lucretia and the infant to be relocated. They will be safe and a long way away from the sadness that she has known here." Isabella raised a worried eyebrow. Chanel reassured her. "Don't worry. The person I am entrusting them to is a longtime friend of mine." "Where are they going?" Isabella asked. "South America. To a whole new beginning ." Isabella was momentarily stunned silent. Chanel chuckled. "What's wrong, dear? Max and I told you I have friends and connections all over. And it's nice to be able to use my influence to help others. I gave my word to Lucretia that she and her baby would be safe and cared for. This is how I ensure that." Isabella nodded in silent understanding as she swallowed hard at the knot in her throat. She had come to feel a sense of responsibility for Lucretia and her unborn child as she felt for her comrades. The sadness came from knowing that in order for Lucretia to go on to safety, there would be no goodbyes. She would likely leave the school through the same tunnels that some of her classmates did. Only this time, the outcome would be a positive one. She shook the thoughts from her mind. She and her comrades were soldiers. Emotions and attachments would only cloud her focus and her judgment. She needed a clear mind to focus on her mission. *"Snap out of it!"* she reprimanded herself. No matter how hard she tried, she couldn't get her thoughts under control. Perhaps a few hours with Goddard would help her blow off some emotional steam. "Chanel, is it possible for me to get a few hours with Goddard?" she asked. "This stuff with Lucretia is weighing on my mind along with other things." "Of course, dear." Chanel soothed. "I will let him know to make himself available you." Isabella gave Chanel a wink and a nod as she poured herself another cup of tea. They sat in silence for a few seconds before Chanel asked the question that had been on Isabella's mind since their lunch with Max. "Have you been preparing for the next mission? Has Max laid out the strategy that you girls will use to infiltrate the baby factory?" "Not yet, but I'm sure he will bring us up to speed soon." Isabella replied. "For now, can you locate Goddard for me? I need to go into this next op with a clear and focused mind." "Of course, dear" Chanel said as she pressed a button on the wall to her right. Chimes sounded and one of the house girls appeared to lead Isabella to Goddard's quarters. It was a short walk down the dimly lit hallway. As the girl opened the door and led Isabella inside, Isabella was anxious to vent some of her pent up emotions. "Miss Isabella is here to see you" the girl announced. "Very well" Goddard said as he dismissed her with a wave. She scurried out of the room, closing the door behind herself. "Welcome back, Little Girl" Goddard said with a sadistic smirk. Isabella glared at him. "You wish!" she taunted him. "I'm sure you prefer dominating young girls as opposed to mature women. Since all those young girls buy into your bullshit!" she snapped at him. "Shut that pretty mouth and get over here!" Goddard fired back as he grabbed Isabella's freshly cut hair and used what remained as a leash to lead her to the bed. He pushed her down on her back on the bed and ripped open her blouse with his other hand. "Be a good little girl and stay put!" Goddard ordered. He reached beside the bed and pulled a few of his favorite implements from his little bag of tricks. Isabella broke into a grin as she saw him pull a few of her favorite floggers and impact implements from his bag. This didn't go unnoticed by Goddard. When he returned his full attention to the bed, a small smile curled his lips. He always enjoyed seeing Isabella struggle to submit to him. The freedom in submission was something she needed from time to time but her natural leadership made her fight it. Hard. It was a part of the way she and Goddard connected. He understood that Isabella was a masochistic. She craved pain. The struggle was her release. The sex acts were just a physical outlet for her pent-up feelings. There were no romantic feelings attached to what the two of them shared. It was purely a pleasure and pain dynamic. One thing that Isabella loved about Goddard was that he could endure as much as he ever doled out. She loved the cycle. He would inflict pain on her and she would do the same to him. This was as close a connection to another person as Isabella could get. Her work and assignments didn't allow for personal relationships or attachments. As Goddard pinned Isabella's wrists above her head with one hand, he ripped her blouse off with his other hand. Tossing the blouse over his shoulder, he reached into his back pocket and retrieved a pair of nipple clamps. There was a noticeable sparkle in Isabella's eye as she tingled with anticipation. These sessions with Goddard were cathartic. They were her form of therapy. She trembled slightly as the cold clamps pinched the pink flesh of her nipples as they snapped closed. "Excited are we?" Goddard teased her as brought a leather flogger down across her taut, pale belly. Isabella let out a guttural moan and begged him to increase his intensity and force. This pleased Goddard. He was well-known for indulging his sadistic streaks and for being relentless. This was exactly what Isabella needed. She delighted in the rough play and rigorous intercourse that followed. Perhaps it was the prolonged stress she had been under that caused her to abandon all her inhibitions and permit Goddard to push the previous limits on the use of anal plugs and beads. At one point, Goddard paused mid-flog and asked aloud, "Are you okay, Little Girl?" Isabella nodded and continued to enjoy the intense combinations of pleasure and pain that Goddard inflicted on her. A session with him could make you think you were in heaven or bring you face to face with the Devil himself. It was entirely up to you. As Goddard brought the flogger down across Isabella's back, he thrust himself into her. She let out a satisfied moan and reached up and around his neck. She brought his mouth to hers and sank her teeth into his bottom lip. Tasting his blood brought a devilish smile to her lips and signaled Goddard to quicken his pace. A few minutes later, they both collapsed into sweaty, disheveled heaps on the bed. Isabella was so spent that she fell fast asleep. Goddard wrapped her in a blanket and carried her back to her own room. He stopped in to inform Chanel to have the handmaids clean up the Red Room and to return Isabella's clothing to its proper place. "How is she, dear?" "She's out cold. Guess she was really feeling stressed" he said. "I tucked her into her own bed. Please tell her that I will be by to check on her when schedules permit it." "Very well, dear. Enjoy your evening." Chanel dismissed him as she turned out the lights in her sitting room. The sunrise broke over the horizon. Upon waking, Isabella's thoughts of her evening with Goddard brought her a sweet sting of pleasure. She dressed in a classic pant suit with pin stripes, felt hat and a matching handkerchief. Lucretia brought in fruit and coffee for breakfast. Chanel appeared in the doorway. "Good morning. Did you sleep well?" "Yes. A bit of exercise is just what I needed." "Leo will drive you to the campus. I had a lunch packed for you. Have a great day, dear." "Thank you, Chanel." "Do not forget that the girls will be here this evening for a strategy meeting to take down the baby factory." "I need to get the girls at the other two campuses to trust me enough that they will open up to me. I was given a brief description of the tunnels, but I think we are going to have to have a pregnant girl inside the school to tell us exactly how it is run." Chanel smiled. "Good idea, Isabella. Let me see if I can find an unwed mother who would be willing to help you." Shaking her head, Isabella made her way out to the car. The canvas bag in her hand was full of sweat suits for her exercise classes. Thinking aloud, she said, "Most of these girls are pregnant, so we'll need to start slowly with stretching before we begin with any self-defense." She skimmed over her file as Leo drove. She realized that the parents of these unwed mothers were all approved by the church. Next to each girl's name was a number. The numbers told how many live births, infant deaths and age of the student. The school was an assembly line for births, recuperation time, conception and pregnancies. These girls were hamsters on wheels. Shaking her head, she reviewed her notes on Lucretia. The priests actually told these girls that they were doing God's work!

They took a vow of celibacy. I guess impregnating underage girls so that the church can sell their babies is an exception! As Leo pulled up in front of the wayward girl's campus, Isabella let out a long sigh. "Here we go!" Stepping out of the car, a cold chill went directly into her soul. Walking up the stairs, she had an uneasy feeling. As she pulled open the door and stepped into the main corridor, she could feel the cold chill of death hanging in the air. She reported to the principal's office to begin her new assignment. Sister Mary Ann greeted her and offered her a cup of tea. "Why is it so cold in here?" Isabella asked. "Our boiler is on the fritz again. The students will fall ill if we don't get that fixed." "Does the boiler run on coal or wood?" "You know about heating systems, Isabella?" "We learned to be prepared. It may need to be cleaned out."

"Harley just arrived. He's down in the basement. Let me see if I can give him a hand." Pulling her coat tighter, Isabella walked to the basement and heard a familiar voice. "Harley, I am Isabella. Can I offer you some assistance?" A voice from behind Isabella's right shoulder spoke up. "I think we have this handled" cracked Max. "Since when do you repair heaters, Max?" "I don't. Harley does. But he's black, so we had to pretend he works for me to appease the small-minded." "So the church is a bunch of prejudiced baby brokers?" "The students need to stay in the dormitories. We put portable kerosene heaters there to keep them warm until the boiler is fixed. We do not have enough portable heaters for the entire school. We asked Sister Mary Ann to keep the students confined to the smaller areas." "What's the issue with the boiler? "This boiler has not been cleaned out in several years. Once I clean out the pipes, it should be safe to restart the furnace." "I will stop in to the office and see what I can find out" Isabella said. When she returned to the office, she found Sister Mary Ann huddled over a kerosene heater with a cup of tea in her hand. "Looks like the students will have a three-day weekend. The classrooms are too cold for us to hold classes as normal." said Sister Mary Ann. "Do you have a lesson plan for me to review?" "Yes. We need to start with stretches and light exercises for the expectant mothers. I will teach the healthy students self-defense and proper fitness regimens. How many pregnant students do you have? How close are they to confinement?" "We normally see fifteen births per year. Currently, there are six mothers that are near confinement. We can go to the infirmary to double check the dates in their charts. If I remember correctly, we have one baby due per month for the next six months. All the infants should be born just in time for summer break. The girls will have time to recuperate before the school year resumes." "Why are students sent here from St. Anne's?" "In some cases, it's academic issues. Some of our students have behavioral issues. Others are disruptive or unwanted by their parents." "Why hasn't anyone spoken to the parents?" "We have many parents who simply have too many children. A child who is disruptive or a bad influence on their siblings is easier to remove than to manage. Puberty also causes rebellion among some young girls." "Sounds to me like parents throw away their children to avoid putting in the extra work it takes to raise them!" scoffed Isabella. "And what about these babies? No one seems to care about them!" "We most certainly do!" scolded Sister Mary Ann. "We find loving homes for the children of these girls." "For a price!" huffed Isabella.   Now see here! Yes, there are fees and medical bills associated with the mothers care, but we do a thorough background check on ALL of our prospective parents! Many of our students have no home to return to, so we place them to work as nannies with wealthy families." "Really? You ship the mentally challenged ones off as slave labor to the laundries once they are no longer suitable for breeding!" "My students are not animals for breeding!" screamed Sister Mary Ann. "How long have you worked here?" Isabella asked.   "I was transferred here a few months ago" answered Sister Mary Ann. "Then you truly do not know about the wayward school?" "I will admit that I have heard rumors, but I chalked it up to old nuns with too much time on their hands." Smiling, Isabella said, "I am here to help the students. Many forms of abuse have happened under the watchful eyes of the Catholic Church." Sister Mary Ann gave a weak smile. "I will do what I can to assist you." "I appreciate it. Thank you." whispered Isabella.   "May I see the student files?" asked Isabella. "I can give you an hour in the office. After that, our new priest is scheduled to arrive. He is Father Patrick's replacement. We will also be getting a replacement for Father Paul. I will get you a cup of tea while you review the files." "Can you give me a detailed account of what happens when a girl goes into labor? What happens, from start to finish of the adoption process?" As Isabella headed toward the office, Sister Mary Ann set about making her a cup of tea. "Thank you. It is cold in here!" Isabella said with a shudder. The sound of Max clearing his throat startled Isabella. Her nose was buried in a file. "Shit! You scared me, Max!" "You need to get out of this office, now! The new priest is coming down the hall." As she hurried to return the files to their proper place, Isabella stood up and straightened her wrinkled clothing. Max announced, "The boiler is back up and running. The school will be warm soon." Shaking hands with Max, Sister Mary Ann thanked him. Handing Isabella back her file, Sister Mary Ann said, "I think your exercise plan will work just fine." Max turned to Isabella. "May I offer you a ride?" "Yes, thank you " "By the way, Max has your employee Harley left" "Yes. He is on his way back to the office." "Good. I am not sure how the new priest will react to seeing a black man here. "He works for me! That should be good enough for anyone!" Slamming the door, Max marched out the main entrance filled with rage. "Why the hell are they so prejudiced against Harley? He is very skilled at repairing furnaces! The color of his skin has NOTHING to do with his abilities!" Smiling, Isabella patted his shoulder. "Sounds like you could use a drink, Max!" "I cannot wait for this op to end! These hypocritical church gob shites piss me off to no end! These self-righteous, pompous pedophile priests need to be drawn and quartered!" "We agree" soothed Isabella. "But nothing is going to stop unless we stop them from selling babies and breeding young girls. This is what we trained for. This is the reason I endured the beatings from the Chancellor. The church does not have the right to turn a profit off the souls of those they were entrusted to save!" Max hugged Isabella as he whispered, "I am beyond proud of the woman you grew up to be." "Are we going to debate politics out here in the cold, or have lunch and a few drinks indoors where it's warm?" cooed Chanel. Pulling off her felt hat, Isabella ran her fingers through her hair. Glancing over, she realized that the file had more paper in it than before. When she opened the folder, she was surprised to find a detailed account of the wayward school's birth and adoption processes. It was her homework for the evening. She needed some lunch and a drink! After changing into more comfortable attire, she joined Chanel and Max carrying the thick folder in her hand. "Light reading?" Chanel cooed. "Sister Mary Ann gave me a report on the birth and adoption process." "Friend or foe?" Chanel questioned. "I am not sure yet" Isabella replied. "The chef brought us quiche, fruit, toast, crepes and mimosas. Max is having a single malt or two. He was incensed over the way Harley was treated at the school today." "It's a real shame that a religion that professes infinite love can be so prejudiced when it comes to the color of a man's skin. We all bleed red!" "You are wise beyond your years, Chanel" smiled Isabella. "I have had girls of color work for me. They were always top earners, good with a needle and thread, great in the kitchen and fantastic nannies. Very easy to please. I love those ladies!" smiled Chanel.

"Eat. You need to keep your strength up. We will go through Sister Mary Anne's notes later" Chanel scolded. Serving herself a plate, Isabella sat down to enjoy her meal. Max joined them with a glass of Scotch in each hand. Cracking a smile, Max exhaled a deep sigh. "I have an idea. But I want the whole team here before I divulge my idea. For now, we can review Sister Mary Ann's notes." As Isabella finished reading a page, she passed it along the table for Max to read. Max piped up. "The church is prejudiced against people of color. White babies bring more money." Isabella sniped. "Business must be booming if the cars I saw hidden under the tarps belong to church members. Someone is getting a major pay day!" Chanel smiled dryly. "That kind of money would take care of my girls for years!" Max said, "The only way to put an end to the "wayward school "is to blow up the tunnels underneath the campuses!" "I will assume we will evacuate all the girls from the school first?" "Of course!" snarled Max.

"I need to see how the pregnant girls are brought through the tunnels, how they deliver the babies and are brought back." "The notes explain how the books are kept.

They include lists of potential parents. The list matches traits such as hair and eye color as well as ethnicity. Babies of color or mixed race are damn near given away. If they are raised as servants, no one notices." "So, they basically sell children for ALL purposes?" "This raises more questions." "No. It proves evil intentions!" "We need to figure out exactly how many of those babies were born from sex with priests."

"Lucretia is due soon. Then we will send her to a new life." "Are any of the new students disabled?" "There is one that is considered deaf and dumb." Chanel looked into Isabella's eyes. "I guess she made the perfect victim. She literally cannot tell anyone. Any student that has any type of disability is treated as though they are less than human. They are deemed unworthy because they are seen as imperfect. These nuns are supposed to embody the love of God but they treat these girls like dirt!" screamed Isabella. "They are just as guilty as the pedophile priests! How much money do the Bishops and Cardinals get from all of this? How about the Pope?!" Isabella shouted. "Calm down, Isabella. Getting angry will not help. We need cool, calm and collected minds. You are trained not to get emotional." "I realize that. These pieces of dirt deserve a beating!" "Finish your dinner and relax" cooed Chanel. "I just get so angry!" cried Isabella. "Yes, I know. Maybe you should spend some time with Goddard to help alleviate your frustration. You always feel better after a session with him. I will tell him to make room in his schedule for you tonight." "That sounds like a good idea" smiled Isabella. As they finished their meal with lighthearted banter, Chanel whispered to Isabella "He has time at eleven p.m." "That gives me time to go over the tunnel blueprints with Max." Rolling out the blueprints, Max showed Isabella where each individual campus and the local hospital was within the tunnel system. He then showed her how each tunnel intersected directly underneath St. Anne's. "If we blow up the tunnels, we need to place charges under each campus. I would prefer to use explosives that will collapse the tunnels. We need to get all the students, staff and infants off all the campuses. This phase of the op will take perfect timing" said Max. "The girls will be picked up for the weekend tomorrow morning. Once everyone arrives, we will design the plan. Get some rest, Isabella. I have some work to do at my office." "Drive carefully, Max." "Always" Max replied giving her a wink. As she returned to her room, Isabella washed her face and changed into a loose-fitting silk pajama set. Smiling at her reflection in the mirror, she sat down on the settee and reviewed Sister Mary Ann's notes. A light knock on the door disrupted Isabella's train of thought. "Yes? "A very pregnant Lucretia entered the room. Goddard is ready to see you now." "Okay. I will be right there. Go get some sleep. I will not need your assistance tonight. You and your baby need rest." "Thank you, Miss Isabella." "On your way back to your room, grab a snack."

"Thank you, Miss Isabella. Goodnight." She knocked on Goddard's door. "Enter!" "Hello!" Isabella shouted. "Chanel explained how frustrated you are about the priests and the babies being sold. And that perhaps some time with me will help alleviate your negative emotions." As Goddard entered the room, Isabella saw that he was wearing a priest's outfit. "What the hell are you doing?!" Isabella demanded. "I am going to absolve you of your sins, Little Girl!" he answered with an evil smirk. Isabella gave him a half-snort. "Oh, really now? I suppose this tells me you'd like to see me on my knees then?" she questioned him as he pinned her against the wall and applied a slight pressure to her throat with his right hand. She let out something between a gasp and a whimper as adrenaline sent her body into overdrive. Maybe it was the stress of her mission, but her body ached for him. She could feel herself bending to whatever he had in mind as he peeled her silk pajamas from her body. Their connection had always been a primal one. Goddard could read her innermost desires as though they were actually printed on her skin. He led her to a stool in the center of the room and bent her over it on her belly. He held the slight pressure on her neck as he thrust himself into her from behind. Her breath escaped her in short bursts. She hardly felt the sting of the flogger as Goddard brought it down across her back again and again. Her pale skin was now cherry red and hot to the touch. The flogger's tassels snapped against her skin again.

This time, it brought a faint trickle of blood from her back. She was too lost in the sensations of her own orgasms and the sensations that Goddard was bringing to her body to notice any physical pain.   The harder Goddard pushed her limits, the more relaxed she became. He teased, licked and bit every inch of her exposed flesh as he thrust into her. She was taken by surprise when he stopped mid-thrust and lifted her off the stool. She instinctively wrapped her legs around his waist as he slipped back into her with a low growl. "Does this please you, Father Goddard?" she asked him with a devilish smile. "Why, yes my child. It is enough to absolve you of ALL your sins!" Goddard laughed as he reached his own release. "You are one hell of a woman, Little Girl!" he said with an air of satisfaction as he fastened his belt buckle. He then applied a salve of lavender and antibacterial ointment to Isabella's back. She winced slightly, but it was more of a reaction to the coldness of the salve than from pain. Goddard then carried an exhausted Isabella to her bed and tucked her in. She slept until seven a.m. The morning brought a new day and a new handmaid. "Good morning, Isabella. "Where's Lucretia? "She was having contractions an hour ago. We could have a baby in the next few hours. Chanel just sent for the doctor. Are you ready for breakfast?" "Yes. That sounds lovely." "Chanel would like you to join her in the solarium for breakfast." "Tell her I will join her shortly."   She dressed casually in a pair of pants and low heels. As she strolled into the solarium, Chanel greeted her warmly. "We have fruit, crepes, coffee and eggs. How was your session with Goddard?"   "He dressed as a priest. I definitely put him through his paces!" Laughing, Chanel replied, "I'm sure it was mutual!" "I heard about Lucretia having contractions. "Yes. I will have to contact my friends so that they can prepare for the arrival of Lucretia and her baby. We will have to get her out through the tunnels. She is deathly afraid of them."   Max spoke up. "I will take care of that when the time comes." "What do you have in mind?" "A sedative in her tea. Perhaps belladonna." "That's lethal!" cried Isabella. "Only in large doses. In small doses, it's a sedative used to help with relaxation and sleep" Max said with a smile.   Running into the room, Elisabeth announced, "The doctor is here, Miss Chanel. "Thank you, dear. If you will excuse me, I must show the doctor to his patient." Chanel walked briskly down the hall into Lucretia's room with the doctor right behind her. "How are you feeling?" Chanel cooed gently. "It hurts!" screamed Lucretia. "This is our in-house doctor. He needs to examine you, dear." Crying, Lucretia whimpered, "Please do not leave me alone with him!"   Chanel spoke softly. "Shh! I will stay right here with you, okay? Try and relax, my child."   After the exam, the doctor smiled. "You are seven centimeters dilated. I will break your water now to move things along." "I feel like I just wet my pants!" cried Lucretia. "It's a part of the birth process. We will have your bed linens changed" soothed Chanel. Lucretia asked, "How is my baby, Doctor? My other baby died. We said prayers for him." "So far, everything seems fine. You have nothing to worry about, young lady."   Chanel escorted the doctor out to the dining area. He lowered his voice to a hushed tone. "She will need an episiotomy. If her labor doesn't progress, she will need a cesarean section. She seems a bit young to be having a baby." "I fully agree with you, Doctor." "Does she have family to help her?" asked Dr. Samuels. "Yes, she will have plenty of help" said Chanel. "I will be back in an hour." Walking into the solarium, Chanel announced, "We need to contact our friends to prepare them for the arrival of Lucretia and her baby. I will be going into town for baby essentials. Does anyone have any requests?" Isabella smiled.   "I will join you. Max, will you please summon Leo for me?" As if by magic, Leo appeared in the foyer. "The car is ready, ma'am." "Max, be a dear and pick up the rest of the team from the school, please." "Yes, ma'am" Max scoffed. "We will have a baby soon. I may need their help with mother and child. We have one hour to get back. Doctor Samuels will be back to assist with labor and delivery."   A woman of color appeared in the doorway. "Yes, Miss Chanel?" "Have you delivered babies before?" "Yes, ma'am." "I need you to stay with Lucretia while I go into town for supplies. "Of course, ma'am." "Doctor Samuels will be back in an hour." Hannah disappeared, scurrying into the kitchen to boil water. The ride to town seemed endless.   Chanel talked as Isabella made a list of what they needed. "We will need several dozen cloth diapers, pins, rubber pants and nightgowns. Undershirts, a bunting set, receiving blankets and several larger blankets in neutral colors. No blue or pink. We don't know the sex of the new arrival. We should pick up a few baby bottles in case she cannot nurse. Evaporated milk and Caro syrup makes a suitable formula. We should pick up a few new dresses for Lucretia. That should cover all the necessities" "That's a tall order" said Isabella.   "We will bring some of it back with us. I will have Leo come back and pick up the rest." Clearing the store shelves of baby essentials was easy. "Do you really need all of that?" Isabella asked. "Some of it is for Lucretia. I thought it might be a good idea to keep baby essentials on hand." "Expecting more babies?" cracked Isabella. "With that many girls, more babies are bound to happen." Leo loaded the purchases into the car and sped home. They made it back in time to see Doctor Samuels walking up the front steps. "I guess we made it back just in time!" joked Chanel. As they walked into the foyer, a blood curdling scream broke the silence. Doctor Samuels laughed. "Sounds like our girl is just about ready to become a mother." "I got diapers, bottles and everything a baby could need!" Chanel said excitedly. As the three of them entered Lucretia's room, Hannah was applying a cool cloth to her head. Doctor Samuels asked, "How close are the contractions?" "Every five minutes or so" Hannah replied.   With a smile, Doctor Samuels said, "Let me have a look. She is at ten centimeters. As I said, she needs an episiotomy for the baby to pass easily out of the birth canal. It's better than having her tear during delivery. Stitching is much easier. I will administer a local anesthetic to prepare her for delivery. I need some clean cloths and a scale to weigh the baby."

Laying out his instruments, the doctor prepared himself for the delivery. "Alright, young lady, at the next contraction, I want you to push." "How?" Lucretia asked. Hannah whispered to her, "Like you are going to poop."   Doctor Samuels said, Now, push. Now breathe" . After an hour of pushing, a loud slap cracked the air followed by a baby's cry. Hannah bathed the baby while Lucretia lay sleeping. Doctor Samuels measured, weighed and did a full exam. He diapered and swaddled the baby boy before handing the infant to Chanel. "Welcome to the world, young man! Your mother has been waiting to meet you. Let's find you something nice and warm to wear. Wake up, Mommy. Your boy is hungry!" Smiling, Lucretia said, "I will name him Samuel after the nice doctor who helped him get born." Doctor Samuels gave her a smile of acknowledgment. "Do you have a middle name?" Lucretia asked. "John" he answered. "What's your last name?" Doctor Samuels asked Lucretia as he filled out a form that documented the baby's birth. "Riebach, I think" Lucretia answered hesitantly. "Samuel John Riebach sounds like a strong name" Doctor Samuels said. He patted Lucretia on the head as he left the room to find Chanel. Lucretia's intellectual deficits were quite obvious and he felt obliged to ensure that mother and child would be safe and provided for. He tapped lightly on Chanel's office door. "Come!" Chanel cooed from behind her desk as she directed one of the handmaids to have the cook prepare a large lunch for Lucretia and another one to show her the proper way to nurse the baby. Chanel made her way out from behind her desk as she listened intently to the doctor's concern. She motioned with two fingers for him to follow her down the hallway. No sooner had the office door closed behind them did Hannah appear, looking slightly disheveled. "Miss Chanel, I had this old cradle brought out of storage for baby Samuel. Max and Leo are setting it up in Ms. Lucretia's room now." "Thank you, Hannah" Chanel said as she and Doctor Samuels continued down the hall. When they got to Lucretia's room, Isabella was already there. "Lucretia, he's beautiful. "He weights eight pounds ten ounces" Lucretia said with a smile. "No wonder you were always hungry! That boy of yours is huge!" Isabella beamed. "The doctor says you should rest for a few days before you get back up on your feet. Chanel bought you dresses and baby supplies. There's nothing for you to worry about." Panic crossed Lucretia's face. "You won't let the nuns take my baby, will you?" "Never!" smiled Isabella as she gave Chanel a questioning look. "The church keeps all birth records. The only proof that families have is the family bible" cringed Chanel. "This allows the church to give infants to whoever has the most money." "This is why the church holds so much power and is so feared!" snapped Isabella. "I will thoroughly delight in blowing up those tunnels!" "It may not be as easy as you think. There is nothing but stone and concrete down there. The arches need several points to place the explosives" Chanel explained. "I am impressed, Chanel. You understand demolitions." "There's much to learn from pillow talk. I have read University textbooks on a variety of subjects. We had a patron who was a professor. He brought me several books." "That's why your pillow talk has depth!" Isabella said with a smile. "I have studied advanced courses in literature, architecture, poetry, political science and government. Sex only holds a man's attention for so long. Men enjoy talking to a woman who is knowledgeable on a variety of subjects. I have a vast library and I require my girls to read up on subjects that they are interested in. I pay for tutors for the girls who need them." Isabella chuckled, "You are one worldly Madam!" "There is nothing that compares to an education! The girls here who are under sixteen attend school for three hours every morning. Sex is mechanical. The brain needs stimulation too!" "I see" smiled Isabella. "What subjects did you enjoy in school?" "Logistics, hand-to-hand combat, history and science." "No daydreaming for you. You are first and foremost a soldier!" "I do my job. I couldn't wait to graduate." "Did you not enjoy my lessons?" Chanel questioned. "At first, I saw no need for them. After a mission or two, I discovered that all the "girly "lessons could be helpful depending on the mission. I now understand the reason for the brothel training." "Good" smiled Chanel. "We would never have put you through anything that wasn't necessary." "When will the girls arrive?" "Max will pick them up. We have our hands full with Mom and baby." "Where will she go?" Isabella asked, addressing the elephant in the room that was on everyone's minds. "Max and I have taken care of that. He will be a more hands-on part of this operation because you don't have much experience with demolitions." "We get to see

Max's precision and expertise? That will be a nice change from him giving us the orders." "Never underestimate Max. He has been a highly trained operative for many years. Leaders ask for his advice on delicate matters." "Max handles delicate matters?" "In the United States, he would be equal to a four-star general." Smiling, Isabella snickered. "I am looking forward to seeing Max in action!" "We should prepare for Lucretia's departure in a few days. She should not be here when the fireworks start. She's too emotionally fragile" whispered Chanel. "You're right" said Isabella. "How did things go with Goddard?" "Exemplary, as always. I am feeling much more relaxed" replied Isabella. "I am glad to hear that" said Chanel. "Why do you take such an interest in me, Chanel?" "Your potential is vast. You could take Max's place when he retires!" "Thank you for the vote of confidence, Chanel!" "You are a natural leader. Your comrades listen to you. That is vital in teamwork." "Excuse me" Doctor Samuels interrupted. "Yes, Doctor?" "Lucretia will need rest. Please have Miss Hannah help her with nursing, swaddling and the basics of baby care. She needs plenty of fluids and nutrition to help produce enough breast milk." "Thank you, Doctor." "I will stop by tomorrow after my rounds." "If you will write up your bill, I will pay you for your services" Chanel said. "We will work something out" Doctor Samuels said with a smile. Peeking in on Lucretia, Isabella saw that mother and baby were sleeping soundly. Max whispered, "Let's talk after I pick up the girls." "Of course, Max." "Hannah, did Doctor Samuels speak with you about increasing Lucretia's intake of food and fluids?" "Yes, sir. I will make sure our new mamma stays healthy. I see she needs some teaching." "Yes. She can learn, it just takes some time for her to catch on." "I understand" smiled Hannah. "A few days isn't giving her much time to learn everything she needs to know" said Isabella. "Agreed" said Max. "But we need to get her out of here before we blow up the tunnels." "Okay, so we have two and a half days before we complete the op? That's cutting it close. We need to get all the girls out of the wayward school. What about the students at St. Anne's?" "Yes, we should evacuate them to be on the safe side.

The boys' campus is far enough away that they should be safe." "I need to get away for a bit. I will return with the team." "I just want you to know that I share Chanel's views about you taking my position one day. Isabella, your leadership skills are great. Your comrades would die for you. That kind of devotion cannot be bought!" Max gave Isabella a heartfelt hug and she almost believed he meant it. "Later, Max" she said as she left the room. She changed into workout clothes and made her way to the exercise area. There was a heavy bag, jump ropes and mats on the floor. As she hit the heavy bag, Isabella heard a hoarse whisper. "Need a practice buddy?" Goddard stood behind the heavy bag. "How about a little hand-to hand in the ring?" "You must be a glutton for pain, boy!" "You don't have what it takes to truly hurt me!" "Bring your best, God!" "Sounds to me like your frustration is showing again!" Jumping up and down in the ring, Isabella gave Goddard the nod to join her. Taking a defensive stance, Goddard landed a few punches. Smiling, Isabella brought her right foot across the bridge of his nose. As she brought her left foot across the opposite side of his face, Goddard screamed, "My nose! You broke my fucking nose!" "It's not so easy to punish me when I'm not tied down, is it? Fight me, you pansy waist!" Wiping his face, Goddard sneered, "You will pay for this! I have been gentle with you, but no more!" Laughing, Isabella taunted him. "You're not so tough without a weapon, are you?" As God got to his feet, Isabella brought her right foot around to his cheek. "Damn, you cheated!" Trying to regain his footing, Goddard felt his legs give out from under him. Isabella seized the moment. She jumped on him, pinning his arms down as she punched his face again and again. "Stop!" Isabella was too consumed by her anger to realize that Max had jumped into the ring and was pulling her off Goddard. Without thinking, she landed a full force punch to Max's nose. Max turned and punched Isabella's jaw. This knocked her out cold. Max barked at Goddard, "Throw her in a tub of cold water! She needs to cool down!" Chanel appeared and said, "I will have a tub filled." As Goddard carried Isabella to the tub, the handmaid said "I'll take it from here. Just set her down. I will disrobe her." Hannah brought Goddard a bucket of ice for his face. Chanel handed Max three fingers of Scotch and some ice for his nose. After downing the Scotch, Max said, "Damn she hits hard!" "That is how you trained her." "Yes, but she struck her superior officer!" "How many times have you done the exact same thing?" "Point taken, Chanel. We need to finish this operation. Her emotions are fucking with her head! We need our logical, no nonsense Isabella back." "This just proves she is human. She has a heart. The priests and nuns are never accountable for harming children in order to line the church's pockets. That's what's troubling her." "The exploding tunnels will create chaos. The police will have to investigate. The church will not be able to cover this up. I will make sure they get all the irrefutable evidence they will need to shut down the wayward school." "Perhaps after the op is completed, the girls could have a holiday. They've earned it, Max." "I am sure they will be happy to return to their day jobs" laughed Max. Chanel said, "I bet they won't attend church for a while. And they will never look at a nun or priest the same way again!" "Agreed!" smiled Max. "How are we doing on Lucretia's arrangements?" "She will be ready for transport in forty-eight hours."   "Where are the girls?" "Settling in. After dinner, we will cover the day's events, plans for Lucretia and then we will discuss the op."   "You have all weekend to discuss the op" chimed Chanel. Max frowned. "I have to give them a crash course in explosives and demolitions. One mistake with this stuff and you not only die, but you take other people with you. They need to be focused, Chanel." "I understand, Max. They are so young to be doing demolitions." "I agree with you. That's why I will be setting the charges. They will not be alone in this. I will take responsibility for this operation. My experience will guide them. No mistakes!" said Max. "I am glad they have you as a handler, Max" Chanel said as she kissed his head. "Let's go check on Lucretia." Holding hands for several moments, they made their way to Lucretia's room. Hannah smiled at them. "Good evening to both of you. Our girl has a good appetite. So does young master Samuel. She took naturally to nursing." "Good. When things quiet down, get her up and walking." "Yes, ma'am." "Now to deal with Isabella" cracked Max. Knocking before they entered, Chanel called out, "How are you, dear?" "Max hits pretty hard for an old man!" Laughing, Max bellowed, "I knocked you out!" "I am sorry for hitting you, Max." "If you were a member of the secret police, you would be brought up on charges!" "I understand, Max." "Get dressed for dinner, now!" "Yes, sir! How is Goddard? I hope I didn't hurt him too badly." "The doctor had to set his nose. You must learn to control the emotions that you bottle up. Any more of these outbursts and you will be sent to prison! I will not tolerate my people going rogue! Is that understood?" "Yes, sir!" Laughing, Max quipped "I guess you don't need a bodyguard!" he said as he closed her bedroom door. Dressing her sore body was difficult but Isabella knew that she had brought this beating on herself. As she slowly ambled down the hall, she thought about Max's words. Would he really have her sent to prison for doing what the school had trained her to do? *It's their fault I am a violent killing machine! But I am not a machine. I have deep emotional scars that don't allow me to feel love, happiness or joy. That fucking school made me this way! I will never have a husband or children because I am incapable of love. I am, and will be a soldier for the rest of my life!* Shaking her head, she entered the dining room. Anastasia screeched, "What the hell happened to you? We were told Max had to pull you off Goddard!" "Yes, he did. I hit Max and he knocked me out cold." "Wow! Who knew old Max was so tough?" laughed Anastasia. "Any time any of you ladies want to go a round or two with me in the ring, all you have to do is ask!" "Enough shop talk, let's enjoy dinner!" scolded Chanel. After the fourth course, Max was ready for Brandy and a cigar. "Baby Samuel is so cute!" "No babies, Ingrid!" "Yes, Chanel." "At least the nuns didn't take him away" chirped Rena. "Samuel John Riebach is so chubby! He deserves a good life!" "Ursula piped in. "Yes, he does" smiled Isabella. Chanel cooed, "Lucretia and the baby are going to Colombia to live with a family who will teach her to be a mother while she earns money as a nanny and a housekeeper. With her being moved to safety, the nuns cannot steal her baby." "Can we give him a present before they go? We were planning to go into town tomorrow after our briefing with Max." "I think that would be fine" replied Chanel. Rena looked into Chanel's eyes. "Lucretia having a new life is worth it, right, Chanel?" "Yes, Rena. Anytime we can help someone have a better life, it's a success." "Not all our ops have happy endings" said Rena. "That is true. The good you girls do always outweighs the bad" Chanel said. "Now that you have been brought up to speed on the day's events, I'm sure Max wants to discuss the op that will take place in two days after Lucretia is safely away." "Monday?" "Yes. I believe that is the day that Max has laid out." "I would like you ladies to join me in the solarium. I understand Chanel has brought you up to speed." "Yes, Max." "The plan is to evacuate both the wayward school and St. Anne's. Once that's done, we will place explosive charges at the top of the walls in the tunnels underneath each school. That's enough for tonight. I need to acquire some supplies."

"We planned on going to town to buy a baby gift for Lucretia." Anastasia whispered. "Be back by lunch!" scolded Max. "Understood." Anastasia nodded. Chanel cooed, "Make a list so that you are not wandering about! Same for you, Max. You're going to need a shopping list!" snarled Chanel. "I cannot acquire what I need from the local shops!" Max snarled back. "We will need a reason for evacuating the schools. I can fudge tests for a gas leak" Max assured Chanel. "On Sunday evening, we move Lucretia and set everything in place. Monday morning we blow the tunnels."

Isabella nodded in agreement. "Get some sleep, ladies." As the door slammed shut, Chanel said "I will check on mother and child and the rest of the house. We need to check on the clients and girls on the floor." Hannah announced "Mom and baby are sleeping soundly. I will retire so that I can be awake for Master Samuel's night feedings." "Fine" smiled Chanel.   Strolling through the house, she greeted a few clients, offered a few drinks and light conversation. After closing at two a.m, the house was quiet. Chanel did a final walk through before turning in for the night. She was thinking about the next forty-eight hours and preparing herself to say goodbye. She knew that the girls could die trying to end the tyranny of the church.   Her fondness for Isabella and her comrades kept her focus blurred. *"I love those girls as if they were my own. I truly love Max too. God, keep them safe. Amen."* As morning crept across the sky, the soft sound of a crying baby brought Chanel to her feet.   Quietly opening Lucretia's door, Chanel's heart warmed seeing Lucretia nursing her son. Hannah spoke. "I will get you your coffee, Ma'am." "Take your time, dear. I will sit with mom and baby. "After changing his diaper, Lucretia offered baby Samuel to Chanel with an innocent smile. Looking into Samuel John's eyes, Chanel whispered, "You will be a great man" as she laid him gently in the cradle. "How do you feel?" Chanel asked Lucretia. "Much better. Walking is getting easier." "Good. On Sunday evening, you will be leaving to join your new family."   "Are you sure they want us?" asked Lucretia. "Of course, dear. I know them personally. They are good people." "I trust you, ma'am." "I would never lie to you or put you in harm's way" Chanel reassured her. "Rest now. Breakfast will be ready soon." Hannah appeared. "Miss Chanel, coffee and breakfast in the solarium." "Thank you, Hannah." The solarium was brightly lit by the new day. Chanel inhaled the aroma of freshly brewed coffee.   "Good coffee is like an old friend. Warm and welcoming." "I agree" smiled Hannah. "Miss Isabella is awake. She did not sleep well."

"Send her in." Hannah nodded and waved Isabella into the solarium as she exited. "Are you losing sleep over anticipation of the final phase of the mission?" "Yes. We lack experience using explosives." "Max will guide you" smiled Chanel. "He has been doing that since before you were born."   "I am impressed with his knowledge and military experience" replied Isabella. Chanel laughed. "We are both professionals!" Ursula, Rena and Anastasia wandered in yawning. As they poured coffee and helped themselves to breakfast, chatter began. "Looks like it will be nice and warm today. Can we borrow Leo to drive us into town?" asked Rena.   "Of course. He will be here at nine to pick you up." "Fantastic!" cried Ingrid. "Chanel, what do you suggest as a gift for Lucretia?" "A nice long travel case for her trip." "We found material in storage last night. We stayed up and made a pretty baby bag." "I see your lessons paid off!" "I made a soft pillow and blanket" smiled Ursula. "Now we just need a few rattles and toys to complete our gift. We used your sewing machine." "Sounds like you made yourselves at home" Chanel clucked. Anastasia let out a long sigh. "We may never get to do this for our own children, so we put in time for Samuel John." "I found some yarn and made a wrap for Lucretia so she will remember us" Rena said. "I am very proud of the women you all have become" smiled Chanel.   As Max listened to their conversation, he realized that the girls knew the risks of their mission. They knew they might die. The love they showered on Lucretia and her son showed compassion within them that many older people lacked. They were wise beyond their years, but still naive in other areas. *"I will not fail them!"* thought Max.   He spoke sharply. "Ladies, don't forget we have lessons this afternoon. Get your errands done! "Yes, sir! "Coffee, Max? "Yes, please Chanel. "The girls scampered off to dress for their trip into town. Isabella remained silently sitting at the table. "Is something on your mind, Isabella? "Max asked. "I would like to go with you to acquire supplies. I need to understand what I will be working with. "Are you sure? "Yes. It's my responsibility as team leader to know and understand all aspects of our operations.". "Good. I love your initiative! "Max smiled. "I presume that work clothes are appropriate for today's lesson? "Yes "answered Max. "I will be with you shortly "Isabella replied. As Isabella left the solarium, Chanel frowned. "Are you sure about that, Max? "Yes. Knowledge gives you the advantage. Hands on learning is always best retained. I made a few calls. I know where to go to get what I need. I overhead the girls talking about what they made for Lucretia and her baby. They still have hearts. That's detrimental in our line of work! "Max vented. "Emotions distort their judgment. Humanity should be discouraged! "It was that humanity and those emotions that caused Isabella to take out the pedophile priests. "I agree. But they will have to make difficult decisions. They cannot protect everyone!" said Max. "I will handle the placing of explosives and setting the charges" said Max. "They will participate. But with so many children to account for, they will be sent to evacuate the schools. I will inform the principals of the 'gas leak' so they can ensure no students are in or around the campuses." "Do you have a plan?" "My dear. I always have a secondary plan just in case!" Appearing in the doorway, Isabella announced, "I'm ready, Max." "What the hell are you wearing?" "Hannah let me borrow some pants that belonged to her son and a cotton flannel shirt. No frills. I can get as dirty as needed. No worries." Smiling, Max said, "You show true leadership." Laughing at Isabella's attire, Anastasia asked "Do you have a side job as a mechanic?" "No. I will be with Max acquiring supplies, not picking up guys!" Max announced with a smile, "Time to get moving!" Leo appeared in the foyer. "Ma'am, I'm ready to take the girls to town." "Girls, go get in the car." Isabella came rushing back through the door. "I need a work coat!" Goddard offered her one of his. "Will this work?" "Looks good. Thank you, Goddard."

Anastasia snipped, "Christ! Before you know it, Isabella will be wearing coveralls!" "God, no! We just got rid of those hideous habits!" pleaded Ursula. Chanel asked, "Do you have your lists?" "Yes, ma'am. I thought stationery or a journal might be nice for Lucretia." "That sounds lovely" smiled Chanel. "Remember, you need to be back by lunch time." "Yes ma'am." On the drive to town, Isabella asked Max how many kinds of explosives there were. "Too many to count. It depends on what you want to do. Each one requires different ingredients. Some can even be made from manure." "Really? There's plenty of shit from farms all over!" "That is true." "Chanel says you have been doing this longer than I have been alive." " That's true. I must be good at it because I have yet to blow myself up! Glycerin is made from boiled down chicken fat. Household items can be used to create explosives if you don't have access to the proper supplies." "I find this fascinating, Max. You covered explosives briefly in class, but we didn't get to blow anything up." "I see. We could set up a demonstration so that you can acclimate to the sights, sounds and see what happens." "Sounds like a good idea to me." "We will need to make several stops. Listen and observe."As Max walked into the first of their destinations, he picked up dynamite. Their second stop was similar to a military supply outpost. Isabella listened quietly. Composition B or C was all they were able to acquire. Max chose Composition C.   With each stop, he added to his haul of supplies. When the cargo area of their vehicle was filled to capacity, Max announced "This will be a mix and match. No one place had everything. Now the fun begins!" "If you say so, Max!" While Isabella learned about explosives, her teammates were shopping for baby toys and a few things for themselves. Each girl selected a gift for Lucretia. Anastasia selected a leather purse and a brush and comb set.   Rena chose a diary. Ursula chose stationery and Ingrid chose a hat. Pleased with their purchases, Anastasia said, "These are things an adult would use. I think Chanel would approve. Her travel case will hold all her belongings easily." Rena scowled. "I have concerns about Isabella. She's been more volatile than normal."   "Agreed. But I think all of this crap with the church has gotten to her. I can't wait to go back to our day jobs. The Catholic Church has left a bad taste in my mouth. They have never been Christian!" As Leo loaded up the car, he listened in on their conversation for a minute. Clearing his throat, he said, "Excuse me, ladies. I could not help but overhear about your purchases. Does the young mother have a wool coat for cold weather?"   "We do not know. That's a good question to ask Chanel." With a soft smile, Leo said, "I picked one up. Here. It has a fur collar. It will be my gift to Lucretia." "Leonardo, you are a sweet man! Chanel would be pleased with the generosity you have shown." "We should get back." Leo joined in laughing and joking with the girls.   "So Leo, how did you get involved with Chanel?" "After my family died, I needed a job. I have experience as a chauffeur to military officers. I understand the need for discretion. I was hired on the spot." "I see" smiled Ursula. Pulling into the driveway, Ingrid announced, "Max is already here." The girls came bounding through the door giggling.   Chanel appeared. "I see you did plenty of shopping!" "Leo also bought a gift for Lucretia. It's a winter coat with a fur collar to keep her warm. It is his contribution to preparing Lucretia for her trip." Smiling,

Chanel looked into Leo's eyes. "That's very commendable, Leo." "Can we show Lucretia what we got her?" "We can take the gifts to her after you wash up for lunch." Lucretia joined them in the dining room for lunch. Unable to contain their excitement, the girls began presenting her with gifts. Lucretia was overwhelmed with emotion and began to cry. "No one has ever treated me so nice before!" she exclaimed. "No tears. Just happy thoughts" cooed Chanel.   Max smiled and handed Lucretia a card. Her hands trembled as she tore open the envelope. "I've never seen so much money before!" "It's just enough to hold you over for a while" Max reassured her. "Thank you, Mr. Max!" "Now I will show you your new wallet!" "But first, let's eat" squeaked Lucretia. "I'm starving!" After lunch, Chanel helped Lucretia back to her room. She helped her organize her travel case with all the gifts she had just received.   Max announced, "We will meet at the garage. I can teach you everything I know. But seeing is believing."

          Driving to a secluded area with an old shanty on the property, Max assembled a small charge. He told the girls to get behind the car. "Can you see clearly?" he asked. "Yes, sir." Max touched off a stick of dynamite. It decimated the shanty. The sound was deafening. "Any questions? Do I have your undivided attention?" "Yes, sir!" "If you make a mistake, you will die! Mistakes equal death! Let's go back to the garage and discuss the plan. Shall we?"   When they were in the garage, Max laid out the plan and explained how crucial the evacuation of the schools was. "A controlled demolition will bring the tunnel and the wayward school down in one shot. There is less debris and less chance of bystanders getting hurt. This will cause enough damage to put the school out of commissioned permanently." "Question. Can we leave a priest down there?"   "As much as I would enjoy that, it's not part of the plan. We have an accelerated timetable. Once Lucretia is on her way, we will set the charges in the tunnel. Once the charges have been placed on the interior wall and the schools have been evacuated on Monday morning, I will touch them off. Any questions? We start late Sunday. Isabella will assist me in preparing the charges. We will walk the tunnels and I will show you where I will place the charges. You are dismissed! I will see you at dinner." Chanel glared. "Was that display necessary, Max?" "Yes. They need to respect the explosives they will be working with." "I understand." "Cockiness gets you dismembered and dead. I need to go back to my office after dinner to work on the diagram for bomb placement. Do we have a time set to meet Lucretia's new family?" "I need to check the message I have, but I believe the hand-off is set for ten p.m. She needs to be fed and packed for departure by nine pm to be on the safe side." "Yes, Chanel." "No sappy goodbyes either!" "With an accelerated timetable, we have a limited amount of time to complete the task. The team needs a good night's sleep. Tomorrow will be a long night!" The door closed with a slam. Chanel was worried. Mistakes would be lethal and the girls' fondness for Lucretia and her son could certainly cloud their judgment for this mission. Chanel walked the house and did a bed check. She observed Isabella intently studying a group of tables and papers. "Burning the midnight oil?" Chanel asked. A weak smile crossed Isabella's lips. "I'm refreshing my knowledge on chemicals for making explosives." "Do you need anything?" "No. I will be going to bed shortly." Sleep eluded Isabella. It always did before an op. Chanel woke to find Isabella sitting in her personal library with a steaming cup of coffee and books in hand. "Light reading?" asked Chanel. "Quantum physics." " Now that is guaranteed to induce sleep. Go and catch a few hours of sleep or you will be useless to Max."

After breakfast, the girls went to the basement for a workout. The solarium filled with bright sunlight as Chanel barked the day's orders to the staff. They were told to prepare a light dinner to send Lucretia off with a smile. A bit later, Lucretia appeared in the doorway. "Good morning, Chanel." "Good morning, dear. Looks like you're much steadier on your feet." "Yes, I am. Thank you. Hannah has already packed my travel case." "We need to get you on the road to a new life far away from here. Our goodbye dinner has been moved up a bit earlier." As Max entered the room, he said "Looking much better, Lucretia." "Thank you, sir. Excuse me. My little darling should be up for his feeding."

"Coffee, Max?" "Please, Chanel. So, where is my right hand?" "Isabella was up all night refreshing her knowledge of chemical combinations in explosives. When sleep eludes her, she reads up on quantum physics. She has a bad case of insomnia, Max." "I see." "I told her to catch a few hours' sleep or she would be useless to you." "Good. Where is the rest of my team?" "Physical training in the basement." "I need to time how long it will take to walk the tunnel and add time for escorting a mother and child. Once I have timed this, I will know for certain what time we should leave." "Fine. The goodbye dinner starts at five p.m. Hannah has already packed her bag." "Care to walk the tunnels with me, Chanel?" "No. I have a million things to get done before sending my girl off!" "Do you not enjoy my company?" "I do not enjoy strolling through dark, dank tunnels!"

Max kissed Chanel's cheek before he headed out. Checking the time on his watch, he ran at an average pace to the end of the tunnel. Remembering that Lucretia had just given birth, he added time. Once he reached the end, he sprinted back to the entrance and checked his time. "Ten minutes. Not bad for my age!" Sweating profusely, Max made his way to the basement.

"Damn, Max! You look out of breath!" cracked Rena. "In the ring! Let's spar!" "Pick on someone your own size!" cracked Isabella. "They're already tired. I just had a rejuvenating rest!" "Fine" smiled Max. "Gloves or bare knuckles?" Isabella asked. "Depends on what kind of beating you're willing to take!"   Climbing into the ring, the sparring began. Isabella landed several punches that Max barely covered. Max landed hard on the mat. "You're getting too old, Max!" cracked Isabella. With that, Isabella's legs were swept out from under her and she landed hard on the mat. Max choked her out. "Goodnight! Sleeper holds are great!" Max laughed.

"Get up! We have work tonight! I need to get cleaned up for the goodbye dinner. Bye, Max!"   Max wiped his hands and face as he walked back to the garage. Assembling bombs required quiet, patience and skill. Max created ten bombs. *"This needs to be done while the students are sleeping"* he thought aloud. "I will call the schools at 7:10 a.m. and advise them of the gas leak. The team will then assist with the evacuation of the students and staff. Charges will detonate at 9:15 a.m. We will be on our way home by noon."   On his way to get cleaned up, Max was certain that his plan would go off without a hitch. A relaxing bath helped soothe his sore muscles. Dressing in a sport coat, black sweater and trousers, Max was ready for the evening's events. He arrived at Chanel's at 4:45.   The pre-dinner drinks were already flowing. "Scotch, Max?" "You know me well, Chanel." "Dinner is just about to be served." Lucretia was noticeably nervous throughout dinner. As dessert was being served, tears flowed from her eyes. "Do we have to go away?" she asked, swallowing hard.   Chanel cooed, "I explained this, dear. Max is going to escort you to the plane." "Will you be there, Chanel?" "No, dear. Max will be with you." "I am afraid!"   Lucretia sobbed. Isabella spoke up. "I will go with Max. You know I would never allow you to get hurt." "Thank you, Miss Isabella!"   "Finish your milk, dear!" Chanel scolded. As Lucretia slurped the last few drops from her glass, her eyes became heavy and she slumped in her seat. Goddard quickly carried her to her room. Smiling at Max, Isabella asked, "Who am I carrying?"

"Baby Samuel" Max answered her. "We sedated Lucretia since her exit will be through the tunnel and I didn't want her to get upset and draw attention to us being down there" Chanel said. "My friend from Colombia, John will be there to meet you and to escort mother and child onto the plane. He said that he would be bringing a nurse with them for the journey. Hurry along. Make sure that both of them are dressed warmly." Chanel said as Goddard quickly wrapped Lucretia in her new coat and made his way to the tunnel with Max and Isabella right behind him.   Isabella was swaddling baby Samuel as she walked, trying not to wake him as she broke into a brisk run dragging Lucretia's travel case behind her. Within a few minutes, they had reached the exit of the tunnel. In front of the three of them was a private plane. The lights glowed against the darkening night sky.   Max led them to a six- foot, seven inch tall, thin man with salt and pepper hair. "John, old friend! Please take extra care of our young mother and her son" he said as Goddard handed a sleeping Lucretia over to John and motioned for Isabella to do the same with baby Samuel. John snapped his fingers, and a nurse appeared beside him as he carried Lucretia onto the plane. Isabella held the baby close for a few seconds as she breathed in his scent and kissed the top of his head. She handed the baby over to the nurse and watched as Lucretia's luggage was loaded onto the plane.

Max handed John a file folder and an envelope. There were no questions asked. Lucretia and her son were gone. On the walk back through the tunnel, Max said, "At least that part of our job is done!"

Looking into Max's eyes, Isabella broke the mood. "Double time it back to Chanel's! IF you can keep up!" Darting off in a fast paced run, Isabella left Max in the dust. As she reached the entrance to the tunnel, she turned her head to see Max directly behind her. "Ready for a drink?" "I need a Scotch and a cigar" smiled Max. Walking through the foyer, Chanel greeted them. "Did it go well?" "Yes. She is safely on the plane. I need a Scotch and a cigar!" laughed Max.   "Was he able to keep up?" laughed Goddard. "He did pretty well for a man of his advanced age!" joked Isabella. "Black op protocol" Max said, looking in Isabella's direction.   Disappearing from sight, Isabella relayed the outcome of the mission to her team.

As the house filled with guests, Max met with the team in the garage. He was dressed from head to toe in black. He lowered his voice. "We are going into the tunnel that is directly below the wayward school. Pay close attention to my instructions!" Handing out knapsacks, Max said "Each of you are carrying explosives. Walking will not detonate them. Once we get to the tunnel, I will give you further instructions." They moved silently along the walking path. They moved directly to the infirmary entrance, down the stairs and into the tunnel entrance.

After opening his blueprints, Max led the team to a spot he had marked. "This is Composition B. In order to take out the tunnel and the school, this is what we need to do. For this to be a controlled demolition, we need to place charges on top of the wall, every ten feet on both sides of the tunnel. When detonated, it will collapse the tunnel. This will make the school's foundation unstable. Then we will go to the second floor of the wayward campus and place charges halfway up all four of the interior walls. Doing so will cause the most damage. It will take years to make the buildings usable again."

Max carefully observed the team's placement of the charges. "At 7:10 a.m, I will inform the school of a gas leak. Report to your normal assignments. They will evacuate the school as their safety protocol dictates. Everyone must go to the other end of campus near the boy's school. Any questions? I will detonate the explosives at precisely 9:15 a.m. You should be home by noon. Excellent job tonight! Let's return to Chanel's."

Too excited to sleep, the girls chatted as they packed their bags. "Tomorrow is it! Finally! Set the alarm one last time!" smiled Rena. As they chatted, Chanel appeared in the doorway. "Would you like to join me in the library for a nightcap?" "Yes, ma'am." Assembling the girls, Chanel cooed "I will miss you. You will be returning to your day jobs. I have truly enjoyed watching you blossom into young women." "We will miss you too." Isabella lingered in the library. "What's on your mind, dear?" "Do you think Max believes in what we do?" "Yes, I do. Sometimes things go beyond black and white or protocol. Your job reaches beyond the government and its laws. Never forget that you are an elite team. You are special. Never doubt that, dear. Now, get some rest."

Monday morning arrived cold and crisp with the promise of a new day. Alarms went off at 5:30 a.m. Dressed for the day's tasks, the team assembled in the dining room for breakfast. Sipping her coffee, Isabella prepared her team for the evacuation. When they reported for their daily jobs. Each girl reported to their assigned area. Sister Mary Ann announced over the intercom "All staff please report to the office!" "Here we go!" thought Isabella.   Sister Mary Ann announced, "We have gotten word about a gas leak. We need to evacuate all students and staff. Here are the exits. Start with the dormitories. Clear the second floor, then the offices. When the school is clear of students, the fire brigade will check for leaks. Let us begin." A headcount showed that St. Anne's campus was clear. Before the all- clear was given for the wayward school, a charge detonated followed by a deafening boom.   The screams of terrified children filled the air and cut directly into the soul. Anastasia glanced at Isabella and signaled that a student was missing. As the tunnel began to implode, Isabella realized a new student, who was deaf was not with the others. She asked the faculty and her team if anyone had the girl with them. Sister Mary Ann's face was stained with tears.   "She must have wandered off looking for her doll and blanket! She must have gone back inside the school!" Isabella ran at a neck breaking pace toward the wayward school. After twenty paces, she saw the frail child wandering toward the commotion. She hadn't heard the warnings or instructions for evacuation. That didn't change the fact that there were several more charges that were going to detonate. Soon.   Isabella ran toward the child and intercepted her as if she were a football. She then threw her body on top of the child while making the sign for "okay". She was trying to explain to the girl that she was there to help. Anastasia's stomach dropped when she saw both Isabella and the child thrown several feet following a concussive blast.   In a matter of seconds, medics flooded the scene. As debris covered Isabella and obstructed her line of sight, she struggled to make some kind of sound to let people know she was alive.   Ingrid screamed, "Max! I see her shoe!" Max and Ingrid ran toward the pile of debris. They quickly cleared the rubble and

Max wiped Isabella's face gently. "Do not move!" he whispered. "I covered the girl to protect her" Isabella gasped.   The medics gently lifted Isabella's broken body to find a scared and bruised child huddled beneath her. Isabella whispered to Max "She's deaf."Clutching her doll, the girl was lifted onto a stretcher. Both Isabella and the girl, named Katarina were rushed to a hospital to be stabilized. Max called in a military transport to take them both to a top secret facility. The rest of the team regrouped back at Chanel's. "Max says you are to wait here for further instructions" Chanel informed them.

Chapter Five: Chipping Isabella

As the helicopter touched down, Isabella was loaded in along with two medics and a doctor. Max told them he would join them shortly. He needed to check on Katarina. Storming into the local hospital, he demanded to know how the girl was. "She is doing well. A few bumps and bruises, but she will fully recover." Max exhaled a deep sigh as he left the hospital and drove to Chanel's. He was disheveled and covered in dust. Hannah greeted him and led him to the shower. As he stood under the steaming hot water, he braced himself for the questions he knew were coming. He stepped out of the shower and dried himself off before dressing in freshly pressed clothes.   He ran his hands through his salt and pepper hair as he walked into the solarium. The team was already there waiting for him. Before any of them could utter a sound, he said, "You will return home. Resume your day jobs. I had Isabella transferred to a military hospital. They specialize in treatments for head injuries. I expect all of you to carry on as normal!"

Anastasia cried, "I want to see Isabella!" "She is sedated. Visitors are not permitted. I will inform you as I know more. Day jobs resume tomorrow morning. I will let you know when your next op begins." "How do we work without her?" asked Ingrid. "You have worked without her before! I expect you to handle the job you are assigned! Do I make myself clear?" "Yes, sir!" "Leo will drive you back to the school. Finish out the day. I understand your concerns but I have never lost anyone under my watch and I don't intend to start now! Ingrid, the school is eager for you to return. Have a safe trip, ladies!"   As Leo loaded their luggage into the car, Rena looked back at Max. Fear welled inside her. Isabella could die. Anastasia slipped her arm around Rena. "We have always known we were expendable." As the door closed, Chanel ordered that her coffee and brunch be brought to the library. Pouring Max three fingers of Scotch, Chanel cooed. "This should soothe your nerves. I had the files delivered to the police as you instructed.

There will be a major investigation. They are bringing in extra hands for this one. I have been advised that the Archbishop and a Cardinal will make an appearance. "Good! We wanted to ensure that the explosion could not be explained away!" Clearing her throat, Hannah announced her arrival. She brought a large brunch. Chanel playfully swatted Max's hand as he reached for the bottle of Scotch. "No more of that until you've eaten something!" Scowling, Max conceded. "I will eat, but under protest!" "That's my boy!" smiled Chanel. "I have not been a boy in many years. As you know, Chanel." "Easy, tiger! Or I may demand that you prove it!" Max raised his eyebrow. "I do have some pent up energy that needs to be expended." Smiling, Chanel rubbed the top of Max's thigh. Hannah spoke up. "Ma'am, Harold is on the phone for Max." "Thank you, Hannah." Max walked to Chanel's desk and lifted the receiver. "Hello?" Harold's deep voice announced, "Allow Isabella to die!" "No! Why would you want that?" "She knows entirely too much about the schools and our Sleeper program. Head injuries have unpredictable outcomes." "There are experimental options. The Swedes have had successful results. Killing one of my operatives is a last resort! Am I understood, Harold?" "You seem to have lost your objectivity, Max. You're emotionally bonded to the team." "They have been our best and brightest to this point." "If her comrades can control her, Isabella could be placed in a different job where she can still be useful to our cause. Max, if this is not a plausible scenario, you will have her put down! If you cannot do it, I will end her myself! Good day!" Max slammed the phone down onto its cradle. Chanel put her arms around Max. "See what the doctors say before you make a decision. Harold has always had issues with Isabella because he could not break her will." "I need to catch transport to the medical facility. It departs in two hours." "Would you like me to accompany you?" With a smile, Max said, "You have plenty to do here. I will see you when I get back." Max turned and made his way to the designated pick- up location. As Max crawled into the heliport, he smiled. "It's been a long time since I've taken one of these for a ride" he said. "Have you qualified on one of these,

sir?" "Yes. It was part of my training." "Care to take the stick?"   Laughing, Max
said "Absolutely!" Flying came back to him as naturally as breathing. Max felt relaxed
for the first time in several days.

Bringing the plane down on the landing pad was as smooth as ever. Nurses were
waiting for Max. They hustled him through a maze of corridors. Arriving outside an
isolation room, he was told, "You need to gown up, sir." After putting on the gown, he
was ushered into Isabella's room. She was sleeping peacefully. Max looked at the
machines that were monitoring Isabella's heart rate. Doctor Rickman appeared and
suggested Max join him in his lab.   "Head injuries can be unpredictable but I see no
reason why she will not wake up. Her memory may be fragmented. The concussive blast
shook her brain up. She had some inter cranial bleeding. We relieved it. Because of her
job, one option is to place an experimental chip in her brain. It will change her behavior
and her attitude. It's a form of mind control, if you will. By changing the frequency
waves, we can change undesirable behaviors. Adding an ocular implant, we\ you will see
everything that she sees. We will be controlling her brain functions remotely. For
example, if she is reading files at her desk, you will read everything that she does. Think
of her brain as being partially hibernated. By changing frequency waves, you can
activate all her training as an operative. If necessary, she could be reactivated." "I do not
like the idea of the ocular implant. It would invade her privacy, bathing and dressing.
The brain implant might be an option to control her memory. This way, she will not have
to be put down."   "She will need therapy to re-learn walking, talking and eating. It will
ensure that she does not have any permanent disabilities. The brain implant will help
control aggressive or violent behavior in the field. What other training has she had?" "Au
pair training to handle children. Office management and feminine jobs." "We can
stimulate that region of her brain to make her more docile. Shall we wake her to see what
we are working with?"   Max watched as the nurse added medication to Isabella's

intravenous line to slowly bring her out of sedation. "I must warn you, she may not wake immediately. Her body has been under tremendous stress." After an hour, Max noticed Isabella's foot beginning to twitch. Her fingers started to clench. "She must be remembering the explosion" said Doctor Rickman.   Max gently patted her hand to let her know that she was safe. "Isabella, you are fine. The mission is complete. It's time to go home."   The machines clamored with loud noises and bright lights. Clawing at her intravenous lines, Isabella swung wildly. Doctor Rickman ordered that she be given an injection. As the orderlies held her arms down, the nurse jabbed a needle in and quickly pushed the plunger. As the drugs hit Isabella's bloodstream, she sank back onto her pillow. She whispered, "Max!" "The girl is fine and you are safe. Just rest." Looking into Doctor Rickman's eyes, Max said "I do not see her returning to a normal life without the implant to control her impulses." "Are you sure about this? There are side effects to the side effects." "Could they be any worse than that?" "The side effects are temporary. If she cannot be contained, we will have to put her down."   "By signing this, you are acknowledging that this treatment is experimental. You're assuming responsibility for the patient and allowing us to monitor her for research purposes." "So basically, she is a Guinea pig. If the treatment works, you take the credit. If it goes bad, I get the blame? Fine!" screamed Max as he signed the paperwork.   "When will this be done?" demanded Max. "At six a.m. Implantation will take several hours. We will attach the implant to her brain and stimulate the damaged areas. Then we wait. As she wakes, we monitor her memories, motor and language skills. We will then determine if she can live in society or if she should be institutionalized. Go to your quarters and get some rest." It seemed as though Max had barely closed his eyes when a nurse appeared in the doorway. "Doctor Rickman said to let you know we will begin the procedure shortly. We have done scans so we know where to place the implant and which frequency to use to keep her calm. Get some coffee, Max. You're going to need it. Her brain bleed is better. Isabella seems to heal fast. This is a good thing. She does have scar tissue. Have there been other head injuries?" Max scowled. "She had disciplinary issues during her training." "If she has always had a propensity for violence, this will slow that down but it will not take that away completely." "I understand" replied Max.   "This is not a miracle fix. It's an experimental option." "Let's just get on with it." "This procedure was originally done on soldiers. The research goes back to the 1800's. It's classified as behavior modification." "Mind control!" scoffed Max. "I would like to observe the procedure" Max said. "My nurse will take you to get into surgical scrubs and scrub up."

Seeing Isabella's skull opened up for surgery distressed Max. Doctor Rickman explained how each part of the brain performed a specific function. As he pointed to the diagram of the brain on the wall, he demonstrated the effect of electrical impulses on the brain. The doctor attached the implant to the outside of Isabella's brain and applied a low frequency. This lit up the area of Isabella's brain that had taken the brunt of the damage.

Doctor Rickman noticed a small lesion and said, "We may as well fix that while we're at it." He tested the implant one last time before closing Isabella's skull. Isabella was then wheeled into a room filled with monitors and cameras for observation. "The anesthesia usually wears off within four to five hours. A nurse will stay with her until she wakes up. Then we will see how we did. Let's go get a bite to eat. Tell me, Max, how our girl got so gravely injured?"   "We evacuated a school and a deaf student went back to get her doll. Isabella was going to get her when the explosion happened. She used her body to shield the child from flying debris." "Isabella sounds like a hero to me" smiled Doctor Rickman. "I can see that you care for her. We will not let you down." Small talk filled the air as concern filled Max's face. "Shall we check on our girl?" "Yes" smiled Max.   Doctor Rickman immediately looked at Isabella's charts as he entered the isolation room. He dismissed the nurse for her dinner break. He checked the monitors. "Our girl is moving her toes. That is a good sign." He checked her pulse with a laugh. "Nice and strong."   He took his stethoscope and listened to Isabella's heart and lungs. "All clear! Good signs." He took a sharp, pointed object and ran it across

Isabella's right foot. He received a kick. "Her reflexes are intact" chuckled the doctor. "Let's see if we can wake her." After adjusting her intravenous line, Isabella began to stir. Putting her hands up to her head she screamed, "My head is killing me!"

"Hello, Isabella." Squinting, she squealed, "Max!" "Take it easy. I'm here." "What about Katarina? Is she alright?" "Yes. She is fine. You shielded her from flying debris and got hurt. You have a traumatic brain injury. It caused a brain bleed. They had to relieve the pressure in your head." Doctor Rickman stepped in to explain that they had drilled a hole in her head. "No wonder my head hurts!" "We need to monitor your motor and language skills so we know what kind of therapy and rehabilitation you will need." "Where are the girls?" "Who do you remember?" "Anastasia, Rena, Ingrid and Ursula." "What do you remember?" "We have office jobs." "Anything else?" "I hate frilly dresses!" "What do you remember about me?" smiled Max. Smiling again, Isabella said "You taught me to drive and helped us get our jobs." "Anyone or anything else?" "A pretty lady named Chanel. She has a big house with red velvet walls and gold trim. It hurts my head to remember." Doctor Rickman smiled. "Let me have you start on a soft diet. If you tolerate that, we will start you on solid food. After that, we will get you up and walking." "I will be back" soothed Max. "She has no memory of the school or her training." Max scowled. "She may never regain those memories. Or they may return all at once. Time will tell" said Doctor Rickman. "You need to prepare yourself for the possibility that she may never be the same. I recommend a nice, quiet job away from operations." "I see" replied Max. "There is a strong possibility that she will never be a functional soldier or operative again. "I understand" Max said in a whisper. Doctor Rickman looked into Max's eyes and grabbed him by the shoulders. "At least she's alive!" Max shook his head. "I guess I cannot ask for more than that." "Compose yourself before you go back in there!" "You're right. Thanks, Doc." Max smiled at Isabella as he entered the room. "What is this crap?" Isabella asked scowling at the tray in front of her. "Looks like eggs, oatmeal, coffee and juice." "Not what I was hoping for,

Max." "They need to be sure you can tolerate this before you get meat and potatoes. Eat up! You need it. You have been sleeping for days. Muscles atrophy when they aren't used. It may take a bit before you get steady on your feet again."   "Max, will you take me for a walk?" "Let's see if those legs of yours will work. Shall we?" Finishing her meal, Isabella thought she could swing her legs over the side of her bed. It was more difficult than she anticipated. Doctor Rickman explained "Your brain has to remember to tell your legs what to do."   Max assisted the orderly with getting Isabella to her feet. Doctor Rickman said, "Stand for a few minutes. Let your brain tell your feet to take a step." After several unsuccessful attempts at walking, Isabella's frustration was beginning to show. "We will try again later" soothed Max. He covered Isabella's legs before leaving the room. She began to doze off and dream.   She began tossing and turning as the dream took form in her mind. She could hear a little girl's cries. Without thinking, Isabella threw back her blankets, stood up and began searching for the little girl. Max was about to yell for help when Doctor Rickman said, "Do not startle her. If she's having an auditory hallucination, we need to guide her back to bed." "Is she sleepwalking?" asked Max. "Yes. It can be a result of trauma. In any case, we know she can walk." After getting Isabella back into bed, Max joined Doctor Rickman in his office. "Drink?" "Yes, thank you."   "Sometimes we over think getting our bodies to do what we need them to. In her dream, Isabella heard a child crying. Her natural instinct was to help the child. Her brain was on autopilot, so she walked without thinking about it." "I will have to leave in a few days to check on the other girls." "Isabella could be here for several weeks. You should plan accordingly. Once she stabilizes, she will be moved to a normal room. I will start her on a regimen of physical and occupational therapy. We need to test her language and fine motor skills. We will evaluate her abilities to walk, talk, read and her hand-eye coordination. This will help us gauge what her limitations will be. Encourage her friends to write her letters. Seeing them may help her memories to resurface. She seemed fond of Miss Chanel. Perhaps she could be her first visitor. We will start with a week of therapy. Then we'll introduce visitors on an individual basis. I don't want to overstimulate her brain. It could undo all her progress with therapy. Bring in some of her personal possessions. They will stimulate her other senses and bring back memories." "I understand" replied Max. "May I use your phone to keep Chanel apprised on Isabella's condition?" "You could send a telegraph or a letter. I will arrange your transport home in a few days." "I'd like to be present when you tell Isabella." "It might upset her" cautioned Doctor Rickman. He dialed a few numbers and handed Max the receiver before leaving the office and closing the door. Max dialed Chanel's personal line while exhaling a deep sigh. "Hello?" Chanel answered. Her tone oozed sexual tension. "Chanel, it's me, Max." "Hello, darling! How's our girl?" Max gave Chanel a brief explanation of the experimental procedure. "She may never function as an operative again" Max said wistfully. "Well, she's alive. That counts for something." The concern in Max's voice told Chanel that he wasn't sure he had made the right decision for Isabella. "Max, you made the best decision possible given the circumstances. Don't second guess it. She may never recall the school or her training" Chanel cooed. "That may be a good thing. Without her memories, Harold may not deem her to be a threat." "She will have to be reassigned after therapy." "I have an idea about that. We can discuss it when you get back. I need to make a few calls." "You mean call in a few favors?" Laughing wildly, Chanel asked "Whatever do you mean, Max?" "You have buckets of shit on all the government officials!" "I will ensure that she has a protected assignment. One that Harold can't monkey fuck around with!" Snorting, Max replied "Understood. I'll see you tomorrow. Goodnight!" A wave of relief washed over Max as he walked to his quarters for a much needed rest. Chanel's ideas danced through her mind. If Isabella was to be assigned as an Au pair governess, she would be protected by diplomatic immunity should Harold decide to play dirty. "Hannah, bring me some tea, please." Opening her desk drawer, Chanel pulled out a large ledger. As she turned the pages, she made notes on which of her diplomatic connections had children.   They would need child care during the upcoming summer break. Beside each name, Chanel had a list of each diplomat's sexual proclivities. She placed asterisks beside the names she thought would make good employers for Isabella. Chanel smiled. "Which of you will do as I ask?" she thought aloud.   Double asterisks meant the wives had proclivities of their own. Sipping her tea, she noticed a large shadow in the doorway. "Come in, Goddard. What can I do for you?" "Have you heard from Max?" "Yes. Isabella had to have brain surgery. She is doing much better."   "I heard she sustained a head injury." "Yes, that's true." "They say she may not remember us." "It's a possibility. Recovery takes time."   "She and I have a unique relationship, ma'am." "It's okay to care about her, Goddard. We all do." "Isabella is special." "Goddard, are you in love with her?"   Goddard tilted his head and breathed deeply. "As much as I can love anyone in this line of work. Let her know she's in my thoughts." "Max said she can have gifts and personal possessions."

"When you visit her, will you bring her a gift from me?" "Of course I will" smiled Chanel. Goddard returned a moment later with a silver music box. "It will cheer her up."

"How lovely. That's very sweet of you, Goddard." "Max says she is not impressed by the hospital food." Hannah poked her head around the corner. "I will make her a basket of her favorite treats!" Chanel laughed joyfully. "I'm sure she will love that, Hannah." "Will her comrades be accompanying you to visit her?" asked Goddard. "No. Max will bring in one visitor at a time so she isn't overstimulated." "Thank you. Goodnight."   Max slept soundly for the next eight hours. As the morning light crept through the window, he awoke feeling more rested than he had in days. He dressed quickly and packed his bag. After arranging a late afternoon transport back to Chanel's, Max was ready to have breakfast with Isabella.   As he strolled into her room, Isabella gave him a look that said "You're late." "How are you feeling this morning?" Max asked. "Good." "Are you ready to start your physical therapy?" "Yes. I could use a good physical training session." "I agree." smiled Max. "Breakfast looks like bacon with biscuits! Now we're talking!" After breakfast, Isabella turned to Max. "You're leaving today?" "Yes. I am leaving this afternoon. I have to check in on your comrades and let them know you are improving. I'll be back at the end of the week with a surprise visitor. You need to cooperate with the therapist." "I will" Isabella replied.   "Is there anything you would like from home?" "A nightgown and my housecoat. Pants to wear for therapy and a journal." "Anything else?" "Snacks to keep in my room!" Laughing, Max said, "I will see what I can do!" "And slippers, please. These floors are cold." "Done. Let's take a walk to your therapy session."   After lunch, they will test your language skills to see what you remember." "The faster I progress, the sooner I get to leave, right?" Doctor Rickman laughed. "That's the plan. But if you over do it, you can be set back to step one." "Pace myself. I get it. Who is Goddard? I remember fighting with him." "He helped you manage your anger. Sometimes you could be a handful. Are there any other memories you want to ask about?" "Why do I have scars on my back?" "I would like to know too" said Doctor Rickman.   "You were defiant in school and were sent to the Chancellor's office frequently. He whipped you for disobedience. You challenged all your teachers." "Was his name Harold?" "Yes, why?" Isabella tilted her head. "I just know I hate Harold!" "Sounds like your memory is coming back to you." "Do I have parents?" "Your parents sent you to a private boarding school."   "They gave me away?" "No." "Did they sell me?" "No. They sent you to school so you would marry well." "I would never consent to that!" "You should talk to the doctors about these feelings." "Why?" "To help process your feelings."   "If I do that, can I go home?" Doctor Rickman smiled. "We operated on your brain. That's major surgery. I want you to be completely healthy before you leave us." An exasperated sigh escaped Isabella's lips. "I will trust your expertise in this matter." Max patted her on the shoulder. "Get well, kid." "What's on the list for today?" Isabella asked. Doctor Rickman smiled. "Another physical therapy session, a walk with Max and a session with our psychiatrist. Then dinner, a stroll through the halls, snack and bed." "Either this is a military hospital or a prison. Every minute is scheduled." Max consoled Isabella by saying "Sticking to a schedule helps time pass quicker. I have given permission for you to be evaluated by a psychiatrist." "Why?" "Because after one session, you will know if he really knows his shit!" "I will take your faith in me as a compliment." Doctor Schwarzkopf performed memory and IQ tests. Then he and Max chatted for a while. After Doctor Rickman relayed Isabella's history to his colleague, Schwarzkopf explained "Her IQ is genius. Her memory is not fairing as well. Her short-term memory is about fifty percent. Long term is at around twenty percent. Even with daily therapy, I cannot guarantee any improvement. Time will be a huge indicator of her success. Traumatic brain injury can cause permanent memory loss or leave the memories that remain like Swiss cheese. I will have a report for you when you return." "Thank you" Max said as he shook the doctor's hand and walked away. He peeked in on Isabella. She was sound asleep. He would return in a few days. As Max boarded his transport, he saw a familiar face. "Hey, Boss! Wanna drive?" "No, thanks. I have a lot on my mind." "Alright." As they flew over the trees, Max enjoyed the view. "Where would you like me to land, sir?" "The field behind the hospital." "Sure thing." Once his feet hit the ground, Max was on his way to his office. There were messages piled on his desk. Pouring a drink, he sat back in his office chair. He rifled through the pile of messages and disregarded any that he deemed unimportant. There were several from the Archbishop, the school principal and from parents of students who attended the wayward school. He had too much on his mind to deal with returning all these messages. He ran his fingers through his hair in frustration. After another drink, he dropped onto the couch, eyelids drooping and slowly closing. Jolted awake by the door crashing open, Max sat up to find Anastasia, Rena, Ursula and Ingrid standing in his outer office. "Long night, Max?" "It's been a long few days." "Chanel told us about Isabella's surgery. How is she feeling?" "Better." "Can she have visitors?" "Yes. One at a time so as not to overstimulate her." "Will she be back to doing ops soon?" Max let out a long sigh. "Her memory is severely damaged.

She may never be the same. Time will tell. Until we know for sure what Isabella remembers, the four of you will be working together. I will have you do some simple ops until we know if Isabella will be able to return to her duties or if she will have to be reassigned. I will keep you informed. How does it feel to be back to your day jobs?" "Fine. When will Isabella be released?" "In three to four weeks if everything goes well. She's already giving her medical team a hard time." "They will release her early because she will make them nuts!"   Max laughed. "I agree! I will bring each of you to visit her. Here's a list of things that she requested. Can you pack her a bag for me?" "Yes, sir." "Thank you. Return to your housing units." Watching the girls through his office window, Max thought *"They will be devastated if Isabella cannot return as team leader."* Shaking his head, he knew that losing Isabella would decimate their self-esteem. They depended on Isabella. He rubbed his temples in an effort to fend off the headache that had started behind his eyes. Max phoned Chanel. "I have a terrible headache." "No worries, Dear. I will send Leo to pick you up. Rest until he arrives." "Can we touch base tomorrow when I feel better?" "Certainly. Go home. Take some aspirin and go to bed. Leo will bring you dinner." "Thank you, Chanel."   As Max made his way home, he felt a wave of nausea wash over him. As Leo pulled the car over, Max jumped out. He bent over and heaved several times. Leo drove him home at a snail's pace. As Max attempted to unlock his front door, he dropped to his knees. Another wave of nausea hit him. The dizziness was disorientating. He tried to stand again. Opening the door, Leo carried Max into his bedroom. Chanel turned down the bed and Leo laid him down gently. Removing his shoes, Chanel covered Max with a blanket. "Leo, please start a fire to take the chill out of the house. The wood pile is behind the house." Chanel unpacked her basket. She brought chicken soup, breads, cheeses and chocolate cake for dessert. Chanel called Doctor Samuels to come see Max. After examining Max, he mixed a powder with water. "Have him sip on this until it's gone. It should help with pain. Keep the shades drawn. Check on him every few hours. I will see you tomorrow.

Keep him covered and keep cool compresses on his head." "Leo, I will stay with Max."
"Ma'am, I will stay too, in case you need me." "I'll be fine, Leo. Could you bring in some
extra wood before you go?"   Leo left under protest. Chanel sat quietly and tended to
Max. She fell asleep in a chair and snored softly. As Max awoke, he saw Chanel's
silhouette. As he sat up, a vague memory of retching on the side of the road flashed in
his mind. "How did I get into bed?" "Leo carried you. The doctor prescribed a powder to
help with headaches. Are you ready for some food? Let's start with some coffee and
toast. Would you like jam or marmalade?" "Go home, Chanel. I'm fine." "Absolutely
not! Once I see you eat something, I will feel better. Leo will be here shortly. Until then,
you're stuck with me!" "You have quite the maternal side." "I wouldn't bet the house on
that, Max! Let me warm you some of Hannah's chicken soup. It cures all. Stress over
Isabella could be causing your spells. You are very close to her. On that note, I have a
list of potential employers for her. These assignments include diplomatic immunity." "I
will look it over when I am feeling more steady on my feet." "Here, eat the soup slowly.
Have some more bread."   Leo appeared in the doorway. "The doctor is here."
"How is my patient?" "He is somewhat better. I will be on my way" Leo said. "See you
this evening, Max."   "How's the head? Take this powder. Mix it with a glass of water
when the headaches start. Do not mix it with Scotch or any other alcohol. I'd like to do a
scan of your head to check for injury. Report to the hospital at eight a.m. tomorrow
morning." "Will do. How is Isabella?" "She's doing well. I'm looking forward to seeing
her again. "I have tried to prepare her friends for the reality that she may never be the
same again." "Give her our love. I will see you in the morning. I'll see myself out. Take
it easy. No combat for a few more weeks" laughed Doctor Samuels. Finishing the soup,
Max laid back and closed his eyes for what he thought was a few minutes. He slept for
several hours. When he awoke and tried to stand, he couldn't get his balance. Leo
knocked gently before entering the bedroom. "Miss Chanel was concerned about you."
"Hey, Leo. Can you help me phone the doctor?" "Sure thing." After a short

conversation, Max asked Leo to drive him to the hospital. Leo helped him outside and into the car. After several tests, Doctor Samuels announced, "You have a severe concussion and vertigo from the explosion. You need a few days of bed rest."

Chanel appeared in the doorway and chimed in, "And I shall see that he gets the rest he needs." With a smirk, Chanel declared, "You are coming home with me! That's final!" Not up to arguing, Max conceded. "That's fine. We need to contact Isabella's doctor." "Already done" Doctor Samuels said. "No flying for at least a week. I will leave you in Chanel's capable hands." Doctor Samuels winked. A frustrated sigh escaped Max's lips. "I sent Leo back to retrieve your shaving kit and pajamas. I have a lovely smoking jacket for you back at the house." "I admit, Hannah's chicken soup put me out." "She has never given out her recipe. It's been passed down through her family for generations." Laughing, Max said, "She has voodoo dolls of all of us!" "No, love. She knows who cares for her." Doctor Samuels brought a wheelchair into the room. "Leo is here." "I am not an invalid! I do not need a wheelchair!" "Humor me, Max" said Doctor Samuels. As Max got to his feet, a wave of dizziness washed over him. "I think you might be right, Doc." "I'll see you in a week. If all is clear, I will allow you to fly again." Growling, Max said "Fine!" Wheeling Max out to the car, Leo said "It's not wise to argue with Miss Chanel." "I see that, Leo. "Let the women fuss over you. It makes them feel important." "I understand Leo. Do you like your job?" "Yes sir." "The ladies are much nicer to look at than old men." Laughing, Max whispered, "I would agree." "What are you boys gossiping about?" Chanel pressed. "Nothing, ma'am." "Sure, Leo." Helping Max into the back seat, Chanel quipped "Home, Leonardo!" "Yes ma'am." Waiting in the foyer, Goddard and Sebastian were happy to help Max into the house. "I see we have a house guest" smiled Goddard. "Where should we set him up? " "My chambers will be fine." Looking at Max with a satisfied smirk, Chanel cooed "I have always wanted to get you into my bed, Max!" Max scowled. "My bed is the largest. You will have plenty of room. There is a desk, a settee and a table for meals. We will start with small walks until you're steady on your feet again. "Yes, Boss!" "You are learning, Max!" cackled Chanel. "The wash basin is in the corner. You will not be disturbed. Get some rest. I will leave so you can change clothes." "Where's the Scotch?" "No alcohol! Those pain powders are strong." "Morphine normally is!" cracked Max. Closing the door behind herself, Chanel went to check on Max's dinner. He enjoyed the new silk smoker's jacket. Recuperating at Chanel's would be much better than recuperating at home alone. The smell of her perfume lingered in the hallway. A soft knock on the door interrupted Max's thoughts. "Come in."   "Dinner will be ready in twenty minutes." "Was my briefcase brought from home?" "Yes, sir. Leo put it on the desk." "Thank you." "Would you like me to fetch it for you?" "Yes, please."   As she handed the briefcase to Max, a smile spread across the handmaid's face. "Anything else, sir?" "No, that will be all. Thank you."   Max reached for his briefcase. A sharp pain shot from behind his eyes. Chanel had been watching from the doorway. "Dinner, pain medication, then bed for you! You are not ready to return to work!" Chanel took the briefcase and put it back on the desk. Hannah brought in a tray with a light dinner. "He will need a glass of water to take his medicine." "Yes, ma'am. Might I say, my potion works better than those modern powders" Hannah said. "I'm willing to try anything to get back on my feet" Max said. "Try my remedy tonight. If you don't feel better tomorrow, you can go back to the other medicine." "Thank you, Hannah." "I will go prepare a batch with my special herbs."   Chanel arranged Max's tray. "Try to eat, Max." After eating what his stomach could tolerate, Hannah appeared. "Here, Mr. Max. Drink this tea, then bundle up under your blankets. You will feel better in the morning. You will start to sweat. I'll keep cool compresses on his forehead."   Chanel smiled. "I will sit with Max until you return, Hannah." Concerned, Max looked at Chanel. "Don't worry. She's a great nurse. If she were white, she would work in the hospitals. The color of a person's skin should make no difference. Skilled is skilled." "Agreed. But some folks here are still prejudiced against colored people. There are people of all nationalities who work for me. I give everyone equal opportunities. Colored women work harder in all areas especially when it comes to keeping happy homes." Hannah returned to Max's room. "Clients are beginning to arrive." "Take good care of him, Hannah." "No worries, Miss Chanel." "Take off your housecoat, Mr. Max. Get comfortable. You will be asleep soon." As Max drifted off to sleep, Hannah pulled his covers tight. Beads of sweat formed on his forehead. Hannah placed a cool cloth to his face. Hannah started humming a soft tune and broke into prayers for Max. This was her ritual. By three a.m. Max was cool and sound asleep. Hannah smiled. "My work here is done." Relieving Hannah, Chanel watched over Max. Reclining on the settee, Chanel too fell into a deep sleep. The rising sun crept through the heavy drapes and woke Max. Gently pulling himself into a sitting position, he smiled. "I feel good!" Throwing his feet over the side of the bed, Max stood without any dizziness. He took a few cautious steps before walking to the water closet. He shaved his stubble. Still feeling good, he put on his new smoking jacket. He smiled at Chanel as she slept. Hannah knocked on the door. "I see you are feeling better" she said with a smile. "Yes, Hannah. Thank you." "Two more nights drinking my tea and you will be cured." "Could you bring some coffee, please? You should bottle and sell that miracle potion." "No sir! It's been in my family for generations." Chanel spoke. "Hannah was right. You look much better." Hannah went to get coffee. Chanel said, "Small walks until you get your sea legs back. I don't think you're ready to fly yet. Having any dizziness?" "None!" "Start with navigating the room. Then we'll take a walk to the library." "If it makes you feel better, I will go slowly."

As Isabella was preparing for her second day of therapy, Doctor Rickman knocked on her door. "I need to speak with you. Max's doctor called. He suffered a concussion and vertigo in the same explosion that injured you. He cannot travel or fly for at least a week. So it may be a while before he comes back." "How did no one know Max was hurt?"

asked Isabella. "Adrenaline makes your body keep going even if you are in pain. Once his body relaxed, he began to feel the pain in his head." "Will he be okay?" "Yes. Rest is crucial after a head injury. He cannot fly until the vertigo clears up. This does not excuse you from your therapy." "I will be doing so well when he returns, he will think it's a miracle!" "Sounds like a plan. Now, we know you can walk, let's try running with some small weights. I'd like to work on your muscle tone. Easy and building up until you can run ten miles." "Ten miles seems excessive to me." "You were in good physical condition before you were injured. That helped more than you know." "When will my hair grow back?" "That could take several months."

"Shorter hair seems to be in fashion. Max was supposed to bring me pants." "Yes, I remember that. I had a friend bring you some undershirts and exercise pants. They are used by soldiers. The nurse pinched you some female undergarments so you'll be more comfortable." "Thank you, Doctor Rickman." "Let's get to work. Our nutritionist will have you on a diet that helps build muscle." "Does that mean more meat?" "Yes, it does." "It's about time!" "Nuts, cheese, and vegetables. Cut out sugars." "Can I have coffee and tea again?" "Yes. In moderation." "How about soda?" "One per week. Juice and milk are better options. Can you follow this diet?" "Yes. It's better than a soft diet! Hey, Doc? I'll race ya!"

After speaking with Doctor Rickman, Max knew he did not have to rush back to visit Isabella. His first walk went well, but by lunchtime, he needed a rest. By four o'clock, Max was rested enough to resume walking the halls. After dinner, he made it to Chanel's library. "Good evening, Max! How are you feeling?" "Better but sore." "Max, your body and brain have been on adrenaline auto pilot. When you finally slowed down, your body let you know you were in pain. Now you are recuperating and need rest. I have compiled a list of suitable employers for Isabella in case she is not able to be an operative anymore. This will keep Harold from having our girl killed." "Thank you for being on the ball. Harold would have considered my injuries a sign of weakness and pounced." "Would you like a book to take back to your room?" "You have many first editions. Mark Twain always made me smile." "Edgar Allen Poe, good choice. Let me walk you back to your room. If you're a good boy, I'll give you a back massage." Laughing, Max said, "Is that all?" "I wouldn't want you to have a setback from playing too roughly!" "Ha!" scoffed Max. After dinner, Hannah appeared with her magic tea. "Drink this and crawl into bed" she said.   Max did not even get four pages into his book before he fell fast asleep. He didn't move a muscle until morning. Waking with a stretch, he felt rejuvenated. "Maybe I will join Chanel in the solarium "he thought. He slipped in quietly behind Chanel and reached for a cup of coffee. "Damn you, Max! You startled me! I was just about to have Hannah check on you! How about a walk around the grounds today? I will find you some clothes. If you can make it around the grounds twice, I will stop mothering you." "Sure you will!" teased Max. "You love barking orders!" "Now, Max. That's not true" cooed Chanel. "Did you peruse my list for Isabella?" "I did. All are great potential employers for Isabella." "I'd like her to be placed near me or in the United States." "We had planned on sending our girls there. This all depends on how well Isabella recovers. You should be prepared. Harold will tell the bosses Isabella needs to be put down."   "If she doesn't remember the school or her training, she isn't a liability. The brain implant will help control her." "Did they say what would happen if her memories returned?" "No. Her brain is like a short wave radio" Chanel said. "I suppose if she were undercover, you could send her messages through the implant." Hannah broke the silence with a tray of coffee and pastries. "I am looking forward to our walk around the grounds. I could use the fresh air. I hear that we will have an early spring. Forty degree weather will be a nice change."   "I agree" smiled Max. "Mr. Max, scrambled eggs, bacon and toast." "Thank you. I will get fat if I spend too much time here!" Goddard spoke up. "Not on my watch! Later, we will work the heavy bag and do some light sparring." "Sounds good to me!" Scowling, Chanel reminded

Goddard, "he is recovering. Take it easy." "Yes, ma'am." "I mean it, Goddard! Do I need to remind you who's in charge?" "A trip to the red room?" Goddard spoke sarcastically. "No. You would enjoy that too much. How about kitchen or laundry duty?" "Understood, ma'am." "That's what I thought!" "Do as she asks, or you'll end up cleaning toilets! Or worse, chamber pots!" "That's disgusting!" growled Goddard. "I'll meet you in the basement in forty-five minutes" smiled Max. As Goddard left, Chanel quipped "Got to keep the help in line! Goddard is full of himself!"   Finding his way to the basement, Max pulled on a pair of gloves and started hitting the heavy bag. After several hits, Max's arms began to feel like lead. "We will only do one round of sparring. Then a massage."   After several minutes of trading punches, Goddard scowled. "You need a rub down." He rang for Katrina to come and massage Max before he burst into Chanel's office. "What is it?" "I think there's more wrong with Max than the doctor said." "Why do you think so, Goddard?" "His arm strength and his stamina is gone." "He was not supposed to be training so soon!" snapped Chanel.   "Take a walk with him. You'll see. I'm right." "Your concern is noted."   Max took a nap before lunch." Chanel went to his room. Opening the door slightly, she heard a soft snoring sound coming from his bed. At two o'clock, Max ambled into the library. "Sorry, dear. I fell asleep." "I have called Doctor Samuels. He will be by this afternoon." "Why? I feel fine." "Let's take our walk. Then Hannah will fix you a snack." They strolled arm in arm enjoying the warmth of the sun in silence. "What's on your mind, Chanel?" "Nothing." "Since when do we lie to each other?" "Are you sick?" asked Chanel. "Not to my knowledge" smirked Max. "Honestly, it does seem to be taking longer to recover from the concussion. Maybe it's old age catching up with me." "No, you're like a fine wine. You get better with age" smiled Chanel. "Thank you, my dear" Max said as they reached the front door. "See? We completed our walk with no problem. Now I'm ready for a snack!"   A tray filled with fruit and cheeses was set in front of Max. "How about a nice cup of tea?" "I'd prefer wine to go with my cheese, but tea is fine." Hannah brought him a glass of sweet tea with a lemon wedge. "Ah, Refreshing! Stop mocking me!" "No alcohol until the doctor says otherwise."   Doctor Samuels said, "That is correct, Max. I'm told there are some concerns about your overall health." "What makes you say that?" "I'm told your arms feel like lead." "Yes. After punching the heavy bag."

"I rechecked your scans. You have a large amount of scar tissue on your frontal lobe. You may have suffered a small stroke, but it's more likely been caused by the number of times you've been hit in the head. Fights, combat and explosions. You're actually lucky to be alive. Maybe you should consider an office job or retirement." "I have a desk job. I am a handler. I give assignments and handle paperwork for ops. I very seldom go into the field. The explosion was an accident." "Stay out of the field! You're sixty years old!" "Thanks, doc!" "If you don't follow orders, I will take you off active duty!" "Yes sir." "No sparring for at least a month. Walking will help rebuild your stamina. Let's see how your vertigo is doing. Stand up. Walk to the doorway" Doctor Samuels said as he attached an eye chart to the wall. He examined both of Max's eyes.

"Touch your finger to your nose. You need glasses." Doctor Samuels said with a smile. "They should help with the disorientation. Come in to be fitted in the morning. Once I place the order, you should have your glasses in two weeks. That should help the headaches to subside."   Shaking hands, Doctor Samuels said, "See you first thing in the morning. I will help you choose a pair that compliments your features." "Great" scoffed Max. "Now I have week eyes, sore muscles and arms that feel like lead." "Maybe a tonic would help" suggested Chanel.   "Enough! I need target practice!" "Ha! How can you shoot a target that you cannot see?" teased Goddard. "Sod off!" screamed Max. "Careful of your blood pressure, old man!" snarled Goddard. Max went back to his room growling with every step. He slammed the door.   "Goddammit! He has no respect for me!" After slamming around Chanel's room, Max thought about what he would do if any of the team were to behave that way. Laughing at himself, he realized that he would have disciplined any of the team had they acted that way. "Harold considers needing glasses as a sign of weakness! I cannot have that!" Taking a deep breath, Max crossed his legs and attempted to meditate. "Screw this sissy shit! I need to shoot a large target!" Looking for his pistol, he began to tear the desk drawers apart. There was a light knock and Chanel glided into the room. "Looking for this?" "What the fuck Chanel?" Max glared at her as she caressed the barrel of his pistol lovingly. "I took the gun from the desk. You were so enraged. I felt it was a necessary safety precaution." "I am an expert marksman! I never miss!" "Normally I would agree with that evaluation of your skills. But the need for corrective lenses may impede your expertise." "Rub it in, Chanel!"

Touching Max's arm, Chanel said, "Needing glasses does not reflect poorly on you as a leader or a soldier." Max's eyes clouded over. "What if my impaired judgment is the reason Isabella got hurt?" "I refuse to accept that, Max. Isabella protected an innocent child who was deaf! That is how she sustained her injury." She hugged Max with the grace of a goddess. "So, that's what's been bothering you? You did not lose her. She will work for our government in a different capacity." "She was one hell of an operative!" cried Max. "She always will be" Chanel consoled him. The next two weeks passed slowly for Max. Glasses, fittings and scans of his head filled his days. He was excited to get the all clear. He couldn't wait to see Isabella. He was not prepared for the surprise that awaited him. As Max's transport touched down, he found both doctors Rickman and Schwarzkopf waiting for him. They were beaming with pride. "What's going on?" Max questioned. He pulled his coat closed as a bone chilling wind blew through the laundry area. Pulling open the heavy door, neither doctor spoke. They pointed to a darkened corridor. As Max reached for his pistol, Doctor Rickman said, "That isn't necessary, Max." As he opened the door, fluorescent light hit him right in the face. "Ouch!" "Thought you'd been given the all clear?" "I have." As his eyes adjusted to the light, he saw Isabella doing laps around the physical therapy room. Followed by shadow boxing and a full range of exercises. Max applauded. Isabella smiled and took a bow. Running at full speed, Isabella leapt at Max, hugging him. They both landed in a heap on the floor.   "I'm sorry, Max! Are you alright?" "Yes, Isabella. I am fine. I see you are doing well." "One more round of tests tomorrow. Then I can go home! Let me have a bath and we can have dinner!" Isabella actually skipped down the corridor. Max looked at both doctors. He was full of questions. "The chip has not impeded her physical progress in the slightest" smiled Doctor Rickman. Max looked at Doctor Schwarzkopf. "What about her memories?" "She should see a therapist as her memories return. But as of now, she is not a danger to anyone. The chip will help discourage behaviors that are not acceptable. We have no further reason to keep her here. Give her a week with her comrades. Then she should be ready for a new assignment. I will come see her before her new assignment starts." "Thank you, Doctor."   "She is on medication for anxiety. She takes it at bedtime to help her sleep. After dinner, she reads and medication is passed out at nine. Testing will begin at eight a.m. You should be on your way home by noon." "Thank you, gentlemen for all the help." "The implant should be checked monthly. We will show you how it's done and how to adjust frequencies." Max nodded. "I should get to Isabella's room." "She is having a snack in the cafeteria. I will show you the way." Putting his bags in his room, Max headed to meet up with Isabella. "I took the liberty of filling out the dinner card, Max. I hope you don't mind." "Not at all, Isabella. How are you feeling?" "Good. The exercise helps." "Physical training has always helped you to clear your mind" smiled Max. "I remember teaching some type of physical education. I also know self-defense. That's all I can remember besides having friends. We attend school together. We have jobs and live together." "You remember quite a bit.   "The school is almost a complete blank for me. Except that there was a fancy ball .I wore a gown. I don't like girly dresses." "You are correct. Chanel had a difficult time getting you to wear dresses." "I have so many scars! I must be a trouble maker." "No, Isabella. You stood up for what you believed in. The Chancellor tried his best to break your spirit, but he did not succeed!" "I must be a tough girl!" "Yes, but only when provoked." "Was I a good person?" "You still are." "There's so much that I cannot recall!"   "You

will in time. Eat up. You have a big day tomorrow." "Glasses become you, Max."
"Thank you, Isabella. Let's take a walk before lights out." As they walked the corridors
in silence, Isabella looked into Max's blue-gray eyes and said, "You did not cause my
injuries. I am glad I protected that girl. I'd do it again in a heartbeat, Max. What I am is
because you have been a great teacher and mentor." Tears welled in Max's eyes. "Damn
glasses! Making my eyes water!" The nurse interrupted by announcing it was time for
evening meds. Walking Isabella back to her room, Max said, "See you tomorrow." Max
made his way to Doctor Rickman's office. "I knew you would need to call for transport."
"I need to phone Chanel to prepare for Isabella's homecoming."

"We called transport for you. Chanel will have everything prepared for Isabella's
arrival. The girls will be there after work." "Thank you, Doctor Rickman." "Let's go over
testing the implant and adjustment of frequencies. You can even send her messages using
Morse code." "Wow!" "She is our first human trial. "Explain!" growled Max. "If this is
successful, it will be a new way for operatives to continue being useful to the
government. Their training will not be lost because of head injuries. It will be beneficial
on all sides." "I see "said Max. "Normally, protocol dictates that an injured operative be
terminated. That's a waste of resources. This way, the operative is still useful. Harold
wanted her terminated. This is a new opportunity for Isabella. It could become the norm
for treatment of soldiers with head injuries."   "I hope you are right, Doctor
Rickman ." "Get some sleep, Max." Walking back to his room, Max said a silent prayer
for Isabella. Max laid back on his bed, trying to relax. The Scotch began to take effect as
a warm, fuzzy feeling washed over him as he drifted to sleep. Max slept in. A nurse
came in with coffee and a smile. "You are missing a great show. Isabella has broken all
of her previous records."   Max stood quietly and watched Isabella crush every
obstacle the doctors placed in her path. Doctor Rickman nodded to Max and beamed
with the pride of a parent. Wiping her face, Isabella squealed, "What's next!" "Nothing.

Get cleaned up. You're going home." "Her test results are better than we could have anticipated." After her shower, Isabella found a pale blue dress, head scarf and a purse and shoes on her bed. Isabella was confused. Nurse Betty explained, "They're from the staff. You're our success story." "Thank you!" cried Isabella. After putting herself together in her new outfit, Isabella turned to find Max standing in the doorway. "I have your prescriptions. Are you ready?" Isabella put her arm through Max's. "Yes, I am. Oh my God! A helicopter!" "Wanna fly it?" "Yes sir!" Controlling the stick, Isabella squealed in delight. "Okay" Max said, "That's enough. My turn!" The pilot just shook his head. "Look over there! That's Chanel's place! Are you ready?" "I believe so" said Isabella. They landed in the field adjacent to Chanel's property. Max waved the pilot off. Walking up to the manor, Max gave Isabella a reassuring squeeze as he opened the front door.

The Governess: Teaching the children

Stepping into the foyer, Isabella grabbed her head as pain shot behind her eyes. As the pain subsided, Isabella found Max, Chanel and the entire house staff staring at her. "Too much excitement, I guess. I flew the helicopter! You should see Max's skills! "Hello, dear!" smiled Chanel. "I sort of remember you. There was a dance here when we were in school. We wore gowns. "Yes, you are correct. Let me show you to your room so you can rest." Chanel rolled her eyes in Max's direction. The look he returned was cold and calculated. "Elizabeth will be the handmaid assigned to you. I still have your clothes from your last visit here."   Joining Max in the library, Chanel began to pour two glasses of Scotch. "She has fragments of her memories. Does she remember that this is a brothel?" "I have no idea!" screamed Max. Goddard appeared in the doorway. "Isabella doesn't remember me, does she?" "Honestly, I have no idea. Take it slow. Answer all of her questions. If you're not sure about something, call for me and I will handle it. The girls will arrive at six o'clock for dinner. I have made the preparations for her new assignment. I explained to the team that she has virtually no memory of them. Time spent with them may bring back some of her memories."   As Goddard left the room, tears stung his eyes. He knew that Isabella's lost memory was out of his control. But he truly did care for Isabella. As Max looked over Chanel's list, he marked the names that he thought would be the best matches for Isabella. "We will start contacting them in the morning. Two of them are stationed at nearby Embassies. "Madam Chanel, here's the dinner menu." "Thank you, Hannah."   "Hannah, Isabella will need a light snack to have with her evening medication at nine p.m. Perhaps some biscuits and a glass of milk or a cup of tea." "Yes sir. Isabella will have a lovely dinner to welcome her home. Leo just arrived with the girls."   Bounding through the foyer, Anastasia asked, "Where is Isabella?" "She is resting in her room." "We have waited so long to see her!"   Before Max could advise them of Isabella's current state, Rena ran down the hall and burst into Isabella's room and jumped on the bed. Ingrid hugged her firmly. Looking confused, Isabella said "Hello." "Silly girl, it's me, Ingrid!" Ursula whispered, "I am Ursula." Rena and

Anastasia said, "We are your comrades, best friends and schoolmates."   A flash crossed Isabella's face. Then she smiled. "Here are a few photographs." Max listened at the door. "This is when we passed our driving tests. You tutored us to ensure we passed." "That makes sense to me now. Am I good at physical defense?" "Yes! Your abilities have put grown men to shame!" "You're not afraid of anything!" squealed Rena. "Max and I flew a helicopter today!" smiled Isabella. "You're a crack shot. Excellent with guns too." "I like hunting?" Isabella questioned.   The team laughed aloud. "Nothing escapes you!" "I remember an altercation with a large man called Goddard." The girls looked to Max for direction on how to broach the subject. Max nodded. "Goddard was one of your training partners. He has a few scars from your skills." Looking over the photographs, Isabella asked "were we bodyguards?" "In a way. We helped people solve problems."

"What happened to the little girl from kindergarten? Her father died, so I helped her get into a private school" smiled Max. "My memory has big holes in it, like Swiss cheese. Are we teachers?" "No, but we have done some tutoring." "I understand." "You helped boys who were small and defenseless to gain strength and confidence by teaching them self-defense which helped them do better in their academics too" giggled Anastasia. "Do you girls still train?" "Yes. We run and do calisthenics to stay in shape." This made Isabella feel more at ease. Chanel rang the bells, signaling that dinner was served. Max took some teasing from Anastasia about his glasses, but dinner went smoothly. Leo drove the girls home after dessert.   Looking around, Isabella asked Chanel a pointed question. "Why do all these people live here, Chanel?" Max choked on his Brandy. "I am a Madam. This is my house." "Is this a house of ill repute?" "It is a brothel."

Waves of anger, frustration and confusion washed over Isabella. "I remember some things. You were there." "I have always been there to help you girls learn." Chanel looked like her head would explode. Chanel cooed, "I have always taken the girls to town for properly fitted clothing, shoes, hair styling and makeup. Most of your teachers were male." Isabella whistled a sigh of relief. "Thank God! I thought I had been a prostitute!"

"No. My staff are consorts. They attend functions with the guests who need an escort. Dignitaries and the like. My consorts fill a need in the community. My men and women are well-read, multilingual and are current on all world events!" Chanel barked.   "I meant no offense, Chanel. I have very little memory so I ask questions." "I understand that. But NO ONE looks down on my consorts. They are my family. I will not tolerate a snotty attitude toward them from you or anyone! Understood?" "Yes, ma'am."   Max escorted Isabella back to her room. "You need rest." Hannah brought in a light snack before bed. "You owe Chanel an apology." "Yes, sir. "Goodnight."

Knowing Chanel was angry, Max prepared for a scolding. Drinks were poured as Max entered the library. "I am truly sorry, Chanel!" "She needs to be placed, immediately!" "Doctor said in a week." "Isabella needs to go back to work. A governess position will keep her close but occupied." "She truly doesn't remember!" "I realize this! Her tone tells me that she needs to be reminded of her position. She is no one special! She works for her country, as we all do! We will start calling employers in the morning! You are dismissed, Max!" Chanel's cold and abrupt dismissal told Max that Isabella was no longer welcome there. Goddard stopped Max in the corridor for a word. "I assume you've heard." "Yes, I have." "Chanel loved Isabella as though she were her own child. Isabella's words were a slap in the face for Chanel. She was defending her family!" "I understand."   "No you do not! Chanel believed that she had a purpose in training those children for their assignments as operatives. Her maternal guidance has softened with her age. But her dedication remains unchanged. All that she does is for God and country. She has forsaken having a husband and a family for the cause."   Max had an epiphany. "I will deal with this in the morning." As Max headed to his room, there was an ache in his heart that only Chanel could soothe. Leaning back on his pillows, Max thought for the first time about Chanel as a woman he could date. She was a Madam, but she was beautiful. The stress of Isabella's injuries had brought to the surface emotions that had long been left on the back burner. Max smiled as he drifted off to sleep.

Loud talking awoke Max. Dressing quickly, he grabbed his glasses and ventured toward the sounds of raised voices. Chanel was passing out orders in her commander in chief voice. "Was that a battle cry I heard?" laughed Max. Hannah appeared with coffee and pastries. "What's all the noise about, Chanel?" "My staff seems to disagree with my assessment of last night's events!" She handed Max four manila folders. "These families are the best suited for Isabella. I will expect your decision by lunch!" With a sour expression, Max suggested they retire to the solarium to speak privately. "No. We will use the library where the phone is." Hannah's worried expression betrayed her feelings. "We need to start preparing Isabella for her duties as a governess." "Chanel, why have you become so bitter and nasty?" "I spoke with Harold this morning. If Isabella does not excel in her new assignment, he will give the order to have her terminated. He considers her a loose end. He suggested sending in her own team to do the job. We have become too attached to see the objective clearly." "I will handle Harold!" snapped Max. "He feels you should retire!" "Over his cold, dead body!" hissed Max. Shaking his head, Max's anger glowed. "Who the hell is Harold? No one! He sucked up to get his position!" "I have arranged for Isabella to taken Au pair refresher course at the Embassy's staff quarters to ensure she knows what her new job entails." "I should accompany her when she is placed. Think of it as a small vacation. Chanel, Isabella has asked for a word." "Send her in, Hannah." "I have come to say I am very sorry. My comments were out of line. Questions seem to come out before I can stop them." "I truly understand. Get dressed. Leo is taking you to a refresher course on Au pair duties." "Why, ma'am? "You are being assigned as a governess to get back into working a regular job again. Hurry along. Breakfast will be served in twenty minutes."

As she left, Isabella gave Max a look that was filled with hurt and shame. "That was cold, Chanel." "Sometimes you have to be cruel to be kind. Harold wants her dead. I need to distance myself, Max." "I'm sure you're right. Harold deserves to be put out of his misery!" "She has to learn to function without you. Choose the family. We will take her to meet them." "I have chosen the D'Agati family. Michael is the Italian Ambassador. He deals with military security. I will call to get the necessary paperwork. Is Friday good for you, Chanel?" "Wednesday is better. My house is very busy on Fridays and Saturday. We will tell Isabella after dinner this evening." "Should we disclose her injuries?" "Yes, Michael will understand. Harold will only give her a week or two to acclimate to her new assignment before he calls for her death to be the team's net op. They would have no choice but to kill her." "That is so wrong!" screamed Max. "It would show the team that they are expendable soldiers. He would have Isabella do the same to them." Frustration made Max's blood boil. Walking the grounds after making his phone calls helped Max put his emotions into perspective.   As Leo pulled into the drive, a shiver ran down Max's body. Walking toward the back door, Max breathed hard. Entering through the kitchen, he grabbed a towel to wipe his brow. Isabella was squealing with pride and waving a Certificate of Completion. "I am certified!" "That is wonderful, dear" smiled Chanel. "Get washed up for dinner." Chanel called Max to the library. "Michael is awaiting us at the Embassy. He will take her to meet his family."

With a ferocious appetite, Isabella cleared her second serving of dinner. "We will have dessert and coffee in the library, Hannah." "Yes ma'am." As Isabella took a seat in the library, Max looked with empathy into her confused eyes as he began. "You have been chosen to serve as a governess for a diplomat and his family. The D'Agati's are an affluent Italian family who made their money in military security. Michael Sr. and Francesca Marie. Michael Junior is fifteen. Katherine Marie is thirteen and Nathan is five years old. We have a file for you to read. Chanel and I will drive you to the Embassy on Wednesday morning." "Did I make you or Chanel angry, Max?" "No. Why would you think such a thing?" "I feel like I am being punished. Why can't I go back to my office job?" "You have had a head injury and you don't remember your job." "I know! You don't want me out in public!" "This job will help you adjust to working again." "Are you ashamed of me?" "No, dear" smiled Chanel.   Tears filled her eyes as Isabella excused herself. She ran towards her room. Goddard watched her, hoping that she would notice him. She did not. Bursting into the library, Goddard demanded, "Max! What the hell did you do to Isabella?!" Visibly hurt, Max turned to look out the window.

Chanel looked into Goddard's angry eyes and said, "If Isabella cannot function as a governess, Harold will order her comrades to kill her. It will be a lesson to them. If they cannot serve, they have no purpose." "I will kill Harold myself!" screamed Goddard. "He scarred Isabella for life!" "We can only help to prepare her for her new assignment."   Grabbing Max by his shoulders, Goddard snarled, "Are you going to let that son-of-a-bitch Harold kill my girl!?" Turning on his heels, Max snarled, "You mean our girl?" "No, Max. SHE IS MINE! If you had the balls, Harold would have been dead years ago so that he couldn't sadistically torture new students! Let me explain, Max. If Harold orders Isabella killed, I will kill him!"   Exhaling a long sigh, Max said, "Understand something, Goddard. I am their handler. But I will not allow Harold to give that order. He will hit the ground before he finishes the sentence!" "Let's hope it doesn't come to that" said Chanel.   Goddard slammed the door as he left the library. Chanel began to pour drinks and handed Max a glass. After he downed the Scotch in two gulps, Chanel poured him another. She then whispered, "Max, you know what needs to be done. It will be your decision." No one realized that Isabella had overheard the conversation between Max and Goddard. Holding the file, Isabella decided that she needed to know everything, even if remembering was a problem.   She went to find Goddard. Knocking on his door, she could hear loud moans that she thought were dire pain. Goddard answered the door. "Yes? Are you lost?" "No! We need to talk!" "Come in." Isabella walked over to his chest of implements and softly caressed the wood.

Turning to Goddard, Isabella said, "I heard the conversation between you and Max. I have less than twenty-four hours to get a crash course in "me "before I am shipped off to a new assignment. Will you help me? And why the hell does Harold want me dead?" "I will do my best to answer your questions." "We weren't just office workers, were we? That school was not a normal school, was it? Why was I taken to a military hospital that specializes in research and development procedures? What is Chanel's connection to the school? Where did I learn my self-defense skills? Why am I drawn to you and this room?"

"No, you weren't just office workers. You are sleeper operatives. Those were your day jobs. The school was advertised to poor families as a finishing school that would help their daughters to marry well. You work for the government as an operative soldier. You sustained head trauma. They were not sure if you could return to duty. They placed a chip in your brain as an experiment. Chanel administered brothel training using her consorts so that you girls could use sex to extract whatever information was needed from influential people. Or so you could escort diplomats to important functions. She also taught you how to dress, apply makeup and navigate high heels. Your self-defense skills come from combat training from the school. You also studied weapons and bomb-making. The scars on your back are because Harold could not break your spirit. Parents received a monthly stipend and a dowry because they were told that their daughters married well. You are drawn to me because of the torture training from the school. You associate pleasure and pain as one and the same. It is my specialty. Not many men can handle the beatings that you can dish out. As far as Harold wanting you dead, if you do not perform as an operative, he believes you are no longer useful and should be terminated. How do you feel, Isabella?"   "Like I want to punch something!" "I will show you what we did to help you relieve stress." "Can we go slowly?" asked Isabella. "Of course. Let's start with a massage." "That sounds reasonable."   Noticing the whips and floggers hanging on the wall, Isabella asked "What are those?" Taking down a flogger, Goddard slapped Isabella's back. "It doesn't hurt! There is a tingling sensation." Picking up a whip, Isabella moved it in an upward motion. With a flick of her wrist, she heard a loud crack. With a gentle smile Goddard asked, "Would you like me to reintroduce you to the pleasure and pain area of training?"   Fear crept across Isabella's heart. "I will only take you as far as you are comfortable." "Was I the one who hit you?" Isabella asked. "Only in training." "Is that why you were wearing a bandage?" "You broke my nose, but I deserved it. Are you ready to try some pleasure \pain therapy?" "I'd like a few minutes." "Fine." Looking into Goddard's eyes, Isabella asked "Did someone hurt you? Is that why you work here?" Laughing, Goddard said "I have also had training. Like you, my parents could not afford to feed me. I worked on a farm. They beat me instead of feeding me. Chanel found me outside of a laundry begging. I was a big kid with big muscles and a nice smile. Chanel brought me home with her. I started out doing chores and caring for animals. She noticed that older women drooled over me. Chanel sent me to school, then to consort training. I have escorted queens and princesses. I am paid well and Chanel is a mother figure to me. She saved me from a life of hopeless despair. I do understand how you feel and your point of view."   "I think I am ready to try" said Isabella. "Where would you like to start?" asked Goddard. "I will trust you" said Isabella.   Goddard reached down and picked up Isabella. He carried her to the bed and laid her down gently before undressing her tenderly. Her skin flushed warm as Goddard's hands made their way over her skin. He kissed her gently but with a slight force.   Her breath caught in her throat. Emotions flooded her mind and her head began to spin as the sensations of sex with Goddard overtook her senses. She lost herself in the rhythm of their bodies thrusting and collapsing into each other over and over again until they were both exhausted, sweating heaps. For Goddard, this was a very vanilla session. But he didn't want to frighten or injure Isabella any more than she already had been.

Isabella looked at Goddard with questions filling her eyes. "Why didn't Max tell me about my past?" "You sustained a traumatic brain injury. The doctors told him not to overstimulate you. To let your memory return gradually and freely." "Thank you for this, Goddard. Goodnight."   As she walked to her room, Isabella felt strangely at ease and relaxed. Sleep came easily. Hannah knocked on her door at eight a.m. "Breakfast is served." "Hannah, I will be leaving for my new assignment in the morning. Can you help me prepare my travel bag with clean clothes?" "Yes, Miss Isabella. "Thank you."

Putting on a house dress, Isabella took her file to the solarium. "Good morning, dear" smiled Chanel. "Good morning. Where is Max?" "He went to the office to catch up on work." "I have studied the file. I will be ready for my new assignment." "You seem calm and more relaxed, Isabella."   "I spent some time with Goddard last night. He answered some questions for me." Smiling, Chanel patted Isabella's hand. "I spoke with Goddard. He told me about your questions." "I don't remember much. But now, I understand more about my thoughts and feelings. I now understand why my success as a governess is so important."   Chanel cleared her throat. "If you cannot function..." "I know. Harold will have me killed." Scrunching her lips together, Isabella said, "Maybe Harold needs a trip to Goddard's room. Someone should give him some permanent scars! But I don't think punishment or pain would change his perspective about operatives. To him, we are not human. We are weapons. If we are no longer useful to the cause, we are disposed of like garbage." Chanel spoke softly. "We did not want to overwhelm you." "I understand. But as long as Harold is alive, we all have targets on our backs. He will have us taken out like trash." "I see that talking to Goddard has helped to clarify things for you." "Chanel, thank you for saving him. Goddard is a special man. I'm starving!"

As Isabella loaded her plate, Chanel could see that a great weight had lifted from Isabella's mind. As Max stood in the foyer listening to Isabella, he knew what must be done. "Hello, Max!" "Hello, Isabella. How do you feel about some target practice or practice driving a car in case you have to take your charges to school?" "You will let me drive?" "Sure. You already have a license." "Can I shoot a big gun?" Laughing, Max said "we'll see how you do. Eat up so we can head out." "Let me change into pants, Max!" "Hurry up!"   After shoveling food into her mouth, Isabella ran down the hall at full speed. She knocked Hannah over as she opened the door. "What in the world?" Hannah questioned. "Max is taking me out to practice driving! I need pants! "Isabella squealed. "Here are some gray flannels and a sweater. "Oh darn! I need a hat! My hair hasn't grown back from my surgery."   "Slow down. Here's your felt hat. Try these low-heeled shoes." "Thanks, Hannah!" Running behind her changing screen, Isabella squealed with delight as the day's prospects danced in her mind. Max looked at Chanel. Chanel asked, "How much did you hear?" "All of it." "Did you speak with Michael about Isabella?" "Yes. She will be hired on a trial basis. Unfortunately, Harold knows this too! He is counting on Isabella cracking under the pressure, or her training coming back to her. Either way, he will decide Isabella's future." "Do you think the girls could carry out an order to kill Isabella?" "I have no idea. They have the skills, but they also have emotional attachments. I am not sure. I have to consider what's best for them as their handler."   "What is that, exactly?" "Isabella may be right, Chanel." "What do you mean, Max?" "It may come down to Isabella and the team or Harold." "We could run that school much better than Harold does!" snapped Chanel. "I agree. But he will never give up that prestigious position without a fight." "What do your superiors think? "They are sitting back waiting to see who survives." Max poured another cup of coffee and shook his head. "This will be hard on all concerned." "Except Harold!" snapped Chanel.   She whispered, "Just accept what needs to be done for the preservation of our family. Who's next? You know damn well Harold was in on the church's profiting off children and sexually abusing them in the name of religion!"

Isabella entered the foyer smiling brightly "Did I enjoy driving?" "Yes. You were the best in the class. We will start out slowly around the field. When you're comfortable handling the vehicle, we will go onto the road."   Three hours of driving practice led to another three hours on the shooting range. Smiling, Max gave Isabella a gentle shoulder squeeze. "Your skills are returning nicely. We should get back before Chanel starts to worry." Fruit and cheese were being served in the solarium. Isabella wolfed down a plate full before Chanel could finish a sentence. "Get cleaned up for dinner" Chanel said.

As Max smiled, Chanel glanced in Isabella's direction. "How did our girl do?" "Driving and shooting came naturally. She was a duck to water. Tomorrow we hand her off to the D'Agati's." "I spoke with Michael. He said that the current governess will show Isabella everything she needs to know before going on holiday. Does Isabella know this is a temporary assignment?" asked Chanel. "We will explain it to her before she gets to the Embassy." "What about Harold?" "I will handle one problem at a time!" snapped Max. "You already know that no matter how well Isabella does, it will never be good enough for Harold. He wants her eliminated!" "I guarantee he will die first!" snarled Max. "I hate to point out the obvious" whispered Chanel. "But Harold is your superior." "Superior asshole!" screamed Max. "I agree" said Chanel. "I would never tell you how to do your job. But you aren't in the best condition to have a physical confrontation with Harold." "I have the girls." "Yes, but that may be a conflict of honor for them." "Harold tortured Isabella. Those girls will do whatever it takes to protect her. Goddard and Sebastian stood quietly in the doorway. Looking at one another, they said in unison, "We would happily assist you if it was needed." Laughing, Max said, "I just might take you up on that." "We are ready!" "Thank you, gentlemen. I may call on you if Harold gives the order on Isabella." Goddard gave Max a deep stare. "No one hurts Isabella!" Hannah announced, "Dinner in ten minutes." Isabella announced her presence with "I had fun today, Max." "So did I!" beamed Max. "Don't anger our girl! She's a crack shot!" As they chatted, the bells sounded to indicate that dinner was served. Chatting through dinner, Max decided to tell Isabella about her new assignment. "We will drive you to the Embassy and you will meet Michael D'Agati Sr. You will accompany him to his home and meet his family. This is a temporary assignment while his governess is on holiday. It will last a few weeks. My superiors will be following your progress." "I will do my best" smiled Isabella. "I see that!" Isabella excused herself to have a bath and an early bedtime. Max said, "I explained Isabella's head injury to Michael. I did not mention the chip in her brain. Too much information might taint their view of her abilities as a governess. I will stay in contact with both Isabella and Michael to make sure things run smoothly." "I have been meaning to have lunch with Francesca" said Chanel. "Looks like we have all our bases covered" Max said. "I am stopping by the office then going home for a good night's rest" said Max. After Max departed, Chanel checked the appointment book and greeted clients. As the evening came to a close, Chanel tallied the cash receipts and totaled each consorts earnings. She placed the cash into individual envelopes and locked them in a drawer. Turning out the lights, Chanel walked to her bedroom saying a prayer for Isabella. Sleep eluded Chanel. She was worried about Isabella. She walked to the kitchen to make a cup of tea. A soft light shone above the stove where Hannah stood in her nightgown. "I thought you might need some tea, ma'am." "You always know what I need, Hannah." "We have been together many years, Miss Chanel." "Yes, we have Hannah" cooed Chanel. "Are you worried about Miss Isabella?" "Yes I am." "She will be fine, ma'am." After tea, Chanel went to the library. Sitting in her settee, she was asleep within five pages of her book. As the morning peeked through the stained glass, Chanel began to stir. "I must have fallen asleep in here!" Shaking her head, Hannah appeared with a tray of coffee and pastries. "Breakfast should be ready in thirty minutes. I have Miss Isabella's travel case packed. She is ready to go." "Thank you, Hannah. I will get changed." Hannah had asked Goddard to bring Isabella's travel case to the foyer. Isabella came bounding into the dining room, where Hannah had breakfast waiting Chanel joined Isabella for coffee. "How are you feeling?" "Good. I am ready to take on my new assignment." Isabella was dressed in pinstripes and beaming with pride. Max came bustling into the dining room. "Coffee on?" "Yes sir" smiled Hannah. Leo announced, "The car is out front and ready,

Miss Chanel." "Thank you, Leonardo. Coffee?" "Yes, please."   Max held the file on Isabella's new assignment and quizzed her. She got every answer correct and felt confident. She began to relax and so did Max. The drive to the Embassy took two hours. When they stopped for fuel, Isabella stretched her legs and noticed that all the elegant homes in town that were filled with children. "Penny for your thoughts" smiled Chanel. "I never noticed how many of these large houses were filled with children and families." "Are you concerned?" "No. I just never noticed it before."   The drive became monotonous. The hills went on forever. As they got closer to town, the streets filled with people. Pulling into the Embassy parking lot, Max announced "We are here." Walking into the large marble lobby, Chanel looked for Michael D'Agati's office. As the receptionist looked up from her desk, Max smiled. "We have an appointment." "Which one of you?" Isabella spoke up. "I am the new governess for Mr. D'Agati's children." "Just a moment please." She pressed a few buttons on the phone. Michael came out and shook hands with Max. He kissed Chanel's cheek. "This must be Isabella." "Yes sir."

Shaking his hand, Isabella nodded. "This is a temporary assignment. Our governess, Hilda will be going on holiday. You will be filling in for her during that time. I have arranged for Hilda to spend the next forty-eight hours helping you acclimate to our home and our schedules." "Yes sir."   Walking Max and Chanel to the door, Michael reassured them that Isabella was in good hands. Michael led Isabella to his car and they drove up to a gated drive. Michael said, "We are here." Isabella noticed the perfectly manicured lawn, fruit trees and benches around the lawn. Pillars adorned the front porch. Michael opened the door and led Isabella inside.   "This is my wife, Francesca. These are the children. Michael Jr is fifteen. Katherine is thirteen and Nathan is five. This is Isabella. She will be filling in for Hilda while she is on holiday." Hilda smiled. "Let me show you to your quarters. The staff has our own kitchen area. You will tend to the children. You can be seen but not heard. Any correction of behaviors is to be done away from visitors. Here are the children's schedules. No changes are to be made without approval from Master or Missus. The older children play sports and have music lessons. Katherine has a dance recital this weekend. Nathan is very shy. He prefers books to people. He has a pet snake. He is more withdrawn. His parents have busy social schedules and they travel often. The children are kept busy. But they miss their parents greatly. As long as you keep to their routines, you will do fine." Looking at all the schedules, Isabella's mind whirled with crazy thoughts. "I will leave you to unpack. I will have you join us for dinner and Nathan's bedtime routine. We retire to our rooms after nine pm unless the children need something. You get one day off every seven days. I will return in seven days, but will not be back at work for another three days. I will see you at six p.m. for dinner." Closing the door, Hilda left Isabella to unpack. Isabella thought to herself, "What havoc did I wreak to deserve this assignment?" After she had unpacked, Isabella wandered the halls. She peered into Nathan's room. She saw a small boy who looked lost and sad. Nathan said quietly, "They want to send me to military school to toughen me up." "Why? You are a smart and beautiful boy." "I am not the son my dad wants. Money covers up many things. But not the disappointment in your parents' eyes because you can't meet their expectations" Nathan said sadly. "You are very smart for your age" said Isabella. "Only because my best friends are books" said Nathan. "It sounds like dinner is ready. Shall we go?" Reaching out her hand, Isabella walked Nathan to dinner. "I see you have been getting acquainted" Hilda said. Everyone took their places at the table. Francesca engaged her children about that day's activities. Hilda nudged Isabella. "Staff eats in our kitchen" she whispered. "Mother, can Isabella join us for dinner?" Nathan asked. "Of course, dear. Isabella, join us" smiled Francesca. "Tell us about yourself, dear." "I went to a private school. I was injured trying to protect a deaf girl." "We were told you had a traumatic brain injury." "Yes. I do not remember my childhood or schooling. My friends showed me photographs from when I got my driver's license. Max was in the photographs."

"Were you hospitalized for very long?" "The doctors said I would need a month of rehabilitation. I was discharged after two and a half weeks." "You seem to have overcome a lot of obstacles." "Tell me about the family. What's everyone's favorite food?" Katherine smiled. "Seafood. Junior loves steak and mashed potatoes with gravy." Nathan smiled, "Chocolate cake!" "What do you enjoy outside of school?" "Dancing, swimming, watching movies." Nathan responded, "Reading books." "We have a television" smiled Francesca. Michael Sr. said, "I enjoy hiking and boating." "Shopping "smiled Francesca. Nodding, Isabella began to understand why Nathan was so sad. There were no family activities. Gifts replaced love and parental attention. The governess was their emotional support system. Hilda seemed cold and very detached from the children. "Homework, children!" quipped Hilda. "Yes, ma'am." "My homework is done "Nathan said. "You may watch television for an hour." "Can Isabella watch with me?" "I need to show Isabella around." Nathan looked to his father for some support. "I don't see the harm in letting her spend time with Nathan. You have all day tomorrow to school Isabella" said Michael Sr. Grabbing Isabella's hand, Nathan scurried to the family room. He turned on the television while standing next to Isabella. Isabella held her head as pain radiated through it. "Are you okay?" asked Nathan. "Yes, dear" smiled Isabella. "Come sit on the couch with me." The further from the television Isabella moved, the better she felt. The hour sitcom passed quickly. Isabella said to Nathan in a firm but gentle tone, "I believe it's bedtime." "Why?" asked Nathan.

"Please don't make me look bad in front of your mom and dad." Shaking his head, Nathan agreed to bedtime. "Turn off the television when you leave the room" said Isabella. Watching from the doorway, Hilda noticed that Isabella already had a good repertoire with Nathan. But teenagers were difficult at best. *We shall see how she does with them.* Morning came with the sound of Hilda's voice commanding that the children "Get ready for school." Michael complained that he would be late. Francesca was lounging in the solarium with a cup of coffee. All three children ran to kiss their mother before leaving for school. As the children departed, Isabella turned to Hilda ."Are mornings always this chaotic?" "Yes. This is a typical morning. Let's go have coffee in the kitchen and I will give you a tour of the house and the grounds. I'll show you which areas are off limits." "Off limits?" questioned Isabella. "The Master's office and bedroom are off limits. They are only cleaned when the missus can supervise." "Any other areas?" "The library and garage. The children are allowed in all common areas, their bedrooms and the backyard." "So, the house is like a jail?" asked Isabella. "No. But Master has many confidential government files. He also has another room off the garage where the weapons are stored. This rack is for keys. Each set of keys is for the tool shed, pantry, garage, boat house and all vehicles. We have housekeepers, a full time chef and groundskeepers. You are never alone should an emergency arise. There is a list of emergency phone numbers." "Where are the outdoor activity toys for the children kept?"

Hilda looked confused. "Croquette, horseshoes, lawn darts, bicycles." "Tool shed" Hilda replied. "Why is Nathan so sad?" "I believe he is bullied because he is a book worm. He is not athletic in the least. That is why his father wants to send him to military school. If you can encourage him to be more athletic, by all means. Now I must leave you on your own. I need to finish packing and catch my ride to the train station. Follow my guide and you will do just fine." Isabella thought to herself, "These children need to learn teamwork, accountability and to function as a unit. If one of them is attacked, they are responsible to defend the other. No one left behind!" As she made her boot camp lesson plan, Isabella knew what needed to be done. She would teach these children all that she knew and remembered. In the tool shed, Isabella sorted through the outdoor items. She was satisfied with what she found. She went back into the house. Hilda was at the front door, travel case in hand. "Have a wonderful holiday!" smiled Isabella. After having a quick lunch, Isabella was ready to greet the children as they came home from school. Michael Junior burst through the door and announced, "I have fencing practice!" "Take your things to your room." Katherine announced, "I have dance practice and my final costume fitting for my recital!" Getting frustrated, Isabella said firmly, "Take your belongings to your rooms! Snacks are on the table!" A horn beeped, signifying that rides to practices had arrived. Scanning the porch and the front lawn, Isabella wondered where Nathan could be. She found him hiding in the hedges. He was sniffling and gasping for breath. She gently scooped Nathan up into her arms. "Would you like to tell me what happened?" "Same thing that always happens!" "Bully beating you up?" "If it were just him, I would try to fight back. But he brings his friends and they gang up on me!" Nathan cried. "In my experience, if you take down the leader, his goons aren't very brave. Let's get you cleaned up. Then I will teach you some self-defense." After pressing cold compresses to his face, she took Nathan to the makeshift boxing ring. Francesca called out, "Isabella? May I see you for a second?" "Yes, ma'am?" "What are you doing with Nathan?" "He was beaten up at school. I thought I would teach him some self-defense tactics." "That's a proactive approach as a governess!" smiled Francesca. "He needs a confidence boost" smiled Isabella. "His father does not have time for him. They are not close." "He told me his father wants to send him to military school." "I'm afraid so" frowned Francesca. "I will do my best" smiled Isabella. Nathan looked into Isabella's eyes. "Can you help me?" "Yes. Trust me. Get in the ring. Are these yours?" "Yes. Dad got me the gloves, but never had time to teach me." After lacing up Nathan's gloves, Isabella started teaching him simple exercises. As his confidence grew, Isabella added punching sequences. She showed him different kicks and punches. Nathan was impressed that a girl knew how to fight! "We will practice every day." "Thank you for teaching me!" Nathan exclaimed as he gave Isabella a big hug. "Now we should give your big brother a lesson!" On her way to pick up Michael Junior, she felt he needed to learn how to lose a fight or two. Watching Michael Junior and his instructor Stanley, Isabella asked "Mind if I give that a try?" Stanley laughed as he handed his sword and gear over to Isabella. "I won't need the protective gear." A questioning look crossed Michael Junior's face. "Starting positions! En guard!" Isabella allowed Michael Junior a few stabs at her. Smiling, she took every point before pointing her sword at his heart. "Never underestimate your opponent! Now, let me show you how to go in for the kill." Michael Junior was both angry and confused. A woman had shown him up! Nathan stood on the airlines watching. He snickered. "I like having Isabella as a governess!" "We will wait for you in the car, Michael." Stanley turned on the radio. This caused a buzzing in Isabella's ears. Then a pain shot through her head and settled behind her eyes. Arriving home, Isabella announced "Get cleaned up for dinner. Homework after." Isabella kept touching her throbbing head. It would be an early night. Michael Junior announced at the dinner table "Isabella has great fencing skills!"   Michael Senior looked at his son. He was filled with confusion. "Her schooling has begun coming back to her. Father, she is no ordinary girl!" fussed Junior. Katherine chatted about landing the lead in her recital. "Our costumes have real crystals that sparkle!" "They sound beautiful" smiled Francesca.   "Nathan, I understand you had another altercation at school." "Yes, Father." "Did you at least try to defend yourself?" "No. I turned the other cheek as the Bible says."   "From what I understand, there is a gang of bullies who are targeting Nathan" Isabella said.   Laughing, Junior said, "It's fun to watch." Katherine said, "I tell my friends he was adopted!" Nathan ran from the table in tears. Isabella noticed that the older children received no reprimand for not defending their younger brother. Going to find Nathan, her heart ached for him. This reaffirmed her decision to teach him what she knew. As she comforted Nathan, she promised, "I will help you." "But even Mother and Father do not care about what I endure every day at that wretched school!" "Apparently, no one has taught teamwork at that school!" "No. The bullies are the popular kids. I am not." "Things will change" said Isabella. "No they won't!" sniffed Nathan. Walking into Junior's room, Isabella demanded "Why will you not protect your younger brother?" "He's a cream puff! Eventually, he will get tired of getting his ass kicked and fight back!"   "There are five boys and the ring leader! Does that sound like a fair fight to you?" "No. Nathan cannot hide behind me or Katherine for the rest of his school days." "So you have no empathy for Nathan at all?" "No. We had to learn how to stand up for ourselves. Mother and Father were too busy fulfilling their social calendars to know what we were going through! We have always had just the staff for support. Father brings us out for appearances. Katherine and I found what we were good at to keep us occupied." "So, you excel at sports and Katherine in dance?" "Nathan is so much younger. He got really into books. He can do our homework. He has an extremely high IQ. But the simple things, walking, talking and riding a bike were difficult for him. Archery, boating and sports frustrate Nathan." "I had some classmates that were good at book lessons but struggled with driving and self-defense. Our Chancellor complicated things by doing the following:

If one fails, the group fails

If one of my mates did something wrong, I took the punishment.

I have scars from the Chancellor's whip.

No one was to be left behind.

Teamwork was required to complete the goal

Michael Junior nodded. "That sounds like the military academy." "Here is what's going to happen. I will run this like a boot camp." "You can't do that!" exclaimed Michael Junior.   "I can as your governess. Your parents are going on a three day trip. Give me three days. I will tell your parents how much help you were with Nathan. Deal?" "I suppose. Do you really have scars?" "Yes, I do." Isabella showed him some photographs. "These were taken by the hospital." As Michael Junior looked through the photographs, a look of pain, terror and fear crossed his face. "This is what will happen to Nathan if he gets sent to military school." A screech came from behind Isabella. Katherine grabbed the photographs and thumbed through them. "Are you willing to join our boot camp while your parents are gone for three days?" "Yes!" They placed their hands atop one another and said in unison "Agreed!"   "School is closed for the holiday. We will have plenty of time. Mother and Father leave at daybreak." "Boot camp begins at six a.m. Goodnight!" As Isabella made her way down the hall, Francesca called, "Isabella" "Yes, ma'am?" "We are leaving on a trip in the morning, Dear. It's related to my husband's work at the Embassy. The entire staff will be at your disposal. I sent the cook to purchase extra groceries since the children will be home. No slumber parties or guests while we are away. Homework is to be done. Try to get the children to spend time together."   "I will do my best, ma'am." "You must accompany them anywhere they wish to go." "Yes, ma'am." "Isabella, are you in pain?"   "I have a headache." "Let me fix you up a pain powder." "Thank you, ma'am."   After Isabella had taken the medicine, Francesca whispered, "Get some rest. You have a full day with the children tomorrow." "Thank you, ma'am. Goodnight."   Closing the door, Isabella dropped into bed. The cold sheets felt good against her clammy skin. Falling into a deep sleep, flashes of her school training crept into Isabella's dreams. Combat training was clear along with night ops and self-defense. Learning to drive was foggy. Waking up, Isabella was drenched in sweat.   Wandering into the staff kitchen, Isabella drank glass after glass of water but it didn't quench her thirst. On her way back to quarters, she felt a stab of pain. Holding her head, a memory flashed of being tied to a board while she was being whipped. Blood oozed from her back. Harold screamed, "Admit it!" "I have done nothing wrong!" "You protected a younger student by doing her assignment!" Isabella heard her own voice say, "She's too young to go to a brothel!" Shaking her head, Isabella tried to go back to bed. She wondered why she had pain when a television or radio was turned on. "I need to ask Max about that." As she drifted off to sleep, the pain in her head subsided. Isabella was jarred awake by the D'Agati's preparing to leave. On her way to the kitchen, Isabella was summoned to the dining room.   "This is our itinerary. The name of the hotel where we will be staying. Our contact numbers are listed. The household money is kept here. The car has a full tank of gas. There is a driver should you need to take the children anywhere." "Yes ma'am." "Here is a list of favorite television shows and board games. Any questions?" "No ma'am." "Keep the children on their normal schedules." Waving goodbye to the D'Agati's, Isabella grabbed her cup of coffee and dressed quickly. Sounding revelry, the children complained, "We are on holiday!" "No! Boot camp time!" Nathan was the first to join Isabella in the dining room. Rubbing their eyes, Michael Junior and Katherine joined them twenty minutes later. "We will start with calisthenics and hand to hand combat. This afternoon, we will cover target shooting and self-defense. Let's start with a five mile run!" Complaining, Katherine announced, "This training is harder than dance class!" "Michael, join me in the boxing ring." Gloving up, Isabella showed him defensive strategies. Then punches. Michael announced, "I cannot hit a girl!" "You better defend because I will make you eat the mat!" Isabella landed a punch to Michael's jaw that knocked him off his feet. Getting up, Michael said, "Girl or not, I will whip your ass!" "Take your best shot!" Michael landed a few punches. Smiling, Isabella jumped to her feet kicking and punching. Michael landed on the mat covering his head. Katherine screamed, "Stop! You're hurting him!" "Make me!" screamed Isabella.   Jumping into the ring, Katherine hit Isabella with a whip. Nathan grabbed a bat and swung wildly. Isabella won easily. "This is what should have happened when those bullies beat up Nathan! Blood is thicker than water. If anyone hurts your brother, it's your obligation to beat their asses! Katherine, you have strong legs from dance class. You will excel in martial arts. They are normally used as self-defense."   After showing her a defensive stance, Isabella looked into Katherine's eyes. "Hit me!" Katherine took a good swing, which Isabella blocked. "Nathan, come join us! Now, Katherine, hit Nathan. Nathan, you step in and block. Step back and block! Nice work! Ready for lunch?" "Yes ma'am!"   As they finished lunch, Katherine started dozing off at the table. "Clear the table. Let's get back to work! Let's try some target shooting." Confused, Nathan asked, "Guns?" "First, we will practice with bows and arrows." Setting up targets, Isabella demonstrated archery.

Katherine complained that the safety guard hurt her arm. Michael Junior adjusted the bow to fit her more comfortably. Nathan observed as his siblings practiced. Pulling out his notebook, he wrote an equation. Mathematics were Nathan's strong suit. "See!" whined Katherine. "He's always writing in his notebook!" Isabella looked at Nathan. "Are you ready to give it a try?" "I did the calculation. To hit someone in the eye, you have to adjust for a slight breeze!"   Smiling, Isabella said, "Show us!"   Nathan picked up the bow, adjusted his stance, licked his finger and held it in the air. With a nod, he pulled up the bow, pulled back the string and fired. It was a perfect bulls eye! Nathan was beaming. He finally felt as though he had a skill that was useful to his siblings.   Smiling, Isabella knew she had brought them closer together. Michael Junior rustled Nathan's hair. "Looks like you are useful after all!" "What's next?" "Weapons can be made from nearly anything." Isabella led the children on a tour of both the kitchen and the garage.   "Cleaning solvents like bleach are flammable." Nathan showed his skills by reciting the periodic table of elements from memory. "When you work as a team, each person contributes their abilities. "Big brain Nathan would absolutely fit in in the military" squeaked Katherine. "Yes. The military loves brainy guys. Physical strength is important, but so is intelligence." "Just because I am a book worm doesn't mean I'm not important!" "Exactly!" smiled Isabella.   "Who is ready to try boating?" Michael Junior looked at the sky shaking his head. "Storm clouds are rolling in." "Okay. Change of plans. Back to the house and get cleaned up for dinner" said Isabella.

Katherine winced as she climbed the stairs. Isabella tossed her a bottle of linement. "This will help your sore muscles. Pass it to your brothers when you're done with it. Dinner in twenty minutes." As they sat down to their evening meal, a deafening silence fell over the room. "What did you think of today's training?"   There was no reply. "How about self-defense training?" "That was interesting. Why did you provoke us?" "I needed you to understand that when someone hurts one of you, they hurt all of you. If you stand together, no one can hurt Nathan." "Do you expect us to jump in if he's in a fight?" "Yes! Remember him jumping in the ring and doing whatever he could to protect Michael? We'll practice more tomorrow. I will work one on one with Nathan while you practice archery. Then we will learn a new weapon. Hit the rack!" "Can we watch television for an hour?" "I don't see a problem with that." The children walked to the family room. Katherine flopped down on the couch. Nathan made a dash for the television. As the box came to life, Isabella once again felt the stabbing pain behind her eyes. It was followed by a wave of nausea that dropped her to her knees. "Are you alright, Isabella?" "Yes. I just feel funny whenever a radio or television is turned on."

Michael Junior smiled. "I overhead my parents talking. They said the doctors put a chip in your head to regulate your mood and attitude. They said it would make you normal again." "Yes." "Maybe the radio waves cause the chip to act up." "You may be correct. You're a very smart young man" smiled Isabella. *"I need Max to explain all of that to me more clearly"* thought Isabella. "Ice cream, anyone?" giggled Isabella. Looking at the couch, Katherine and Nathan were fast asleep. "Mikey, help me carry them to bed. I will turn off the television." Isabella lifted Nathan to her shoulder, marched upstairs and gently eased him into his bed. She heard a phone ringing from the office. She ran to open the office door and grabbed the receiver. "Hello?" "How's my favorite Governess?" "Hello, Max. It's good to hear your voice!" "How goes the job?" "I'm doing alright with the children." "Anything to report?" "No. But I do have a question for you, Max." "Shoot." "Whenever a television or radio is turned on, I have pain in my head. Tonight, I had a severe wave of nausea." "I will contact the doctors to see if this is a side effect of the surgery." "Maybe it's the chip in my brain. Michael Junior overhead his parents talking." "I understand. I will find out" soothed Max.

"Where is everyone?" "The D'Agati's are on a three day trip. The children are in bed" "What do you do all day?" asked Max. "We're having a mini boot camp." "What the hell are you teaching those children?! " "Calisthenics, archery and self-defense."

Drawing in a breath, Max asked, "Why self-defense?" "Because Nathan gets beat up by a gang of kids at school." "He's a child, Isabella!" "I realize this. I have just taught him to deflect a punch so his face doesn't get turned into chopped beef! I have also been doing team building exercises. The parents do not encourage them to work together. They have too many social engagements to bother with what goes on with the children. The house staff is raising these children." "I believe you are overstepping the boundaries of your assignment!" "No, I am not. I care for these children." "I will check in again soon. Goodnight, Isabella."   As Max hung up the phone, he knew that Isabella's actions would alarm Harold. Rubbing his head, Max poured himself a large Scotch and phoned Chanel. He explained to Chanel everything that he and Isabella discussed. "She is teaching the children military tactics. Harold's going to hit the roof!" "Give Isabella some room. She may do just fine" cooed Chanel. "She knows about the chip. Michael Junior overhead his parents talking." "Oh, brother! I did some digging. Heidi and Harold go way back. She is keeping him informed of everything." "She is away for ten days on holiday." "I don't believe that! I would wager that she is with Harold right now!" Max said, "We do not know that for certain." "Be prepared, Max. I do not believe that Harold will wait the full ten days." "I will keep in contact with Isabella. Goodnight, Chanel!"   As Isabella checked on the children, she felt something was amiss. She dressed quickly and walked the perimeter. She checked all the doors and windows. When she was satisfied with the perimeter check, she went back to bed.   Drifting off into a deep sleep, Isabella lay motionless. Her breathing was slow and easy. Sunrise came too soon for Isabella. Remembering that boot camp would resume after breakfast, she smiled. Standing on the back porch, Isabella breathed in the scent of fresh air that had been cleansed by the recent rain. Today would be a good day. As the cook started preparing breakfast, a familiar voice bellowed, "Oh, my muscles!" "Did you use the linement like I suggested?" "Yes, but I still hurt!" Michael Junior registered the same complaint.   Nathan bounded down the stairs eager to start the day. "How do you not have sore muscles?" "I'm a kid!" Isabella said, "Five year olds don't usually have aches and pains." After breakfast, we will start with running an obstacle course for time." Isabella ran the course in ten minutes flat. "Michael, you're up!" He ran the course in twelve minutes. Katherine stretched, then ran the course, sharing her brother's time. Nathan tried to complete the course but was unable to climb the rope. Looking at one another, his siblings went to lend him a hand. Smiling, Isabella reminded them how important it was to never leave a comrade behind. "Two more runs of the course and we will start on self-defense." Nathan's agility was improving along with his confidence. After lunch, Isabella set up new targets. After running through the targets, Isabella turned to the children. "Run. Grab the bow and arrows, shoot. Then pick up the BB gun, shoot. Run the obstacle course. Tag me and I will shoot the remaining targets. Then go to the ring and shadow box. You have twenty minutes starting now! Loser has to help the cook!" As each child completed a section of the course, Isabella noted their competitiveness as well as their teamwork when it came to the rope climb. Their form in shadow boxing made Isabella beam with pride. "Now, have a seat and let me show you how it's really done!" Isabella boasted. She had replaced the regular bow with a hunting crossbow, the BB gun with a rifle and a few grenades for good measure. Running the course, Isabella demonstrated precision and skills of a seasoned combat veteran.

"Since none of you beat my time, clean up for kitchen duty" Isabella said. "How do you know all that stuff?" the children asked. "I honestly don't remember much about what I know. I get memory flashes of a school, and the Chancellor tying me to a board and whipping me." With tears in her eyes, Katherine hugged Isabella. Michael Junior and Nathan joined in on the hug. Shrugging off the unexpected hug, Isabella sent Katherine and Michael Junior into the house. Nathan darted off past the gated entrance. Isabella called out, "Nathan, wait!" Then she called his siblings. "I'm afraid I scared Nathan. He ran off." The three of them divided the perimeter and began searching for Nathan. Running down the drive and past the gate, Isabella's instincts led her to the nearby park where you could feed birds. As she approached the bench, she could see the top of Nathan's head. She crept forward slowly so she wouldn't startle him. She noticed that a dog had Nathan cornered. There was a man nearby who seemed to have control of the animal. Curiosity got the best of Isabella. As she got closer, she heard the man command the dog to "stay." Then he told Nathan he would protect him from the dog and he began rubbing Nathan's back. A memory flashed in Isabella's mind of priests molesting young boys. Without a second thought, Isabella ran up behind the man.

Seeing the fear in Nathan's eyes, Isabella motioned for Nathan to move back. She put a finger to her lips. Nathan stayed silent. With stealth like skill, Isabella came up and grabbed the man in a sleeper hold. With a quick jerking motion, she snapped his neck. The dog snarled as Isabella dropped his Master to the ground. She crouched down and growled in the dog's face. The dog ran away whimpering.   Isabella grabbed Nathan and held him close. She whispered, He would have hurt you in unspeakable ways! Never trust a stranger!" "Yes, ma'am." "Let's go home." Turning around, Isabella was face-to-face with Katherine and Michael Junior. "I'm sorry you had to witness violence, but I was concerned for Nathan." "We understand." "I need to clean up the obstacle course. You children head to the kitchen." After Isabella explained what happened to the house security staff, they went to deal with the body and contacted the local Constable.   When Isabella was done cleaning, there was no trace of the boot camp. Cook put the children to work peeling potatoes, taking out garbage and setting the table before excusing them. Whispers from bedrooms drifted downstairs. The children were shocked by what they had witnessed, but they understood that it was done to protect Nathan. Preparing for dinner, Isabella was planning the final team building exercise.   The head of security phoned Mr. D'Agati and explained the day's events. "We checked his record, sir. He is a known pedophile. He escaped from prison years ago. The governess protected the boy." "We will be home by eight a.m. Don't mention it to the staff. We would like to surprise Isabella." "Yes, sir." Francesca pleaded, "Don't be angry, Michael. I asked her to get the children to do activities as a group." "I see" smiled Michael.   Their trip home was long and monotonous. They were exhausted, but happy to be home. The children sat eating at the table. They waited for Isabella to lay out the day's events. "Today we will have a scrimmage of sorts. I have set up a course. The concept is teamwork. First team to capture the flag wins. I have drawn maps with clues for you to follow." A voice behind Isabella asked, "Mind if we join you?" She turned to see Mr. and Mrs. D'Agati standing behind her. "Do you need a rest after your long trip?" "No. Just give us a few minutes to change clothes. We will join you in the backyard." Looking at Isabella, the children were full of apprehension. "What's bothering you?" "Mother and Father never do activities with us! Who picks the teams?" "How about men versus women?" "That seems a bit unfair to have all the muscle on one team" quipped Francesca. "We have Isabella. She's as skilled as any man!" Smiling, Francesca said, "I'd bet you are correct, Katherine!" Isabella walked the course with the parents so there wouldn't be any surprises. She passed out maps, compasses and clues. "One hour! Time starts now!" As both Michael's fought over who would be the team leader, Nathan analyzed his map. Francesca conceded team leader to Isabella. Isabella said, "Each clue gives a piece to the location of the flag. There are traps and misinformation. Teams rely on each member's individual strengths." With each piece, the ladies filled with confidence. At the end was an agility course complete with mud pit. Michael Senior thought that with teamwork, the agility course would be a breeze. He didn't realize that he wasn't as physically fit as he thought. Ego got in the way with the men. Working together to cover the course, the women were ahead. Reaching for the flag, Francesca was knocked out by Michael Senior. He clawed his way toward the flag. Just as his fingers grasped the cloth, Isabella took him out at the knees. Remembering Isabella's lessons, Michael Junior grabbed Nathan and hoisted him up to grab the flag. Nathan snatched the flag then tucked and rolled to escape Katherine's grasp. Beaming with pride, Nathan yelled, "I did it!" "You sure did, son! Let's have some lunch!" The D'Agati's were laughing and covered in mud but they were finally engaging as a family. Walking behind the family,

Isabella was pleased at what she had taught them. The children had school in the morning and would return to their normal routine. Baths and homework occupied the rest of the evening. As a special surprise, cook had prepared pizza from Michael Senior's mother's recipe.   Nathan suggested that they watch television as a family. Smiling, his father said softly "For an hour. Then I have to catch up on work. Deal?" "Yes, Father." Isabella sat in the staff kitchen. She was having a cup of tea when she heard the familiar sound of footsteps on the stairs. The children were going to bed. As Francesca tucked them in, she asked, "What else did Isabella teach you?" "Team building and self-defense. Nathan needed self-confidence. We did archery and Nathan got a bulls-eye!"

Francesca smiled. "It seems she kept you busy." "She told us that if we saw Nathan being bullied, we should always jump in and help him! Blood is thicker than water." Michael Senior stood in the hallway listening to all that his children had learned from Isabella.   He knew that he could never accomplish so much in a few days. Work always got in the way of his time with his children. "I wish we had met Isabella sooner!" Francesca joined her husband in his office. "I did ask her to work with them. Nathan told her you were going to send him away to military school. She helped him gain confidence!" "Stanley's father expressed concerns about Isabella fencing with Junior. She seems to have a wide range of skills." "All the kids talked about her skills on the agility course and with weapons. I have no doubt she could put our security team to shame!" laughed Michael Senior.   "Katherine mentioned that she has scars on her back from a Chancellor's whip. What the hell kind of school did she attend?!" "Her head injury came from protecting a little girl. She has been trained to protect, just like our bodyguards." "That's exactly what I was thinking!" exclaimed Francesca.   "We have to speak to her about how she handled that pervert!" "I read the file on him. He would rape and kill children. She protected our son, Franny." "I agree, but our children witnessed her kill someone!" "That part was a bit sloppy. But aside from that, she's done a hell of a job!" "What about Harold?" "I have nothing but good things to report. And our children love her!" "The children did mention that whenever a television or radio is turned on, Isabella has pain in her head." "I will discuss it with Max so he can tell her doctors. Call her in." Isabella knocked lightly on the office door. "You wanted to see me, sir?" "Yes. Please come in. We have spoken at length to the children. Your obstacle course and confidence building was a hit. As was self-defense and archery." "I'm pleased to hear that "smiled Isabella. "The children were concerned about your head pain." "I am fine. Radio waves seem to bother the chip." "We need to discuss the incident with Nathan and that despicable man. I read his police file. Your instincts were correct about him. Thank you for protecting my son. But the children witnessed the violence." "I am sorry. My training took over. It was literally beaten into me. I will be more cautious in the presence of the children." Francesca spoke softly. "Katherine told me about the scars on your back." "I didn't realize I had them until the hospital staff showed me photos of my back. I had no memories. I am starting to get flashes of memories, but not full events." "May we see the photos?" Isabella handed the file to Francesca. She winced as she thumbed through the photographs. She returned the folder to Isabella. "Was Harold your Chancellor?" asked Michael Senior. "I think so. I don't remember much about school."

Nodding, he said, "You're excused." Closing the door, Isabella headed to bed. When she was sure Isabella was out of earshot, Francesca screamed "Harold is a monster! He deserves the same treatment!" "I agree, Franny. He is only interested in her assignment because he wants to know if she remembers the school." "He will kill her, Mike!" "That's why I will give her a glowing review. She seems like a genuinely sweet girl. Let's get some rest. I will catch up on work tomorrow." As Isabella slept, Max was getting an earful from the D' Agati's security guard. "Thanks for the update" said Max as he hung up the phone. He screamed, "Shit! Harold is going to call for Isabella to be terminated! I may need to call on Goddard and Sebastian!" Pouring himself a Scotch, Max began planning an exit strategy for Isabella. Waking with the sun, Isabella prepared to get the children off to school. The children kissed their mother goodbye with lunches in hand. Their rides arrived. Nathan asked Isabella if she could drive him to school. "Of course I can. But don't you want to ride with your siblings?" "No!" "Are you afraid of the bullies?" "Yes" Nathan said. Isabella smiled gently. "Let's go over what you've learned. Deflect." As Isabella punched, Nathan defended. "Better yet, remember they cannot hurt you if they swing at or kick you. Take out the leader and the rest of them will scatter like rabbits!" "Thank you, Isabella!" At recess, Kenny cornered Nathan. He and his friends encircled Nathan. "Where's my money, nerd?" "I am not giving you anything!" screamed Nathan.   Laughing, Kenny said, "Guess you forgot about the whooping I gave you last time!" Kenny lunged at Nathan. Nathan stepped aside and Kenny landed on the ground. Lester pushed Nathan back towards Kenny. Kenny punched and Nathan deflected. Nathan was holding his own. Nathan ran up behind Kenny and grabbed his neck. He was trying to put Kenny to sleep!   Michael Junior and Katherine jumped in and pulled Nathan off of Kenny. "If you want to fight our brother, you have to go through us!" The circle closed around the siblings. Kenny had a bat! The siblings stood firm until the Chancellor broke up the fight. "What's going on here?" A girl called from the back, "Kenny and his goons started in on Nathan again!"

Kenny screamed, "Nathan tried to kill me!" "No. He used a choke hold." "To my office, now! "   After interviews with several students, the Chancellor figured out that these boys had been bullying Nathan all year. His siblings had stepped in because it was five against one.   "Where did you learn a choke hold?" the Chancellor asked Nathan. "I have been training." "Go home! You're suspended!" "Why? Because I defended myself?"   Rethinking his decision, the Chancellor said, "You and Kenny will meet me in the gym after school. I will be calling your parents." Listening to the phone call from the hallway, Isabella headed to the school. As she entered the school, a flash of memory struck her. She remembered all the abuses she had suffered at school. "Enough!" she thought to herself. Finding her way to the gymnasium, she burst through the door. Her eyes rested on a makeshift boxing ring. Kenny and his goons were name calling. Nathan was in the opposite corner struggling to put his gloves on. "Here, let me lace those for you." "Isabella, you came!" cried Nathan. "Of course! I would never let you down " said Isabella. "He's three times my size!" "I see that" laughed Isabella. "Formulate a strategy in your mind. I want you to get to the inside. Body shots. Then take out his knees! Once you take out his knees, he is your size. You can handle the rest. I am here." "So am I." "Father, you came!" "I am behind you." "So are we" cheered Katherine and Michael Junior.   Me too" smiled Francesca. "Mother!" "Knock his block off!" said Francesca. The Chancellor called Kenny and Nathan to the center of the ring. "This is where the fighting ends! Go to your corners! Come out at the bell!"   As the bell sounded, Kenny came out swinging wildly. Stepping to the inside, Nathan landed several body shots and quickly jumped back just out of Kenny's reach. Nathan snuck in a head shot and Kenny screamed, "You're a dead boy!" Isabella coached Nathan. "Sweep his knees. Once he's down, jump on him and punch him until he stops moving!"Calculating, Nathan nodded. Kenny came back out at the sound of the bell. Isabella yelled, "Now!"

Using a sweep, Nathan took out Kenny's knees. As Kenny hit the mat, Nathan jumped on him and hit him over and over again. The Chancellor pulled Nathan off of Kenny. When the Chancellor turned his back, Nathan came to the center of the ring yelling, "Anyone else! Just leave me alone!" Nathan walked to his corner with pride.

He looked up to see Kenny's father in the ring berating his son. "You're a no good piece of crap pant waist! I will give you a beating when we get home for losing!" Kenny's mother was trembling and bowed her head in shame. She helped her son exit the ring. Before she could stop herself, Isabella said, "What kind of man turns his son into a bully because he is pathetic?" "Shut your mouth, whore!" "Come shut it for me, big man!"   Kenny's father lunged at Isabella. She sidestepped him, laughing. "Is that the best you can do?" Getting up off the mat, he lunged full force swinging at Isabella's face. Her patience gone, Isabella beat him mercilessly until he stopped moving.   Leaning in close, Isabella whispered, "If you lay a hand on Kenny or your wife, I will kill you! Do you understand?" Gasping, he whispered, "Yes. How did you know?" "I have known many men like you who are bullies!" As Isabella walked back to the house, she was pleased that she had brought the family together again. Singing Nathan's praises, the family rejoiced in his victory. Heidi listened intently as her favorite gossipy cook filled her in on the day's events. Heidi excused herself and ran excitedly to Harold's office.

She eagerly reported on Isabella's activities. With a sadistic smirk, Harold made the call to Max. "Send the girls in to extract Isabella. You have forty-eight hours to extract and terminate Isabella! Those are your orders, Max!"   Sending word to Anastasia, the team reported to Max's office. "You need to extract Isabella. Things have gone haywire with her new assignment. Harold wants her brought in."   Anastasia screamed, "I WILL NOT KILL ISABELLA!" Rena, Ingrid and Ursula said in unison, "Neither will we!"Nodding, Max said, "Just bring her to me." "Max, you cannot kill her!" "Relax! I will handle Harold. You just go get Isabella. I will call the D'Agati's and let them know to expect you." "Yes sir."

Times A Changing

Max dialed Michael D'Agati. On the first ring, he heard "DAgati residence." "May I speak to Michael Senior?" "Just a moment, sir." "Hello?" "Mike, it's Max. Isabella will be picked up shortly." "I thought we had her for ten days?" "Harold has called." "I understand. She did a phenomenal job with my children. She showed me what I was missing by working so much. My children love her! I know she broke some rules, but she saved my son Nathan from a murderous pedophile!" "I understand, Mike." "Should I speak to Harold? She truly has no memories of the school." "It does not matter to Harold." "I will give her the message." As he hung up the phone, Francesca looked at her husband with sad eyes. "Harold called Max. Isabella will be picked up shortly. Max takes orders too, Franny." "I hope nothing happens to her." "Isabella?" Peeking from the top of the stairs, Isabella said, "Yes sir?" "Max called. Your friends are coming to pick you up. They will be here in a few hours." "I guess I should say goodbye to the children." The walk to their bedrooms seemed endless. "I guess I got a new assignment." "Did I get you in trouble?" "No, silly!" "Dad said no military school for me. At least for a while. I get to take boxing lessons!" "That will be good for you." "We're going on the boat Saturday!" "Where's Katherine?" "At dance practice." "Tell her I said goodbye." Packing her travel case, Isabella felt a wave of nausea and a pain in her head. Dropping to her knees, she held her head until the pain subsided. Francesca knocked softly. "I wanted to thank you for helping my children. You were a godsend for the time we had you." "I enjoyed my time with all of you. Keep doing activities as a family to keep the bonds strong."   Nathan asked, "Can I meet your friends?" "Sure! I would be honored." "Bursting through the door, Katherine and Michael Junior bickered over who would shower first. "Hey!" "What, Nathan?" "Isabella's leaving us." "Why?" "New assignment" scowled Nathan. The ringing doorbell interrupted the conversation. Opening the door, Francesca said "Yes? Can I help you?" "We're here to pick up Isabella." "Hi!" beamed Nathan. "Nathan, Katherine and Michael Junior, these are my friends. Anastasia, Ursula, Rena and Ingrid." "Hi!" Isabella smiled. "Be good for your parents and be good to each other." "Thank you Isabella." Waving goodbye, Isabella felt a tear roll down her cheek. The drive to Chanel's was deafening. "What's wrong?" asked Isabella. "Harold had you called in." "Why?" "You broke some rules." "He wants me put down?" "Max said he would handle Harold. Max told us to bring you to him."   "That can't be good!" cried Isabella. As the girls drove back, Max was on the phone with Chanel. "I need to hide Isabella." "Do you have a plan, Max?" "I need to bring Isabella there. We should arrive by eleven p.m." "How long did Harold give you?" "Forty-eight hours to complete the task. The girls refuse to terminate Isabella."   "That was to be expected. They are very bonded as a unit. Things will work out, I am sure." Chanel ended the call abruptly and went to find Goddard. She knew that she would have to explain the situation with Isabella and the issues with the chip before he went off in search of Harold and unleashed ungodly mayhem. She knocked on his door. "Enter." Chanel gave Goddard a knowing look. "Harold gave the order?" "Yes. Max and the girls will be here by eleven p.m." "How long?" asked Goddard. "Forty-eight hours."   "I will let Sebastian know" Goddard said. Chanel knew things were about to get dangerous. "Goddard, dear. There have been some issues with Isabella's chip." Concern filled Goddard's ice blue eyes. "Is she okay?" "Truthfully, I am not sure. She has had severe pain when she is near a television or a radio. I am making arrangements for her to be relocated and I will do all I can to make sure that she gets the best possible medical care."   "Very well" Goddard nodded. The sadness was visible on his normally stoic face. Chanel closed his bedroom door and retreated to her study. She exhaled a deep sigh and perused her contacts for a place where Isabella would be safe from Harold's reach. It would have to be someplace out of the country with excellent medical care.   Chanel was certain that Michael D'Agati could and would gladly help them obtain travel documents for Isabella. Chanel told the staff to expect Max and the girls. Hannah set about preparing snacks and a light meal for everyone. Chanel asked Goddard and Sebastian to meet her in her office once everyone had arrived. They nodded in silent understanding.   The look of hatred in Goddard's eyes betrayed exactly how he felt as they walked to the foyer to greet their guests. Tension filled the air and pleasantries were brief. Max and the team followed Chanel and the boys into her office and closed the door before anyone spoke. "As you all know, Harold has given the order to terminate Isabella."   Goddard put his fist through the wall beside the door. Sebastian gritted his teeth. "Settle yourselves! No one is going to hurt Isabella." Chanel said. "I will make arrangements for her to be relocated. She will be safe. I will need Sebastian and Goddard to help with the physical aspects of the plan.   "What would that be?" Goddard asked. "We, or should I say Isabella is going to terminate Harold! It's long overdue!" said Chanel.   Silence filled the room. Max looked at Chanel with a combination of shock and amusement. "It's simple" said Chanel. "Tomorrow evening is the deadline for terminating Isabella. So tomorrow will be the end of Harold's reign of terror. "Isabella, dear that honor shall be yours. Goddard has made his Red Room available. Consider this your opportunity to exact payback for all that he made you suffer. Goddard and Sebastian will be available to dispose of the garbage when all is done. We will only get one opportunity to take him out. Pull no punches. Get this done. Then Isabella will be relocated. I will leave you with the rest of the evening to choose your plan!" Chanel dismissed them and retired to the library. The group dispersed to different parts of the manor. Isabella found Goddard in the corridor. "Hello, Goddard" Isabella spoke softly. He enveloped her in a long embrace. For the moment, he knew she was safe. "Can you show me around your Red Room? Show me how the um, contraptions work?" asked Isabella. "Sure" said Goddard. He led Isabella by the hand to the Red Room. Max, Sebastian and the girls were helping themselves to Hannah's freshly prepared snacks.   Once in the library, Chanel locked herself in and dialed Harold's direct phone number. "Harold, dear. It's Chanel. I got a call from Max this evening." "Do tell" Harold said arrogantly. "He asked me to help him hide Isabella. He and the team refuse to terminate her. You may have to do it yourself. Stop in tomorrow evening. When it's done, we can have a bit of private time to de- stress. You can celebrate." "Very well" said Harold. "And thank you, dear Chanel." Chanel hung up and prayed. Goddard was giving Isabella a crash course in the functions and purposes of each of his implements.   She paid extra attention to his instructions on bondage, knot tying and his collection of razor sharp things. Harold had no idea what awaited him. Isabella said goodnight to Max and her comrades.   Hannah led her to her room. It had been a long and emotional day. She was exhausted. Tomorrow would be just as tough.

She changed into her nightshirt and fell into bed. It was a restless sleep. Morning came too soon. Isabella awoke at dawn and started preparing herself for the day's events. She told herself that killing Harold was necessary. It was the only way to stop him from abusing others as he had done to Isabella. When she had steeled her nerves, she dressed in layers and solid black. She knew that Harold was not going to go down without a fight. She had declined Goddard's offer to sedate Harold before his life was ended. She wanted him to feel as much pain as his body could take before he expired.   She made her way into the dining room where Hannah had a full spread of breakfast options laid out. "Good morning, Miss Isabella. Please sit. I'll make you a plate." "Thank you, Hannah. Would you add a few extra jelly donuts to my plate?" "Yes ma'am. Raspberry or apple filled?" "Two of each, please."   Hannah nodded and set the plates in front of Isabella. She devoured every morsel and was on her third plate when Sebastian and Goddard joined her. "Hungry?" Goddard asked with a smile. "Very" Isabella said through a mouthful of food. "Care to go for a run with us?" Goddard and Sebastian asked in unison.   "Definitely. Has anyone seen Chanel today?" "Not yet today. She told all the staff that she was not to be disturbed. She will come out of the library when she's ready" said Goddard. The three of them left the table and set off on their run. Chanel hadn't slept a wink. She had been making arrangements for Isabella to be relocated.

Michael D'Agati was more than happy to expedite the paperwork for Isabella's travel documents. Now she was trying to reach an old friend she knew who would gladly help Isabella. After an hour, she made contact. She explained the situation and Isabella's needs. Chanel realized that her contact who she had known since the girl was an infant was now a grown woman who was making her own way in a world that had once belonged to her father.   She knew that Isabella would be safe and cared for. It was all that anyone could hope for. Isabella would be met at the International airport. There was no way that any of Harold's cronies could touch her after tonight. Chanel straightened her blouse and stepped out of the sanctuary of her library to face the day's events. As she entered the dining room, Hannah served her a cup of coffee and said, "Good morning, ma'am. Miss Isabella is out for a run with the boys. I imagine they will return soon." "Very well, thank you Hannah."   Chanel knew that physical exercise had always helped Isabella to focus and clear her mind. Finishing her coffee, Chanel could only pray that the plan would go smoothly. After two hours, Isabella, Goddard and Sebastian returned to the manor. Each went in separate directions to freshen up. Chanel had closed the brothel and cleared all schedules. She had arranged a day in town for all the staff that wasn't a part of killing Harold. There didn't need to be a house full of witnesses. Nor was it possible to torture a man and not have the screams heard. She walked the halls checking for any stragglers that may have remained from the previous evening. All clear. Then she peeked into Goddard's Red Room. She saw that he had prepared. The room was covered in plastic and heavy tarps. Some very sharp and terrifying implements were laid out on a rolling cart.   Everything seemed to be falling into place. Everyone seemed to know their places and what needed to be done. All she could do now was wait. And trust that everyone would be able to follow through. Evil wouldn't be easy to defeat but it could be done. And it would be.

Chanel checked the time. One hour until Harold would arrive. She paced the foyer nervously. The minutes dragged on for an eternity. Chanel saw the headlights on Harold's car as he pulled up to the drive. She sounded the bell to alert everyone that the time had arrived. Each took their places. Hannah announced that Harold and Hilda had arrived. That was unexpected, but Chanel surmised that she could distract Hilda while the others dealt with Harold. "Hello, Darling" Chanel cooed. "You should have advised you would be bringing a guest" Chanel scolded Harold. "Hello, Hilda. How are you?" Chanel asked. She was struggling to hide her disdain for Hilda. "Hannah, please bring Harold his usual Bourbon on ice and a glass of red wine for Miss Hilda." "Yes ma'am." Hannah said as she disappeared toward the kitchen. As she poured the drinks, she recalled all the things that she had heard about Miss Hilda. She was one of Harold's spies and she was at least partially responsible for Harold giving the order to terminate Isabella. Hannah decided to exact a bit of revenge for Isabella. The girl had suffered enough. As she poured the wine, she sprinkled a small amount of oleander into the glass before placing it on the tray and returning to the foyer. "How was your trip?" Chanel asked curtly. "Delightful and refreshing" Hilda answered as she sipped the wine. Chanel turned her back and rolled her eyes. "Harold, why don't you show Hilda to the library? I am sure there is something there that will hold her interest while we discuss business." "Certainly, dear" Harold said as he took Hilda's hand and helped her to her feet. Hilda struggled to stand and her words were slurred. "I-I don't feel well" she uttered. Her face looked pale and flushed. Hannah rushed to Harold's side and the two of them helped Hilda into the library. Once she was safely in a chair, Hannah closed and locked the door before leading Harold up the corridor to Goddard's Red Room. "Miss

Chanel will be with you shortly" she said as she opened the door for Harold. He let himself into the room. It had been darkened intentionally. Seconds after Hannah pulled the door closed, Isabella stepped out from the shadows. "Hello, Harold. How nice to see you again" Isabella said coldly. Harold turned and nearly jumped out of his jacket. He lunged toward Isabella and was grasping for her throat. She landed her elbow under his sternum and knocked the wind out of him. "You're dead, you whore!" Harold gasped. Isabella chuckled. "You arrogant prick! If you want to terminate me, do it yourself!" Harold struggled to his feet. It took him a few seconds to realize that Goddard held one of his arms and Sebastian was holding the other one. They lifted him off his feet and chained him to the Saint Andrews cross that hung in one corner of the room in an "X "shape.   As Sebastian secured Harold's ankles in place, Goddard clamped a Heretic's fork collar around his neck. It was a leather choker band with a prong on each side and a spike in the middle. This implement is used to ensure proper posture of the wearer. If they slouch, the spike in the center pierces the flesh under the chin.

Once the boys were confident that Harold was immobilized, they took their leave. Isabella began to rub salt on Harold's exposed chest as she told him about the flashes of memory she had of how he treated her while she attended the school. "I remember the scars! How tough you thought you were as you whipped me!" Isabella screamed at him. "Well, guess what, Harold! You taught me well. I now have a whip of my own!" Isabella shrieked as she cracked the whip across Harold's face. The blow split his skin and blood dripped down his body onto the floor.   Isabella shoved Goddard's dental gag into his mouth as he started to scream out in pain. "Now, Harold. Screaming indicates weakness. Are you a weak man, Harold? Only a weak man enjoys beating little girls!" Isabella took one of Goddard's blades and made several small, deep cuts along his carotid and femoral arteries. She wanted him to bleed out slowly and painfully. She leaned in close to Harold's ear and whispered,   "I remember everything about you and your dammed school!" Harold spit in her face. That was the final straw for Isabella. She reached up, grabbed a handful of his hair and shoved his neck down into the center spike on the collar. There was a sickening pop as Harold's head rolled off his body and onto the floor.   Isabella wiped her face on her sleeve as she left the room. Goddard was waiting for her. He looked at her with concern. "It's done. That sadistic asshole is dead!" Isabella said as she walked away down the hall. On her way out the side door of the manor, she passed Sebastian. He was carrying a rolled up rug to the back of a waiting truck.   "Goddard may need your help" Isabella told him as she ran past him into the field. She ran until her lungs burned. By the time she was ready to return to the manor, the sun was setting in the sky.   Isabella walked back guided by the pink and yellow hues in the sky. When she entered the side door, Chanel was waiting for her. "You must go and get cleaned up. Quickly! Leo is waiting to drive you to your flight!" Chanel hurriedly explained as Isabella washed up. "You are being be relocated. I have arranged everything. Upon arrival in Medellin, you will be evaluated to ensure that your chip is functioning properly. Come! It's time to go, dear!"   Chanel whisked Isabella out of the manor and into the waiting car. A few moments later, she was off to a new beginning. It was the first of many changes to come. The new school year would see Max as the new Chancellor and Chanel as his right hand.